I0823576

PORTRAIT OF AN UNKNOWN WOMAN

Camille de Peretti

PORTRAIT OF AN UNKNOWN WOMAN

Translated from the French
by Hildegarde Serle

Europa Editions
27 Union Square West, Suite 302
New York NY 10003
www.europaeditions.com
info@europaeditions.com

This book is a work of fiction. Any references to historical events, real people, or real locales are used fictitiously.

Copyright © Calmann-Lévy, 2024
First publication 2026 by Europa Editions

Translation by Hildegarde Serle
Original title: *L'Inconnue du portrait*
Translation copyright 2026 by Europa Editions

All rights reserved, including the right of reproduction in whole or in part in any form.

Passages from poems by Georg Trakl in the following pages are taken from *The Last Gold of Expired Stars: Complete Poems 1908-1914*. Translated by Jim Doss and Werner Schmitt. Sykesville, MD: Loch Raven Press, 2011.

Library of Congress Cataloging in Publication Data is available
ISBN 979-8-88966-178-8

de Peretti, Camille
Portrait of an Unknown Woman

Cover design by Ginevra Rapisardi

Cover image: Gustav Klimt, *Portrait of a Lady*, 1916-1917, oil on canvas. Piacenza, Galleria d'Arte Moderna Ricci Oddi. Photo by incamerastock/alamy

Prepress by Grafica Punto Print – Rome

Printed in Canada

CONTENTS

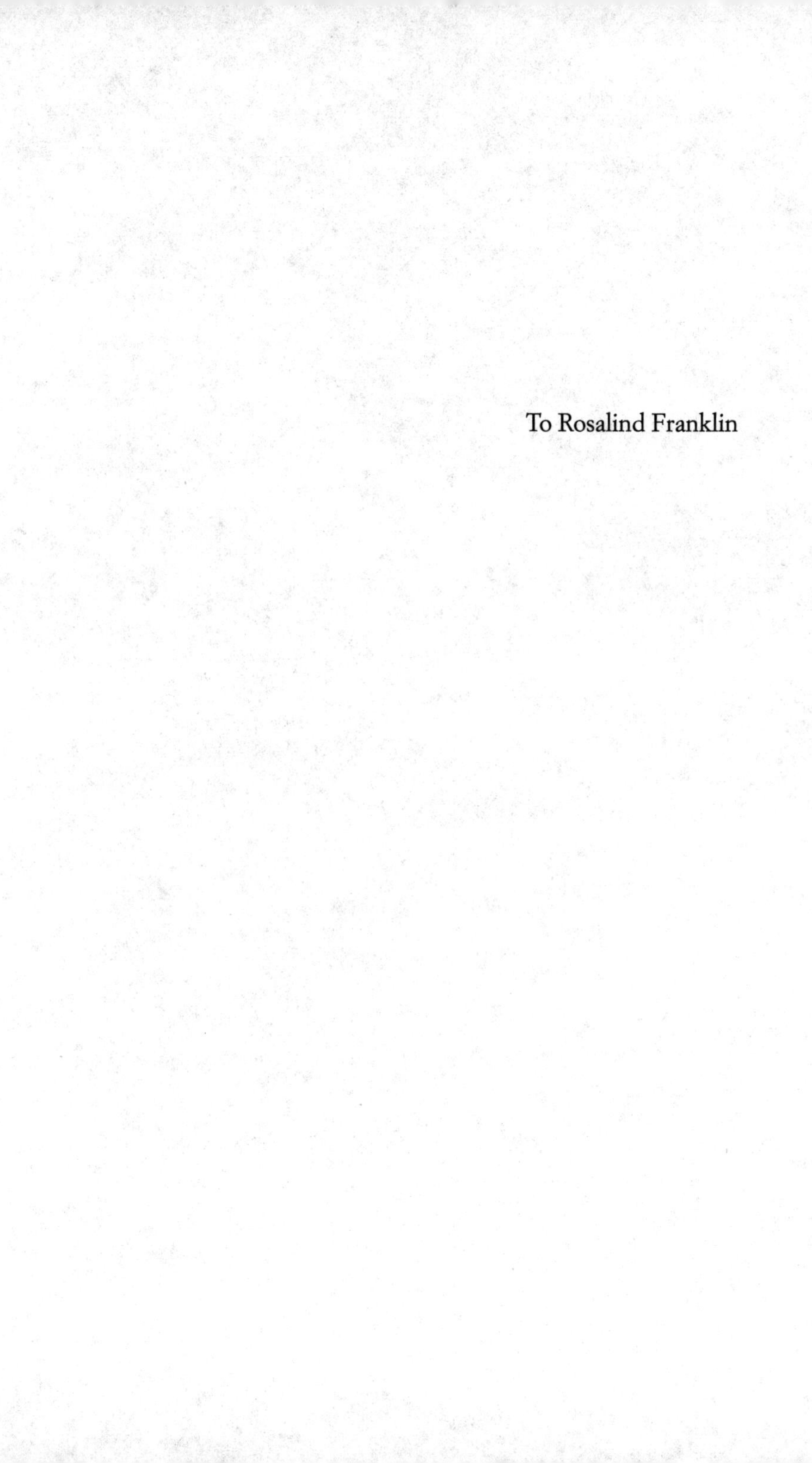

To Rosalind Franklin

PORTRAIT OF AN UNKNOWN WOMAN

The Facts

In 1910, Gustav Klimt painted the portrait of a very young woman, in three-quarter view, with hair loose under a large brown hat, a fur stole around the neck, and seemingly bare shoulders.

This painting, titled *Backfisch* (*Damsel* in English), was exhibited at the Galerie Miethke, in Vienna, in 1916 and bought by an unnamed person, of whom no trace can be found in the records of the time.

In 1917, a year before Klimt's death, and for an unknown reason, the painting was altered by the artist: the hat and stole were removed, the shoulders covered in a white, floral-patterned shawl, and the hair tied back in a demure chignon.

In 1925, in Piacenza, Italy, the art collector Giuseppe Ricci Oddi bought a painting by Klimt titled *Portrait of a Lady*, unaware that it was an altered version of *Damsel.*

It wasn't until 1996 that an art history student at Piacenza University, Claudia Maga, proved that these weren't two different paintings, of which the first had been lost, but one and the same painting, if radically reworked.

Bizarrely, not long after this discovery, on February 22, 1997, the painting was stolen, thus disappearing for a second time.

The investigation got nowhere until the summer of 2016, when a burglar confessed to the Italian police that he had committed the theft. Although the painting was no longer in his possession, he did announce that the person who had commissioned him to steal the work had promised that it would be returned twenty years after the date of its disappearance.

In 2019, the gardener at the Ricci Oddi Gallery of Modern Art discovered, behind some ivy he was about to cut back, a garbage bag containing the painting, which was in perfect condition.

No art expert, no museum curator, no exhibition organizer, no police investigator knows who the young woman depicted in the painting was, or what secrets lie behind the turbulent story of her portrait.

Part One

Swelling to the day and again passing,
The eternally identical tragedy
That thus we play without understanding,
And its insanity's nightly torture
Wreathes the soft glory of beauty
Like a smiling universe of thorns.
—From "Three Dreams" by Georg Trakl

1

Gotta spit to get a shine!"

The boy's eyes widened in disbelief. He must have been around twelve, his complexion pale under the grime smearing his face.

"Spit on their shoes, are you kidding me?"

Isidore stuck to his guns.

"Gotta spit, I tell you, they love it."

Isidore had his own particular style, not a long stream of saliva, but tight movements of the mouth, pffft, pffft, pffft. He expelled his spit like so many tiny marbles, bursting moistly as they landed on the leather, an act that was dynamic, not disgusting. Two years now, he'd been a shoeshine boy, setting up his chair, box, and tin against the Bowling Green railings, which were cast-iron, close-set, and spiked. It wasn't the worst of casual jobs, 10 cents for a proper polish. Most of his customers were generous, some even giving him double the price, potentially making him one of the city's best paid shoeshine boys.

"What's your real name?"

"Gabriel."

"And why does everyone call you Boba?"

"Dunno."

Isidore wondered whether the kid would be up to the job.

To make his polish, he would mix beeswax with soap flakes, turpentine, and boiling water. And a little beetroot juice to bring out the shine. He'd shared his trick with no one. His buddy Ben used banana skins instead. It was Mr. Schmidt who passed his old cloths on to them.

But to get a real sheen, pffft, pffft, you had to spit.

No question, at five minutes per pair, during peak times before the stock exchange opened and after it closed, he could get through up to ten pairs an hour. When a decent laborer was known to be paid 20 dollars a week.

"Work it out yourself . . . I turn round up to thirty pairs a day, so 3, sometimes 4 dollars a day thanks to the gentlemen, that's 18 dollars a week, pal!"

Isidore was bigging himself up a bit, but for a kid like Boba, even 16 dollars a week would have seemed an enormous sum.

"Yeah, well, it's all down to the location."

Isidore's secret was to seem forever pleased and cheerful. And to talk to them. When he smiled, his blue eyes shone with intelligence.

"How are you today, sir, and how's business going?"

He had a sweet little face, luckily, because at nineteen, he really was too old for such work.

Isidore wasn't the type to plan ahead. He made his life up as he went along, and this spontaneity had got him out of a tight corner more than once. Resourcefulness, it's called. And he could roll with the punches and then start again without batting an eyelid. It was just hard luck. His customers, the gents in toppers and front-pleated trousers, thought the same thing: what a waste for a kid like that to do no better than shoeshine boy.

It was with the location that Isidore had been lucky. He'd set up shop precisely when the guy who polished shoes at Bowling Park had quit, and no one had asked him how he'd got the spot or if there'd been an agreement. All the kids who took up this line of work knew it: the pavements belonged to those who kept them. Isidore had been brought up the hard way, no caresses or caprices for him. He wasn't one of those boys nudging model sailboats around the lake in Central Park, with beribboned nannies to watch over them.

"How are you today, sir, and how's business going?"

The man stretched his foot out towards Isidore. He wasn't a regular, but wore the white collar and wide-striped tie of those who worked in the sector. Isidore got straight down to work, with gusto and vigor—the Wall Street bankers liked it that way.

"Business is as good as ever, my boy! Shares going up, up, up!"

"Got some in the RCA?"[1]

"Sure have, my boy, sure have. You interested in technological innovations?"

"I'm interested in everything, sir."

Boba stared at Isidore, goggle-eyed. He had no idea what the RCA was, when, in fact, it was top-tier. Some said that, one day, they'd be able to put radios into cars! And all of Isidore's customers had bought shares in it. In RCA and Coca-Cola, because with Prohibition, shares in Cola had gone up 25% in a month. Could Boba really replace him? He'd just have to. In any case, Isidore didn't want to be a shoeshine boy anymore, that was decided.

Because of Lotte.

Pffft, pffft, pffft. Isidore clenched his jaws and moved his cloth faster. He would smile at his customers, but with the other street kids, the little rats like him, he gave no quarter. If Boba did take over his tin, his box of brushes, his chair, and the golden egg-laying goose that was Bowling Green, he'd have to remain devoted to him.

Isidore could have passed on his site and magic-polish recipe to him, and the kid would have paid him a small cut; but what Isidore didn't want to lose was those hot financial tips. Since he'd made his mind up, since he'd staked everything on the

[1] Radio Corporation of America.

stock exchange, he mustn't mess up. Everyone was speculating, why shouldn't he? Every day, there were headlines about the easy bucks made by unknowns who'd dared to take the plunge. Fortunes made in next to no time, amazing stories. Isidore was no dumber than anyone else.

"How are you today, sir, and how's business going?"

Eighteen dollars a week easily covered the rent on the room he shared with Ben, some half-decent coffee, salami, pickles, potatoes, and a bootlegged beer now and then. He was no great boozer and wanted no trouble with the police. And gin-and-tonic at 35 cents a glass in a speakeasy, no thank you, especially as you risked leaving your sight there. Scary stories were going around town of liquor being adulterated and thinned down with methylated spirits that made you blind.

Eighteen dollars a week, and on Sundays, Isidore and his pal Ben would go dancing at Loew's Theater, in Coney Island. Isidore was no great dancer, but the girls certainly hovered around him and, generally, he obtained their favors.

What crowds there were, on Sundays in Coney Island! It was a mix of workers, students, sailors, traffickers, and baseball players. Folks would come with their families, the children swimming and squealing with glee, the beaches jam-packed, you'd treat yourself to an ice cream, and then there was the Cyclone, the biggest roller coaster in the world! The Cyclone that could scare you silly. Isidore had always told himself that if he took a girl onto it and she didn't scream, he'd marry her. The first time he'd sat in a carriage and found himself perpendicular, holding his head so it didn't tip back, he'd thought his heart would break loose. Twenty-five cents a ride, all the same.

"Thank you, sir, have a good day!"

Boba grabbed a cloth.

"Can I do the next one?"

Isidore nodded, thrusting his fists into his pockets.

"Okay, but don't you forget to ask how business is going, hey!"

If he wanted to quit that line of work, it was for Lotte. A young girl with a thick blond plait, a white dress, and very well polished little ankle boots. She could have screamed on the roller coaster, it would have made no difference; she was perfection incarnate, with the porcelain complexion and rosy cheeks of a doll. The first time Isidore had seen her, she was surrounded by a gaggle of laughing friends. A woman of a certain age seemed to be chaperoning the group. He'd imagined her to be an aunt or a cousin, and the old woman in question had soon spotted the young man and decided to beware of him. But Coney Island was buzzing, and amid all the hubbub and laughter, he'd managed to get close enough to the young girl to ask her name.

"Lotte."

The Germanic sound was as sweet as barley sugar to Isidore's ears.

"Lotte? Delighted to meet you, I'm Werther."

He'd come out with this, quick as a flash, and Lotte's mouth had turned into an "O"—no boy of her age had read Goethe, at least, not as far as she knew.

Since the Great War, German immigrants were keeping a low profile on the American continent, anti-German propaganda was rampant, and in high schools, it would have been unthinkable to teach *The Sorrows of Young Werther* rather than *The Adventures of Tom Sawyer*. Of course, Lotte couldn't have imagined that this was one of the only books Isidore had ever read. For the shoeshine boy, it was far more than good luck, it was fate.

The old woman had soon nipped their enthusiasm in the bud. When a boy started talking literature with a young girl, a roll in the hay wasn't far away. Like the farmer's wife who's spotted a fox on the prowl, she had wanted to usher her silly little geese away. But luckily for Isidore, these young ladies had insisted on having an Italian ice. Sensing his time was limited, he'd asked Lotte which school she went to (Spence, Upper East side), if she'd been on the roller coaster (Only once, her friends had been terrified, but she hadn't), if she often came to Coney Island on a Sunday (Yes, often, especially when it's sunny), then perhaps they'd see each other next Sunday (Perhaps).

He had asked the questions in the right order, so as not to seem too insistent, and had given her his best smile, his special smile, the one that made his customers toss him an extra nickel. And then he'd waited for the following Sunday like he hadn't waited for any other day ever before in his life.

He had immediately become obsessed with her. Needed to know where she was, what she was doing, and where she would go, whether she was thinking of him like he was thinking of her.

His pal Ben had laughed: "Don't know how you're going to find her again in this crowd!" But it hadn't taken Isidore long to spot her among her swirling friends. Just a glimpse of the blond plait, and he'd felt his entire being combust. She was there, and she had seen him, too. He had walked straight up to her, with no shyness, no restraint. Their conversation had instantly resumed, with no awkward silence. He had so many questions to ask her, he wanted to know everything about her, wanted to absorb her. He couldn't look at her too much, because Lotte's mouth, Lotte's shoulders, Lotte's little breasts, which he could make out under the fine white cotton, made him lose his grip. When she'd had to leave, he'd taken her hand and she'd recoiled. Isidore had felt mortified.

And yet, the following Sunday, she had returned. The following Sunday and all the other Sundays. And now, when Isidore appeared, Lotte's friends started to giggle.

The man in the tie slipped 10 cents into Boba's hand. The kid had spat all he could, no one could accuse him of not trying.

"Listen to me, Boba, I'm happy to pass the site on to you, but you're going to have to make them talk."

"Make them talk about what?"

"Well, about their work, about good investments, you know. Like that, in the evening, you can tell me all, d'you see?"

Clearly, Boba didn't see.

Lotte had told Isidore the story of her family. She was the daughter of a German engineer who had landed in New York at twenty-two and was today an oral-hygiene magnate, worst luck. And yet at first, Isidore had misunderstood. When Lotte said "Daddy's factory," he thought the father worked in a toothpaste factory. It took him a few Sundays to grasp that the factory belonged to the daddy in question. He had since bought a tube of "fresh tasting" Chlorodon, which he would religiously spit out into his washbowl every morning with a dreamy expression on his face. He hadn't admitted to Lotte that he was a shoeshine boy, but for some consistency, had said he sold shoes in a store. And like all those who believe in their good fortune without knowing the rules, Isidore was way off the mark: to Lotte, whether a shoe-seller or a shoe-shiner, it was unacceptable. The clear disappointment on the young girl's face had made him feel sick. And yet, at nineteen, trials are to love what wind is to fire: they extinguish the small and fan the great.

"Most of the guys whose shoes you'll be shining work on Wall Street. You must ask them how business is going, like you've seen me do, and then casually say, 'So, what should one invest in right now, sir?'. You stick their reply firmly in your little head, and come evening, you repeat what you've heard to me, that's not hard, is it?"

"No."

Isidore had chosen Boba because he was the kid with the most innocent-looking mug in the Irish neighborhood.

For some time now, he'd been imagining Lotte happening to walk past the Bowling Green railings, and finding himself face to face with her, brush and cloth in hand. He was having nightmares about it. And so it was decided, Boba would do. Isidore would stay with him for two or three days to see how he got on, and then leave the kid to spit in his place.

2

Dense shadows engulfed the second floor room, bearing down on the mother and the open-mouthed infant. Martha heard the morning angelus; it was six o'clock. She reached towards the makeshift cradle, made for her out of a crate by the kind neighbor on the first floor, and took hold of her baby. She lifted her nightshirt and laid the still-sleeping mite against the living warmth of her breast.

The chubby little hands gripped the nipple and a drop of milk seeped out. Silently, the infant began to suck. He was a baby that didn't cry; had never cried. Even on the day he was born. Martha had thought he was stillborn because he hadn't let out a sound. Which might have been better for both of them. She pulled the sheet back up, it was cold. The baby was pinching her hard now, a sensation both painful and sweet. She looked out of the room's only window, dawn hadn't broken. The sucking slowed down, the baby would soon be full. She waited a few more minutes, delaying the moment when she'd have to put her feet on the cold, dusty floorboards. Finally, still groggy with sleep, she felt her way to the candle and lit it with a match.

The room became lighter, and the contours of the table in the corner, and the cupboard in which Martha stored linen and food, could be made out. She bent over to stir the embers in the stove. She would cover the fire every evening and add a small lump of coal in the morning, that was sufficient, the baby was eight months old now, and strapping. She put the kettle on the stovetop for coffee. From the other side of the wall, she heard the neighbor grunting. The man was a brute who battered and screwed his wife indiscriminately. She changed the baby and dressed him.

Her hands were itching. Despite applying a little butter at night, particularly on the thumb joints, eczema still inflamed her skin. At the factory, the most recent recruits were sent to the vats, and the products added to the water left you with rough, red patches, causing unbearable irritation. Martha knew that scratching just made it worse. She would cut her fingernails short, but at night, the itching intruded on her dreams. By morning, her hands had bled and the sheets were stained.

She had a quick wash and rolled her hip-length hair into a tight bun on top of her head, then splashed cold water on her face, which really woke her up. Once ready, she cut a slice of bread, popped the loaf back under the cloth, and drank her coffee standing, with baby on hip. She then put a thick woolly on the little one and threw a shawl around her shoulders, they needed to hurry.

The childminder's house was right opposite the factory, which was very handy. This woman, scrawny as a cat saved from drowning, had seven children in her care, all sons and daughters of feather girls. She wasn't a bad childminder, but she had her favorites. Sometimes cheerful and energetic, sometimes exasperated, she wore a long blue apron covered in traces of snot and tears—the little ones would blubber against it and blow their noses on it, in turn.

"Good morning, Mrs. Prato."

"Good morning, Martha."

"Can I leave him with you?"

The baby reached out to the childminder, who took him with a smile. If only all babies were as easy as this one.

"Yes, that's it, leave him with me, off you go. See you later!"

The price of the childminding included a bowl of soup at midday for the mothers who were still breastfeeding. They would run out of the factory, breasts swollen, down their soup in one, feed their baby, and then be off again, just as fast. It was a good arrangement.

Martha went to join the line stretching out before the factory doors. There were a good hundred of them, buns tied tight in the early morning chill. Work started at seven and ended twelve hours later. Martha was on the vats with two other girls as strong as her. Anna and Zita. The former was freckled and good-humored, the latter stuck her big belly out to act as a counterbalance when she worked the stirring poles.

The vats were installed slightly apart from the main building, owing to the smells they gave off. Smells so noxious that, in the early days, they gave Martha a headache, but then she got used to them. The factory specialized in the processing of plumes for the military. When the feathers arrived, they were already damp and heavy from the mix of spirits and salted water used to disinfect them.

Martha, Anna, and Zita worked on grease removal. They would tip the sacks of feathers into the vats and stir the beige water, made milky by the detergent. Thousands of gray crane feathers that stuck together and got their barbs entangled. Gradually, the swirling of their pointed shafts and tiny tips cleaving the surface became hypnotic, so the direction of the stirring had to be reversed, until, finally, the fragile, clingy things separated from each other. It was repetitive work, demanding great physical strength, but at seventeen, Martha was tough. She wasn't talkative, far less than her two workmates, and yet Anna and Zita had soon taken the new girl under their wing. Maybe she inspired their pity? There was a sad sweetness in the eyes of the young woman, as if her heart were weighed down with a stone of silence.

"Sister of stormy gloom, / Look, a frightened boat sinks / Under stars, / The silent countenance of night."[2]

[2] From "Lament" by Georg Trakl.

Martha had listened to some poets reciting their verses one evening, and found it so wonderful. She had touched beautiful things, not for long, but just enough to know that poetry existed and that it wasn't for her.

She had waited for the end of winter, the baby was six months old, it was high time. She'd stuffed the baby carriage with their few belongings, sewn her meager savings into the hem of her skirt, tied her hair into a bun, and set off early in the morning, going up the Danube with no prospect other than leaving the great, imperial city of Vienna, so crushing in its magnificence, with its immaculate facades, horse-drawn carriages, and roaring motorcars. Vienna with its sidewalks, on which elegant ladies in plumed hats passed those dubbed "girls on the line", because the police restricted the paving they were allowed to solicit on with an invisible line. And Vienna was teeming with brothels, nightclubs, and cabarets. Feminine charms were on sale publicly, at all hours and all prices. For gentlemen in top hats and black frock coats, procuring a woman for fifteen minutes or a night required as little effort as buying a pack of cigarettes. Two hundred crowns for a dancer at the Opera, two crowns for a street girl in dodgy makeup. Martha was no fool, in her situation, sooner or later she would have joined the exhausted cohort of starving, sad women who sold pleasure with no pleasure, and all wound up in hospital. She was pretty, had even posed for an artist. But she had her honor.

Today, she lived the life of a little old lady, clean and proper. She spent nothing, except for food, rent, and childcare. No dancing, no entertainment, no going out, no drinking. On Sundays, she would go to the wash house to do the baby's linen, then to Mass to cleanse her soul and cherish her memories of love in the cool calm of a church. Her sole guilty pride, since she could hardly think of herself as free, was to owe nothing to anyone.

She had pushed the baby carriage some 30 kilometers from Vienna, then stopped at Leobendorf, in front of the red sign of a café. She had walked through the door and asked at the bar whether they had any work. The manageress had examined her from head to foot.

"Go and see at the feather factory, it's on the edge of town, at the end of the main street. They hire your kind."

She was conscious of walking along a beam above the void with a baby on her back. But she knew that factories were less concerned about unmarried mothers, and that in villages, bastard children far outnumbered legitimate ones.

"You should leave me your kid, all the same, while you go and see."

"Really? I can leave him with you? You'll see, he's very good, never cries."

The woman had nodded her head.

"When it comes to kids, I had seven, so . . . crying . . . I'm used to it. But don't take too long, hey!"

The foreman had asked her if she had any experience.

"No, but I'm a hard worker."

References?

"No, but I'm a decent girl."

That had been enough.

Since then, with back bent, she watched the days go by as she swirled the feathers around on the surface of the water. When she got into bed, exhausted, with the baby at her breast, his warmth would send her to sleep, and she often didn't even have the energy to put him back in the cradle Mr. Gruber had made.

Mr. Gruber was very fond of Martha. He was far too old to be her suitor, but she could have asked him for almost anything she wanted, and he would have complied, "just like that, to help out, between neighbors." He would smile sweetly at the baby, and had a charming way of doffing his cap whenever they passed on the stairs, as if Martha were a lady, when she was nothing at all. Several times he'd offered her a little glass of schnapps, "in the name of friendship," but she'd turned him down.

This evening, once again, he had knocked on her door.

"Madam Martha, apologies, I wouldn't want to disturb you, but I've brought you a slice of apple tart."

She had remained at the door.

"Thank you very much, Mr. Gruber, that's very kind of you, you shouldn't have."

The man was smiling at her.

"Is the baby doing well?"

"Yes, thanks, he's a good boy."

"Is he sleeping?"

"Yes."

"Don't give him any tart, hey, because there's rum in it."

Mr. Gruber started laughing, but Martha got the impression that it was forced laughter. She was so tired; she should have invited the neighbor in and they could have eaten the tart together, but something, she couldn't quite put it into words, something intrusive about this man's persistence told her to beware. Of course, he was considerate and affable, and she was so alone; why would she refuse the well-meaning friendship of a neighbor?

Above all, she didn't want to seem rude. Her hand was still on the latch. From the way Mr. Gruber was standing, almost past the door, leaning forwards, very close to her, she felt uncomfortable. It was something subtle, intuition perhaps, a mute discomfort. He kept on smiling at her in silence. Some would have called it a simian smile, though Martha had never seen a monkey in her life. She sensed that he was imposing himself on her, conveying the tacit order that she respect his status as a man. Refusing him would be an awful affront. She should make things easy for him.

She tried to reassure herself, to fight the strange tightness of her throat. She was just imagining things. Mr. Gruber was a friend who wanted to help her because he pitied her, she knew she inspired pity in lots of people. Had she been brave, she would have tried to read that in Mr. Gruber's eyes, because she was naïve enough to think that people's eyes didn't lie. But precisely because she feared seeing something other than friendliness in them, she kept her eyes fixed on the floor. This only made her look sweeter, or more fragile, who knows what the first-floor neighbor was thinking right now of a seventeen-year-old girl who'd got herself knocked up and run away from Vienna with her baby to hide away in a shabby boarding house like the one they lived in?

"Are you feeling alright, Martha?"

He had placed his hand on her arm, and she didn't move.

"I worry about you, you know, it's not easy to be a young mother . . ."

He had adopted a sincere tone; for a moment, she felt reassured, perhaps it was just her who had bad thoughts. Mr. Gruber was so old, he could've been her grandfather!

"Don't worry about me, Mr. Gruber, kind as that is. It's only that the days are long, as you know, I'm tired, I think I need to sleep."

"Of course, I understand, in which case . . ."

This time, he looked fixedly at her, his pupils dilated with desire. A shudder coursed through Martha's body.

"In which case . . . Good night . . . Martha."

Her heart began to pound so hard, she felt sure Mr. Gruber could hear her fear. She still found the strength to say:

"Good night, Mr. Gruber, many thanks for the tart."

She closed the door as slowly as she could, so as not to show that she'd understood. She would fear him now, whenever their paths crossed in the house. She pressed her ear to the flimsy door and heard the firm tread of the man as he went down the stairs, as if stamping on each step on purpose, as if his footsteps were saying, "We will be back."

3

Well into her forties, with peroxide-blond hair and stiff, silicone-pumped breasts bulging under the turtleneck she'd thought *classy*, Michelle had put on her fake pearl necklace and large, clip-on gold earrings to look like Angelica Nero, the formidable businesswoman who broke JR in *Dallas*. But she had to lay her hands flat on her knees because she was shaking. She gazed at her manicured nails, pearly coral, filed into a perfect almond shape. She mustn't let herself be overawed; after all, it was she who was the client.

Whenever she was with her daughter or her friends, Michelle was more the loud-mouth type who lets no one tread on their toes. She'd been through so much in her life. But here, in this carpeted office at the top of a glass tower overlooking Houston's wide, deserted thoroughfares, her throat had gone dry.

Michelle had a typically "her" way of talking about the birth of her daughter. Pearl was "a condom accident," a condom slip-up. Why that particular day? Why that particular client? She would raise her eyes heavenwards and answer herself: "Anyhow, now, what's done is done!"

"Four years later, you say. You don't know the exact date?"

"I can check. We kept the magazine."

"But when you discovered that you were pregnant, you didn't try to check . . . I don't know . . . the registers?"

Registers of what? This attorney clearly didn't know what he was on about. The men who came to Gigi's paid in cash and left no trace; even the regulars never gave their surname.

The attorney seemed doubtful. People were when she told her story, and yet she was absolutely certain, one hundred percent sure, because she had a great memory for faces, had never forgotten one.

When little Pearl was around four, or almost five, Michelle had walked past a newsstand and spotted the face of the guy, now wearing a tie, on the cover of a finance magazine. She'd bought the magazine and brought it home to her daughter, saying: "He's your father, right there!" They'd cut out the photo and put it in a frame, to make it official. The man was the CEO of a major industrial group, and it would have looked bad for this guy to be sullied with a bastard child.

Multimillionaire. She'd played a bit on that, during Pearl's childhood. She'd say to her: "If you're not happy, you can just go and complain to your father!" But anyhow, things never went further than that. Pearl had brought herself up, she was an easy child.

Michelle had never asked anything of anyone, but now, it wasn't for her, it was for her daughter.

"Columbia! That's incredible, that is! Congratulations!"

The enthusiastic tone of the attorney didn't fool Michelle. The shrillness of that *incredible* pierced her like a blade being plunged into her ear.

She got in to Columbia? To study law? With the mother she's got, that's in-cred-i-ble!

Incredible, with a mother who's a prostitute, to pursue such prestigious studies? They could all go fuck themselves! If she'd been perfectly honest, Michelle would have admitted that she hadn't believed it, either. Hadn't believed that her daughter was that clever. She'd never taken any interest in Pearl's education. You didn't have to go to university to make a success of your life. Only those who'd studied thought it important; the rest knew you could manage very well without.

Her story was simple, she'd told it loads of times.

"When I went past the newsstand, I thought I was hallucinating. But it was him alright, and a millionaire to boot!"

"Millionaire or multimillionaire?"

She loathed the condescending tone of the man sitting behind the big, shiny desk.

"You know what I mean . . . very rich, rich enough to pay for his daughter's studies."

Because, Columbia or not, even with a scholarship, the kid would have to take out a loan, and Michelle refused for her girl to start out in life with a thirty-year debt.

"Do you know the precise date of conception?"

"No. Well, my daughter was born in December 1969, so we know it was in March of that year."

"My dear Miss Alvez, with that kind of vagueness, your story won't hold water in front of a judge."

"And if we do a DNA test?"

The man of the law remained silent. At 100 dollars for thirty minutes, Michelle was thinking that his silence was certainly golden.

He was the best attorney in Houston, dark and brooding. *A man of power*. Michelle's heart contracted at the thought that, one day, Pearl would be one of these people, too, if they could play this card right. She'd come alone because the last thing she wanted to inflict on her daughter was the "your story won't hold water" refrain. The first time she'd heard about DNA tests, she'd instantly thought of Pearl's father. She had no desire to be called a liar, and with these new tests, doubts were no longer allowed, guys were forced to own up.

"That's why my question is: does one have the right to force someone to take these tests?"

The attorney paused again. He hadn't expected this vulgar woman to be aware of the latest scientific advances. So far, DNA tests had been used to catch murderers, not men denying paternity.

Michelle saw a flicker of light in the attorney's eyes and knew that her instinct hadn't deceived her: a DNA test was a good idea.

She spent her time listening to the radio or the TV. Was that due to a fear of finding herself alone with her bad thoughts? She needed to hear a voice other than her own, constantly. She devoured all kinds of programs, from reports to talk shows, to interviews, to soaps, and could only sleep with the TV on.

Her daughter was unlike her in every way, especially physically. Michelle had dark-brown eyes and a dark, almost amber, complexion. When Pearl was born, she was so pale, so pink! It was her friend Cynthia who'd said, at the hospital, "You should call her Pearl, she's a real pearl, that one!", and very soon the baby girl had two blue marbles instead of eyes, which was some surprise! Although Pearl had inherited her mother's brown hair, hers turned auburn under the slightest ray of sunshine. Today, she was a pretty young girl of nineteen, with rosy cheeks, a beauty spot high on one cheek, and a slightly sad look in her eyes.

"Hold on, I didn't say that I didn't believe you, I think you're sincere, but imagine what the court would say!"

"But if I'm asking you for a DNA test, it's because I'm absolutely certain!"

"Calm down, ma'am, calm down."

It was her former boss at Chez Gigi, old Max, who'd recommended this attorney to her. Having himself had to battle it out when divorcing his third wife. "Trust me, in family law, he's the tops, my dear."

For a long time, Michelle had done striptease in a bar on the outskirts of Houston, but the nighttime hours exhausted her, and also, she'd been gradually building up her regulars. So she'd worked things out and, with Max's blessing, had quit. Today, she turned over six or seven clients a week. It was enough for her. She wasn't always sensible with money, liked to have a girls' night out every now and then, a bit of cocaine and champagne. Especially champagne, it was *classy*. And then she'd just take on an extra client; she managed her budget day to day. The less she worked, the better she felt, but she wasn't lazy, when she needed to go for it, she went for it.

"A simple detail, was the child conceived in Texas?"

"Yes."

"And she was born in Texas?"

"Yes."

"Right. And your child doesn't have a putative father?"

Michelle didn't understand the question.

"Does your daughter have your surname? She wasn't recognized legally by a man who wasn't her biological father?"

"No, um . . . Yes, she has my surname, and no, I mean she hasn't been recognized legally by anyone."

"Very good, then it might well set a precedent, jurisprudence-wise."

Jurisprudence, that was a word Michelle had often heard on the TV. The attorney thought it important to explain.

"I'm going to do some research, if you authorize me to, but I'm pretty sure that we would be the first to subpoena a man to undergo a DNA test in an action for legal recognition of paternity. No . . . I don't believe there's any precedent, and that's why, of course, the judge will need to be on our side, but . . . but it could prove very interesting."

For me, interesting for me, the attorney thought. Yes, it was surprising that this woman should have come up with such an idea. And if the father really was the boss of the industrial empire she'd named to him, it would be spectacular! That man would be protected by an army of attorneys, and that, too, was all to the good. The horny old multimillionaire, the stripper who'd be seen as a Mother Courage, and the brilliant daughter with a place at Columbia to study law, all the American soap-opera boxes were ticked! They would make the headlines for sure.

"And how much will it cost me?"

"Nothing at all."

Michelle couldn't believe her ears; the attorney beamed at her.

"Nothing at all?"

"I'll pay myself from whatever I get you to win . . . And believe me, I'll get you to win a lot . . . If, of course, you really are absolutely certain."

He studied the client, and his eyes became those of a wolf weighing up the goat's resistance. He had adopted an unctuous tone because he didn't want this case to slip away from him now, but he wanted to see whether this kind of innuendo would destabilize her, whether she was the sort to blub or to fly off the handle. *Are you certain? You, the prostitute who has sex with all those men? You're certain? How can you really know which of them is the father of your child?*

His office had been endlessly visited by liars, smooth talkers, bluffers, impostors, and hoaxers of all kinds. Over time, he had learnt to sort wheat from chaff. At first sight, this woman didn't seem like a compulsive liar, and the fact that she was requesting a DNA test was proof of her good faith. But did one ever really know?

"Your daughter, does she know you've come to see me?"

"No."

"Why not?"

"I first wanted to know whether it was possible."

"Is your daughter tough?"

Michelle would have liked the whole business to be resolved amicably, receiving a check for closing her mouth was more than fine with her. Since she didn't answer, the attorney was suddenly worried.

"I mean, will she be tough enough to face a media storm? Because what you're about to go through, it's going to be *massive*!"

He had jumped up, and Michelle felt even smaller in the deep leather armchair.

"Do you fully understand me? I say *you* in the plural, meaning you and your daughter, *both of you*, but not only you two. After this lawsuit, *all* mothers will want to do like *you*! You will be their model! The first to show them the way! And for all those who brave the unknown, well, the way isn't paved. You'll have to forge ahead. You'll have to face the aggression head-on, not be afraid, not back away."

Seeing his client's alarmed expression, he suddenly calmed down, paced slowly right around the office, stopped in front of her, and took her hand with utmost gentleness.

"My dear Michelle . . . you don't mind me calling you Michelle? You can hardly be unaware that the tabloid press is going to have a field day with our case . . ."

4

A year had gone by, and at the back of a drawer in Lotte's dresser, folded and hidden between two handkerchiefs, lay Isidore's love letters. The handwriting was cramped, careful, childish. It was the bottom drawer, so you had to kneel down and thrust your arms deep inside, to elbow level, to stand a chance of getting hold of the starched hankies, so they could reveal their secrets.

The first time, it wasn't a letter, just a note, a piece of paper folded in four, no bigger than a carousel ticket, which he'd slipped into her hand, and on which he'd written: "*Ich traume nicht, ich wähne nicht.*"[3] To avoid the risk of making spelling mistakes in English, Isidore had chosen to copy out lines in his native tongue from *The Sorrows of Young Werther.* The German had resonated in the young girl's heart like the promise of a love destined solely for her. The following Sunday, she had prepared a reply that she had given him just before they said goodbye, and Isidore had thought the ground was giving way beneath his feet.

And so a secret correspondence had begun. These exchanges of little envelopes, no sooner given, no sooner hidden in the folds of skirts and the pockets of trousers, had immediately obliged the youngsters to be bold. Certainly, Lotte's chaperone was wary of Isidore, but she'd ended up finding him, all in all, pretty inoffensive, since he'd never attempted any physical

[3] I'm not dreaming, I'm not imagining [this].

closeness, at least, not that she'd noticed, and seemed to be a young man who respected propriety. They would part with a simple wave, saying "See you next week!", like good friends. What the chaperone didn't know was that each one was leaving with their own trophy, a piece of the other one that they could hold, touch, and contemplate, as if the ink had come to life. Isidore himself kept these letters carefully under his pillow, and his dreams were restless.

With summer drawing to a close, Lotte clearly wouldn't be going to Coney Island on Sunday afternoons anymore. So she'd suggested to Isidore that he write to her at home (she had enough freedom to receive letters at her address without fearing their interception). Her parents were pragmatic people and, having never fallen under the spell of one, weren't too concerned about the power of an epistolary relationship.

Isidore was crazy about her. So viscerally in love that it was making him ill, a visceral love, and the mere thought of Lotte tied his stomach in knots. The young girl was both the cause of the sickness and the remedy. As soon as he just glimpsed her, a diffuse heat (Where did it come from? The chest, the stomach, the throat?) would start throbbing in his veins, and his organs were reduced to formless magma. It impacted on his breathing and cut his appetite. If only he could have held her in his arms and hugged her, hugged her with all his might, he could have started to live normally again.

As the months went by, he'd finally convinced himself that Lotte was the solution to his suffering; it would be enough for her to say just one word and all his childhood wounds would be healed. Never had Isidore dared to kiss her; just the thought of lightly brushing her lips would make his eyes burn, and he'd see stars.

When he was with her, he was no longer remotely conscious of time passing. Once back home, he could only vaguely remember what they'd said to each other. Despite their social disparity, and although Lotte was a girl (because boys and girls understand each other so little), they were twin flames.

Isidore lived on Mulberry Street. A rough street in one of the city's most disreputable neighborhoods. He'd considered giving Lotte a slightly smarter address, where he'd have wangled collecting his mail, but the risk of one of her letters getting lost was far more unbearable than that of her discovering his seedy abode. And since the young girl made no comment, he'd realized that the mean streets of Five Points were totally unknown to her. He was safe on that score.

Once winter arrived, it was Lotte's idea that they meet up to go ice skating. It was about time as their correspondence had taken a passionate turn and after all those poems on autumn and their hearts being borne by the wind, seeing each other in the flesh would bring them back to reality and temper their fantasies of ethereal love.

Fearing he'd end up on his butt, a fate worse than death, Isidore had practiced furiously. Naturally agile and athletic, he'd soon been able to emulate the other skaters, and, after just three days, he was swirling around with a certain elegance. He'd bought himself a thick woolen jacket, a warm hat, and a scarf with wide stripes to look like a student, because the poor always appear poorer in winter. And then he'd waited for her, imagining how they would glide side by side, hands gripped through gloves, cold breath billowing from their mouths, and the intensity of his desire had scared him.

Lotte had duly arrived, wearing a pink coat with ermine collar, and matching fur hat and muff. She was like a china doll arriving on the ice. The most beautiful girl in New York, and perhaps even in the world! And it was at Isidore that she was smiling. From this day on, the young man's panic of reason, had known no bounds.

In Lotte's eyes, he'd read all that she'd refrained from writing to him. "She loves me, she loves me like I love her," he kept repeating to give himself courage. And every flutter of her eyelashes, every lift of her eyebrow seemed to confirm the devastation between them.

From waking to going to bed, Isidore was haunted by the secret of this love, endlessly thinking about it. And paradoxically, the more entrenched the feeling became within him, the more his bashfulness in the young girl's presence increased, almost paralyzing him.

If the truth of this first love was expressed in Isidore's timidity, for Lotte, it was in her discovery of an unsuspected boldness. She was eighteen and treasured by her parents, particularly her father, who saw her as an angel of beauty and innocence. It wasn't that Lotte was brazen, but having been so spoilt by her father, who ceded to her every whim, she wasn't used to being thwarted in her desires.

Once it was spring again, the young woman's blood reached boiling point. Now that the gloves they'd worn for skating had been cast to the back of the cupboard, her skin could brush against his, and when their fingertips touched, it sent such shivers through her, it was almost unbearable. And one day, Lotte kissed Isidore.

On a Sunday in April, back at the Coney Island fun fair, the two sweethearts were queuing at the Italian ice stall. Lotte's usual friends had gone off to buy cotton candy. Amidst the laughter, the music from the attractions, and the cries of little ones tugging at their mothers' skirts to get a giant barley sugar cane or a cone of doughnuts, Isidore was talking into Lotte's neck, as quietly as possible, as if he wanted his words to enter her soul. He was gazing at her nape and the fine blond hairs that had escaped from her chignon. There were crowds of people around them, a hubbub of laughter and exclamation, but the only voice that mattered was that of Isidore, murmuring into Lotte's ear, and slowly, very slowly, the young girl had turned her head. He had been left almost hanging there, leaning forward. The tip of Lotte's nose had brushed against his cheek, electrifying them both. In slow motion, Lotte's lips had paused at the corner of Isidore's mouth, and without knowing whether they were being seen or watched, the way children think they're hidden when they cover their face with their hands, they had both closed their eyes and shared their first kiss.

Returning to Mulberry Street had been simply dreadful. If he could, he would have struck his own heart. Lotte just had to be his wife, he just had to make his fortune.

When he'd left his site and his tin of polish to Boba, he had gone to find one of his customers, an Irishman he'd always really liked, and who wore fine tweed suits. Isidore had asked him, very simply: "Could you tell me what I should do to invest 1,000 dollars on the stock market?" The man hadn't batted an eyelid; 1,000 dollars was a very great sum for a shoeshine boy, but everyone had their secrets. He had introduced him to a broker and advised him not to put all his eggs in the same basket. Isidore hadn't listened to him. He'd already promised himself he would succeed, succeed absolutely. Like a gambler who enters a casino for the first time, he'd staked all his savings in one go. He had been lucky, beginner's luck.

Boba continued to ask the Wall Street bankers how business was going and which companies to invest in, on Isidore's behalf. The broker and Isidore had become friends—he had a good nose, the lad, and talent. But more than anything, it was the time itself that fostered wild hopes. Over eight years, the Dow Jones Index had climbed by 468%. Even movie stars, such as Charlie Chaplin and Groucho Marx, were speculating. There were hundreds of thousands like Isidore, large and small investors, who *believed*, and the market proved them right in doing so. In just those early days of 1929, sixty new companies had been listed on the New York Stock Exchange!

At first, he'd thought he couldn't do without the advice of those whose shoes he'd polished, but he was wrong. There were good tips everywhere, you just had to take an interest in it all, the days of pot luck were over, and Isidore had become very serious. All day long, he read the papers and spoke with brokers, mainly Irish ones. They would discuss General Electric, General Motors, Philip Morris, Honeywell, and Texaco. He liked technological innovations, became passionate about AT&T,[4] and particularly loved the brilliant Telegraphic Ticketing Machine, which issued the listings in almost real time right across America. He had learnt how to buy on margin and his profits had soared, because now, for one dollar invested, he'd be lent ten dollars. There was almost no risk involved! He had set himself a target. To possess 6,000 dollars.

Since September, prices kept moving up and up, it was crazy how much they were moving up. Wanting to remain faithful to his first lie about being a shoe-seller, he estimated that 6,000 dollars would allow him to buy a business and establish himself as an honest retailer of shoes (best quality leather—elegance and refinement for the modern man—that kind of thing), though, in truth, the plan wasn't quite finalized in his head. With 6,000 dollars put aside, he could claim to provide a future for Lotte.

In the meantime, the two sweethearts faced the greatest challenges in seeing each other. It would have been unthinkable for them to go to the movies together. As for rumors, if he'd waited for her outside school, in full sight of the young girl's giggly friends, that would have been worst of all. So, they had very few opportunities to be together.

[4] The American Telephone and Telegraph Company.

Lotte and her family attended the Presbyterian church on Fifth Avenue. The temptation of seeing her, in the company of her father and mother, of observing her with head bowed, devotedly murmuring a prayer, and then imagining himself before the pastor marrying them, she with a white lace veil over her blond locks, he in pinstriped morning coat and trousers, under the benevolent gaze of Lotte's father, who would have adopted Isidore like his own son . . . the image of this perfect happiness was so vivid that he couldn't resist the pleasure of getting closer to it.

He walked through the porch just before 9:00 A.M. With the sermon starting at 9:30, he wanted to find a position from which he could see without being seen. He'd put on his best clothes, and you couldn't really tell whether he belonged to the lower-middle merchant class or not, he just looked like a handsome, modest, but well-kempt young man, and his shoes were impeccably polished. The nave was divided by three aisles; he decided to position himself up on the balcony.

He was just approaching the stairs when she appeared before him. She was wearing a blue coat and one of those fashionable cloche hats. Edged with a wide burgundy ribbon, it contrasted with the gold of the young woman's wavy hair. Isidore lowered his eyes and noticed the two-tone pumps, possibly kid—he was no expert on women's shoes. He felt lost and immediately regretted having come. He'd have liked to just disappear, but it was too late. He saw Lotte's father, dark-haired with a stern-looking moustache, a side-parting, steel-gray eyes. The small, upturned white collar, spotless, and the fitted cashmere jacket spoke of the wealthy, tough businessman. Lotte's mother was plumper, untidier, her fine fur coat not fully buttoned and gaping. Isidore was surprised, he'd not pictured her like this, graying hair short and curly, pillbox hat askew.

Gradually, clusters of men and women in their Sunday best, and small children who had been told to behave, filled the pews with their respectful murmuring. Isidore found himself facing the inexorable dilemma of his ruin or his salvation. Lotte was still in three-quarter view, so, without thinking, without looking back, he made his escape.

The sunshine flooding the steps outside hurt his eyes, he felt like vomiting, vomiting the harshness of a life that had never allowed him to hope for anything, vomiting this impossible love and his ludicrous dreams of a fortune.

He walked back along Fifth Avenue, head down, *Lotte*, *Lotte*, *Lotte*, those two syllables cadenced his steps. He now had 5,786 dollars, he was nearing his target, but would that be enough? How much did a fur coat like the mother's cost? He felt like praying—don't they say that prayer is the trembling sister of love? But he'd barely looked heavenwards before a feeling of total helplessness overcame him. *5,786 dollars, you're way off the mark, you idiot. A girl like Lotte deserves so much more than that. It'll never work.* He pictured her, radiant behind the counter of their shoe store: "Good morning, sir. Welcome to Shoes for the Modern Man! Which style would you like to try on?" *Shoes for the Modern Man, what nonsense!* And the truth was, he had no intention of becoming a small retailer. He loved the stock market too much for that. No, he must keep going the way he'd started, expand his portfolio, and get to 10,000 dollars, and then, then . . . Recently, a broker had impressed on him the merits of a chemical laboratory that was working on a patented antiseptic for the general public. But it was risky. And Isidore loathed doctors.

"Hey! Hi, Isidore!"

The nasal voice of the kid saved him from the storm raging inside his skull.

"Hey!"

Isidore spotted Boba waving his arms on the opposite sidewalk. He then darted across the road and planted himself in front of Isidore, looking pleased as punch.

"Hi!"

"Hi! How's things?"

"Funnily enough, I wanted to see you."

"Oh yeah? Why?"

Boba, with fists deep in pockets, milked a silence. Isidore found him comical, trying to draw attention to himself like that.

"Because I have some news on business, as you might say."

"Oh yeah? Go on then, out with it!"

"Well . . . um, well . . ."

"Well what?"

He was starting to annoy him, playing hard to get like this.

"Well, you'd do well to pull out, because it seems business risks turning sour."

"Who told you this bullshit?"

"Whoa! It's not bullshit! You're the one who told me to repeat to you whatever I was told, aren't you? Well, just yesterday, I was talking business like you asked me to, and one of the regulars just said, laughing: "If the shoeshine boys know as much as me, it's time for me to pull out!"[5] I asked him what he meant, and he said that too many folks were interested in the stock market, and you mustn't believe in miracles, that the higher it rose, the more vertiginous the fall would be, I remember clearly that he used that word, *vertiginous* . . ."

Isidore felt sick.

". . . and that folks in general understood nothing about business, but if there were too many in the boat, it would end up sinking, and I thought, I must tell that to Isidore, if I come across him."

Isidore remained silent. He had 5,786 dollars. It wasn't enough. He thought again of that miracle antiseptic business. He had to pull it off at least one more time. And anyhow, he had no choice, he didn't know how to swim.

[5] "When the shoeshine boys have tips, the stock market is too popular for its own good." Joe Kennedy.

5

The carriage had finally turned onto Hietzinger Haupstraße, then onto Feldmühlgasse. It was already no longer the city, and almost the countryside. The Master had agreed to receive Franz at 4 o'clock, and Franz was extremely punctual. He walked along the gravel path lined with apple trees made shiny by the rain. The small house looked out onto an orchard that stretched as far as the eye could see. It wasn't at all how Franz had imagined the Master's studio to be.

A light drizzle moistened the air, he checked the painting was well protected. He'd taken care to wrap it in several layers of fabric. He was holding it firmly under his arm, it wasn't a large painting, it must measure around 70 by 50 centimeters, but it was cumbersome all the same. Since he was really afraid of damaging it, Franz walked with care.

The paneled door was ajar. He knocked to make his arrival known, and entered directly into what must be used as a study or a dining room. A table, two chairs, a black-lacquered, glass-fronted bookcase in which statuettes were displayed, and hanging on the wall to his right, a dozen or so Japanese prints of identical size, lined up vertically.

A young woman draped in a kind of kimono that allowed a hint of her naked silhouette underneath, suddenly appeared.

"I have an appointment with Mr. Klimt," Franz said, presenting his card.

She took it nonchalantly and told him to wait; then, making the panels of her kimono billow, she disappeared.

Franz remained somewhat stunned by this atmosphere of muffled silence; he got the impression that, outside, the rain had started to fall again. He had kept the painting in his arms, almost put it down, then changed his mind, thinking that it wouldn't be respectful.

He didn't have to wait long. The young woman returned, her kimono half-open, and Franz was disturbed because he belonged to a world in which, particularly in the middle of the afternoon, women wouldn't allow the merest triangle of skin to reveal itself. Hair tied back but tousled, to say the least, he wasn't used to that, either; she told him to follow her. The panels of her dressing gown furled and unfurled in such a way as to make her look like a butterfly.

She led Franz into a room that must be a bedroom since a large bed took pride of place, but from the pungent smell of turpentine and the tangle of easels and canvases, he concluded he was in the studio.

Gustav Klimt moved towards him. The year was 1917. Klimt was fifty-five and Franz twenty-nine. But at twenty-nine, Franz was still a child.

"Mr. Brombeere?"

Franz bowed.

"Thank you for agreeing to receive me, sir, it's a great honor for me to meet you."

Franz admired all artists, whether they be poets, musicians, or painters, but in his eyes, Gustav Klimt was the greatest Viennese artist of his time, maybe even of all time! The elevated world Franz had grown up in might have been frequently shocked by the flights of fancy of the Master, who, regardless of scandal, would shamelessly paint lascivious, callipygian women displaying their buttocks in murals on official buildings, but Franz knew how incredibly fortunate he was to be allowed into his studio, the holy of holies. And he just stood there with his wrapped-up painting under his arm, a bit sheepish, not knowing where to start.

"Do sit down, let's sit down!"

Klimt had a strong, gravelly voice. He indicated the bed, covered in a cloth with wide black and white stripes, to Franz.

"Let me unburden you."

Klimt took the painting and placed it on the mattress.

"May I?"

"Yes, yes, please do."

Without too much care, Klimt began to unwrap the painting from its various layers of fabric. When the young woman's face was finally revealed, Franz felt slightly giddy.

"Ah!"

Klimt removed an unfinished painting from one of the easels and placed the portrait on it.

It was of a very young woman, in three-quarter view, against a green background. A girl with dreamy blue eyes, and auburn strands of hair framing her face that gave her a rather unkempt look. She wore a large brown felt hat, too big for her, and a cheap fur stole around her neck. A blue velvet jacket was falling off her shoulders, which she had barely covered with a transparent shift; she looked like those "girls on the line" who generally sell their charms.

Klimt remained for a moment in front of the portrait he had painted a few years back, and screwed up his eyes, as if trying to remember the girl who had posed for him in this very studio. Franz remained respectfully silent, not having dared to sit down yet. One didn't sit on the beds of people one was meeting for the first time.

"So, tell me, young man, what can I do for you? Our mutual friend left a great mystery hovering over the reason for this meeting."

"Oh, don't blame him, sir, I was very evasive myself, because I . . . I wanted to remain discreet."

"Alright, I'm listening."

"I bought this painting by you, I mean that it's an honor

for me . . . I admire, I've always greatly admired your work . . . and the fact is that, quite by chance, the fact is that I know this young girl, or rather, I knew her and I wasn't expecting that . . ."

Franz sighed. He might have rehearsed several times how he was going to put his request, but he felt he'd got off to a bad start.

"I wouldn't want to waste your time . . ."

Maybe he should get straight to the point and talk money? No, that would be a gross mistake.

The artist sensed that the young man's discomfiture wasn't feigned.

"Sit down, give me your hat."

Franz sat on the edge of the bed.

"Would you like something to drink?"

"No, thank you."

He was all choked up, wouldn't have thought he'd be this emotional.

"Don't worry, you're not wasting my time at all, tell me all."

"Thank you, you're too kind."

At that moment, Franz realized how much this story had weighed on him, and still weighed on him, and how much he needed to confide in someone. And so he decided to begin at the beginning.

"Martha, the young woman in the painting, arrived at our house in February 1908. She was fifteen and I was twenty. I wasn't a very . . . forward boy, if you know what I mean . . . but the fact is, my parents, particularly my mother, worried about me."

Klimt pulled up a chair and sat facing Franz, crossing his arms on his chest like an attentive listener. Franz continued:

"Two months earlier, on the evening of Christmas Day, the son of one of their friends had committed suicide. He'd contracted syphilis . . . He preferred to die rather than end up paralyzed or deranged, you know? It was awful. Apparently, some sufferers end up totally toothless because they rub mercury on you . . . anyhow . . . It's definitely that tragedy that convinced my mother."

He paused for a while.

"I've never spoken about it with her, of course, but she's a pragmatic woman. She loves me, in short . . . I'm her only son. My family is rich, very rich, always has been. I don't even know where they actually got that fortune from. We live in a mansion, on the edge of Stadtpark. I get on well with my parents, I'm not sure why I'm telling you that, although, yes, to tell you that we're nevertheless different, my parents and I. My father isn't remotely interested in art. My mother pretends—at least, I suspect her of pretending—to be moved by music, but apart from Strauss's waltzes, not much touches her. As for me, I've always had an artistic sensibility. You're going to think me pretentious for saying that, particularly to a great artist like you."

Klimt smiled at him.

"Come now, young man, don't apologize, a painter will never speak ill of an art lover who buys his paintings!"

The two men gazed at the portrait in silence. Franz felt more confident.

"When Martha arrived at ours, we already had a small army of servants. I don't know who actually recruited her, our butler most probably, with my mother's assent. Nothing was said to me explicitly, but I immediately understood why Martha was there. A friend of mine had told me how his parents had lured him away from a brothel he frequented, with a young girl who'd come from the country supposedly to dust the furniture, and who would join him in his bed every night. This isn't something that happens frequently, but in my world, it is done. I hope I'm not shocking you."

He looked questioningly at the Master, but he didn't seem overly shocked.

"It was Martha herself who made it clear to me that she was at my service. Those are the very words she used. 'If you need anything at all, I am at your service.' I would hate you to think that I forced her. She knew what she'd been brought into our house for. I thought she was a virgin, but didn't know she was fifteen years old. She didn't look that young, she came from the countryside. She was pretty, I found her very pretty. It seems ridiculous today, but I fell a little in love with her. A young man of twenty can easily confuse carnal love and love pure and simple. At first, I would go and join her in her room. Our servants live on the top floor. I thought I was being discreet, but of course the other servants knew. She had an amazing body!"

He had said that proudly to the painter who knew women's bodies so well. It was a body in which Franz would drown himself. And a skin of milky softness. He remembered how accommodating she was; she was his, she was his little Martha.

"During the day, she would help our cook. I rarely set foot in the kitchen, and anyhow, I didn't want to be near her in broad daylight. But at night, the house went dark, everything disappeared, and we would find each other again."

He paused to banish the images surging up from the mists of his memory.

"She had told me about her childhood, she was an orphan and had grown up with a sour-tempered aunt and an uncle she loathed who reeked of wine. She had received no education. Out of idealism or egoism, or to convince myself of my high-mindedness, I'd got it into my head to teach her to love beautiful things. I would read poems to her in the evening, on my bed. She would join me in my bedroom, because of the other servants."

He remembered how she loved him to read poems in a foreign language to her . . . *Les Chants de Maldoror* in the original French, and she would listen with her ear pressed to his chest, it must have resonated louder. With one hand holding a book and the other plunged into Martha's long chestnut-brown hair, he was a spoilt young man. Their nights had something sweet and powerfully erotic about them. The scent of her hair turned him crazy with desire, he might well have confessed, it was so long ago now, but he refrained from doing so.

"I wouldn't say we were on an equal footing, I wouldn't say that because . . . because Martha knew to stay in her place . . . but we shared a complicity, we became more than a master and his servant. She was very tender with me, and I with her. It was something we had in common, that need for tenderness. I'd even introduced her to some friends. Can you imagine what madness? One evening, I took her to listen to some poet pals reciting their verses at the Café Central. It's true that everyone had brought along their grisettes, I wasn't risking much, but Martha wasn't like the others, with Martha, we were . . . It was a splendid evening. Yes, without being smitten, I was very attached to her. I wouldn't have admitted it to myself at the time, but I could no longer really imagine my life without her. And the months went by . . . and then one day, she disappeared."

He went silent. The painter was captivated by his story, Franz could tell, and thought it a good sign, this man wasn't insensitive.

"Without warning anyone, neither her masters, nor the other servants, she had gone. I immediately wanted to ignore my grief. It was unthinkable that I, Franz Brombeere, should be upset that some little maid had left me. I tried to be angry, to hold it against her. To be honest, for the first few days, I was mostly concerned, I couldn't bring myself to believe that she'd abandoned me without some misfortune having driven her to do so. I was stunned, I was going around in circles. For the first few nights, I missed her body so much, I thought I hated her. I was full of resentment, I spat on the lower orders you can never trust, and even rummaged in my drawers, I'm ashamed to recall, to check that she hadn't stolen any money or some object of value from me, but no. When

I decided to set off in search of her, it was too late, I had no way of tracing her. I was too proud to ask the other servants for information. And what would they have thought of me? I sent a discreet messenger to the village she was from to question her aunt and uncle. They'd had no news from her since she'd left for Vienna."

As he heard himself speak, he realized how sadly banal his story was. Martha had disappeared one Sunday in May. He lowered his eyes to conceal his distress.

"She was only with us for sixteen months, which isn't long, is it? But when it's your first love, who's counting . . . A first love is for life. I can't have been hers, but . . . that's how it is . . . you don't choose."

It was thanks to a friend that Franz had obtained this meeting. Klimt wasn't one of those accessible men, and he was particularly wary of those who, born with a silver spoon in their mouth, fancied themselves arbiters of good taste. Those who understood nothing about his art, but held the purse strings when it came to how much he would, or wouldn't, be paid for the giant murals that would grace new official buildings. He remembered the young girl of the portrait, she'd sat a dozen or so times for him, she was indeed gentle, maybe a little sadder than the girl in Franz's story, but how can one know?

"You've come so that I help you to find her?"

"No, no, of course not!"

"Because I've no idea what became of her, she was just a temporary model, I didn't even remember that she was called Martha."

At these words, Franz felt a pang of emotion, whether of vexation or relief he didn't know, he couldn't untangle his feelings. It took a lot for him to keep talking, but the Master seeming to have barely known the girl was quite encouraging. He looked at the man: he exuded a particular strength, he was free, Franz thought, whereas he himself, despite the millions he was sitting on, never had been.

"Last year, when I went to the exhibition at the Galerie Miethke and saw the portrait of Martha, you can't imagine what a shock it was. She was so alive, so real! I kept gazing at it, returning to it, and immediately went to see the gallery owner. Actually, no, I waited maybe an hour or two . . . Yes . . . I remember that the thought that she could be hung in any room other than mine was totally unbearable . . . That's what decided me. I played it cool with the gallery owner, who knew me by name. He posed no problem. You can't imagine how relieved I was. And when the portrait was delivered to my home . . . I couldn't look at it . . . impossible . . ."

"Because you still loved her?"

"No. I couldn't look at it and . . . I've never been able to since."

Since Klimt had raised an ironic eyebrow, Franz quickly added, plaintively:

"You're thinking, he doesn't know what he wants, is that right?"

"No, but I don't understand."

"The portrait you painted of her is magnificent. But it isn't Martha, it isn't *my* Martha, it's a . . ."

The words caught in his throat.

"The woman in the painting is a prostitute, well, she displays all the signs of being one, and I've often thought that by running away from our house like that, Martha may well have fallen very low . . . and that it was my fault, you know, because I hadn't been able to see, because I hadn't had the guts to . . . Martha wasn't that, or maybe she actually was when she posed for you, and that I definitely don't want to know, say nothing!"

The Master remained silent. Franz had a flash of inspiration.

"In fact, Master, I've come to request something very specific of you, that you give me back the young girl I was in love with. I would like you to change her."

Klimt looked at him in disbelief.

"Sorry, young man, I don't repaint my pictures."

Franz stood up. He was trembling.

"Sit down."

Franz remained standing, hat in hand. He gazed sadly at the portrait, as if apologizing to it.

"You want me to change it, but I can't. I can't even paint another portrait because she's no longer here to pose. And copying the original—guaranteed not to ring true. Do you know Toulouse-Lautrec?"

"No."

"He was a wonderful French artist. The year I painted this young girl, I'd actually just returned from a trip to Paris. You know, artists influence each other a good deal . . . and when I see this big hat, this stole, I think of his paintings, but you're right, it does look very . . . loose woman."

Klimt was smiling, but Franz's expression had hardened. The artist thought to himself that as well as being sentimental, the young man was touchy. Or was he temperamental due to his upbringing, to being spoilt rotten?

"Calm down, calm down. It's a sweet story you've told me."

"Oh, sir, if only you'd known her better! Martha was so gentle and charming and pious . . . It might seem hypocritical to you, considering the life we made her lead, with me . . . without being married, but she wasn't one . . . of those women."

Klimt felt sudden pity.

"Leave me your portrait, young man, and when I get in touch, come back to see me."

Franz held his hand out to the Master. "Really? You're agreeing to it?"

Klimt tapped him gently on the shoulder, like an adult would a small child, and showed him to the door.

"I'm promising you nothing."

6

That Monday morning, Isidore woke up feeling as if he'd swallowed a stone. He was wary of trusting his intuition, but knew he was too obsessed with money to think he was being rational. Was Boba's tip-off the lucky break of his life? And yet it wasn't the first time he was hearing this refrain. The old bankers would repeat it, each one louder than the last: the market's been bubbling for too long, this crazy buying must be stopped!

But the times were wonderful. A man could buy and sell all the shares he wanted, indiscriminately, and be almost sure of winning. Recently, liquidity was such that a stockbroker had sold a hundred thousand shares in under three minutes without affecting the price by a cent! Transactions were huge, and every day, the scale of the fluctuations would beat the previous day's record.

Isidore stopped himself from thinking mathematically; he needed to predict the behavior of the market, needed to sense where the wind would be coming from. As old Larry would say: "No diagnosis, no prognosis; no prognosis, no profit." Speculating wasn't a game. One mustn't wager, one must anticipate.

He decided to go and find his favorite broker, the one who'd told him about the miracle antiseptic. The guy had a thing for medicine and scientific publications, which he'd dress up however suited him. Isidore wasn't taken in, but he needed to go big before the market came crashing down, if it did indeed come crashing down. He told him that he was ready to stake all the money he had. That is, 5,786 dollars. The broker didn't turn a hair. He'd been there before. Everyone was making staggering gains, the risks were low. They arranged to meet the following day.

On Tuesday morning, Isidore woke up with an urge to vomit. He counted again the wad of banknotes he'd accumulated. Fifty-seven 100-dollar bills, four of twenty, one of five, and one of one. His whole future printed in grubby gray on small rectangles of paper.

Boba hadn't named the harbinger of bad news to him, but that word "vertiginous" continued to haunt him. The broker had told him that, during the Great War, antiseptics had killed more soldiers than they'd saved. He thought of Lotte. If their love was as strong as they both vowed it was, 5,786 dollars would be enough. He could by a small business, a shoe store or the like. He clung again to this simple dream for a handful of seconds. Impossible. Maybe he should speak to one of his former customers? Mr. Livermore, who was so talkative? Or Mr. Peeters, who was always in a hurry? Or then his favorite, Mr. O'Reilly, who had given Isidore the name of the broker when he'd first started?

He wrapped his money in a polish-stained cloth and hid it at the bottom of a wooden box, among some broken and random items. The room he occupied with his friend Ben was drab, no one would suspect that such a large sum of money would be stashed away in it. Keeping the wad on him would have just increased the temptation to do something impulsive with it.

He went out with his hands in his pockets and strolled along Mulberry Street as far as Broadway. It was mild for October. He was walking to a beat, as if wanting to lull himself. He was determined not to let images of his past loom up and terrify him. He passed the russet trees of City Hall Park and carried on down. His plan was simple, he'd station himself beside the building on the corner of Beaver Street, where he was bound to come across one of his former customers, who had always given sound advice.

The sky seemed of an immeasurable height. *The wind is rising*, Isidore thought, and tucked his chin under the collar of his jacket.

Boba looked surprised, almost embarrassed, to see him.

"Don't worry about me, I'm here to meet an old acquaintance."

He didn't want to say too much; luckily, there were plenty of customers and Boba had to knuckle down. Leaning against the railings, Isidore watched him out of the corner of his eye. The kid wasn't doing badly. When Mr. Livermore appeared, Isidore thanked his lucky stars.

"Good day, sir!"

The man recognized Isidore and smiled at him.

"Hello, stranger!"

Isidore tried to control his nerves.

"Could you spare a moment for a rookie speculator?"

Livermore stopped and adjusted his spectacles. In his impeccable suit and slightly tilted brown fedora, he must have been around fifty. Isidore suggested accompanying him up to the entrance of his building.

"I don't want to waste your time, sir."

"Very well, let's walk."

Isidore dived in. He spilled the beans. The man listened to him attentively, now with head tilted. When Isidore had finished speaking, he said:

"Listen, my boy, I've been doing this job for twenty years now, and from my point of view, things are pretty simple. No one can grasp all the fluctuations of the market. In a bullish market, your game must be buying shares and keeping them until you think that bullish market is close to ending. That's why I never give tip-offs to anyone. An individual tip, a particular factor, they're merely incidental. It's the broad trend that really brings in the money. The only secret is, never buy at the lowest price and always sell too soon. But if you sense the trend is reversing, get your shares out, all your shares, get out for good. And if you're not afraid, short. Short heavily."

"Short?"

Isidore had never been a bear. He'd never even considered that approach because many brokers had warned him about it: betting on the market going down really was to risk losing everything. Particularly for a beginner, and particularly since one had the right to sell securities with a margin of just 10%.[6] With his 5,786 dollars, Isidore could sell 57,860 dollars' worth of shares. Selling a thing one didn't *yet* own, that was the key to this sleight of hand. Borrowing securities one didn't own and, once the fall was confirmed, buying back the same quantity of shares on the cheap to return them to the person who'd bet on them rising, the same person who'd loaned his shares to you instead of selling them. If there was a vertiginous fall, it was a guaranteed jackpot. But big profit comes with big risk; if the leveraging went against him, and there was a rise, even by just two points, his opening stake would be swallowed up. His bank would launch a margin call and he'd be forced to cut his positions by buying back, at top price, the shares sold, to return them to the lender.

"Could I ask you one last question?"

"Go ahead . . ."

"You, personally, is that what you're going to do? Are you going to short?"

Jesse Livermore paused for a moment, with a mischievous glint in his eye. Then, placing index finger on lips to indicate a secret, he gently nodded his head.

[6] The "call loan" was authorised on Wall Street from 1926.

"Yes."

On the Wednesday morning, the newspapers weren't headlining anything out of the ordinary. The market was functioning normally and Isidore was totally distraught. A sense of urgency gripped his belly, and yet, since Boba had made his great announcement, things seemed unchanged. Jesse Livermore had the reputation of being a man who had won, but also lost, millions. Isidore couldn't afford to do that. He thought constantly about Lotte. Not seeing her made him sick with anxiety. Autumn truly was the worst season. He had to decide. To short, to short, but to short what? Which stock would nose-dive?

Thursday, and then Friday, trundled along; it was now October 18, 1929. A few massive sales of foreign capital took place, "nothing alarming" commented those who, like Isidore, spent their days sitting in foreign-exchange offices and scouring the sky for any signs of a storm brewing. Isidore wasn't taken in by their cheeriness, he told himself that he wasn't the only one to be wary, and had done well to stash his banknotes deep in a wooden box. Most shares continued to rise in value, but prices were dragged slightly down on the Friday. Had the time come? He closed his eyes and pictured himself in a three-piece suit on his fiancée's arm.

On Saturday, the market closed at midday.[7] Isidore took a final look at his little wad of banknotes and placed it carefully in the inside pocket of his jacket. He then took it to the counter of the Harding Brothers office. Trembling, he signed a bond for the short sale of General Electric shares. A strong and steady stock with a high price—83 dollars when the market opened. With his 5,786-dollar security deposit, Isidore borrowed and

[7] Today, the market is open from Monday to Friday.

sold 697 shares simultaneously. The National City Bank, the US's richest, took a commission of 1.5% from him. So his account was now in credit to the sum of 56,983 additional dollars, so 62,769 dollars in total. His hands were shaking.

From now on, he had to be ready, at any moment, to buy back the 697 shares to return them to their owner. The bank, as a precautionary measure, had fixed the limit price of loss at 87.75 dollars a share. If General Electric fell short of this, Isidore would be obliged to reverse his positions. At a buy-back price of 87.75 dollars, to which the commission of his generous bankers would be added, he would be left with just 690 dollars and his eyes to weep with.

On the Monday, there were new withdrawals of foreign capital, but the General Electric stock, like that of AT&T, US Steel, and Westinghouse, remained steady. The employees of the New York Stock Exchange went about their usual business, their jaunty pace making their ties swing. And yet the market was febrile, and certain stocks were starting to shift.

It wasn't until Thursday October 24 that the first great panic broke out. In the morning, there were only sellers around; whatever the proposed prices, buyers refused to come forward. And so the prices plummeted. But not that of General Electric. Isidore was having palpitations.

Before midday, the Dow Jones had lost 22.6%, which was unheard of. In the foreign-exchange offices, the teleprinters were up to an hour-and-a-half behind on the rates, and no one knew anymore at what price they had disposed of their stock.

Isidore decided to go down to Wall Street to see it for himself. But many others had had the same idea and, very soon, the panic-stricken crowd swelled outside the great building and the police couldn't cope. Would there be a riot? The Visitor Gallery was closed. It was a grave moment. The newspapers hadn't had time to print the latest news, but their hollering street-sellers were spreading the wildest rumors amid the general hysteria. "It's Black Thursday! It's Black Thursday!", "Eleven speculators topped themselves this morning!", "Chicago and Buffalo Stock Exchanges closed!"

An urgent meeting of five of the main New York bankers took place at the J.P. Morgan & Co. head office. These serious men decided that the situation mustn't be allowed to degenerate. When it was announced that the banks would intervene to support the markets, everything swiftly stabilized and the that day's fall was limited to 2.1%. Isidore had held his breath until closing time; if the markets rose again, his mistake would be irreparable.

He had to find Mr. Livermore again, he'd know what to do. The people around Isidore were talking about nothing else, but their words made no sense. Even when he read the paper, he had to start again three or four times because his eyes kept sliding over the columns of the articles without him understanding a thing. All he could think of was General Electric. General Electric and Lotte and Lotte's father, and dollars were swirling in the fog of his anxiety-bludgeoned brain. He regretted not having put a tiny bit of money aside, a tiny bit to at least bounce back with; he'd acted like a moron who believes in his luck, like some inveterate gambler. He saw again the store he could have bought, and this dream seemed all the more idyllic because it was fading away.

The days went by, the cycle sped out of control, and this time, the banks could do nothing. The market was purging itself and those who had borrowed to speculate were, one by one, obliged to liquidate their positions. The fall of the Dow Jones Index was now inexorable.

On Monday October 28, Eastman Kodak lost 42%, AT&T

and Westinghouse 34%, US Steel 18%, and General Electric 48%.

Forty-eight percent! Isidore had sold the stock at 83 dollars and its closing price was 43.16 dollars. He felt nauseous. He couldn't even calculate anything anymore. He was obliged to sit down and take out his notebook and pencil. He had earnt 39.84 dollars per share; 697 times 39.84 dollars made 27,768.48 dollars. In just a single day. To which was added his opening stake of 5,786 dollars. His account at National City Bank, the richest bank in America, was now in credit to the sum of 33,554.48 dollars.

7

The mahogany legs of the dark-leather armchair sank into a deep-pile beige carpet. An armchair of padded leather that made not a sound when sat on, and provided its owner with a sense of calm and reassurance thanks to it being placed in front of a wide window overlooking the treetops of Central Park. A well-worn armchair up in the sky with an aerial view of the deep-green foliage. The armchair of a wise man who didn't like to be disturbed and who had made a success of his life in many respects.

In a few months' time, he would be celebrating his eightieth birthday, and he was both a father and a grandfather. He was rich, respected by his associates and feared by his employees. He felt lonely but was never alone. He was one of those men you could ask things of, obtain favors or recommendations from, whose opinion counted. A number of his friends were already on the downward slope, if they weren't already six feet under, but a few still depended on him and waited for his decisions; he was the majority shareholder on the board of directors. He had spent his life erecting tall barriers around his chairman's chair. And his children? They, too, could rest easy, knowing that they would soon be inheriting.

Behind him there stood a fine bookcase; it was his wife who read books, his wife the leisurely intellectual, while he was building their fortune. So that his family lacked for nothing. So that they were protected. He had done for his wife and children what no one had ever done for him. He kept his origins quiet, and would say that he'd been born at twenty years old, one Thursday in October 1929, when the greatest Stock Market crash of all times made ruined men fly through the windows of skyscrapers. Because people still killed themselves for honor's sake when he was young.

He had seen the world change so much. He had loved progress with a passion. He had contributed to pushing the boundaries with his "menthol freshness," sea-breeze soap, and toning shaving cream. He had even got involved with developing dog food, to please Felicity, who was crazy about mutts.

It was after breakfast. He had opened the mail and the torn-open envelope lay beside the coffee cup and some breadcrumbs on the plate. A legal letter. A letter posted in Texas. From a certain Michelle Alvez. A letter that others might have been shocked to receive, but that had merely made him angry. A great, unshakeable anger. The black rage of an old man who hadn't been angry for a long time, an anger that went back to childhood, perhaps.

By what right did this woman dare? He had two sons and a daughter. Peter, Thomas, and Felicity. He had been a father three times, that had been enough. Children involved a good deal of attachment. And since things always seem to detach themselves, one day or another, children involved a good deal of pain, inevitably. One daughter, only one, Felicity, a name he hadn't chosen but that had suited her because she was a joyful child. "Felicity is our joy," was her parents' frequent refrain.

Since when did one declare oneself to be the daughter of someone? He crushed the paper in his old man's hand, a liver-spotted hand with prominent, worm-like veins. This Michelle, what did she want from him? He tried to delve back into his memories.

It was another time, business was done differently then, you would sign the contract and then go off for drinks somewhere nice, to celebrate. If some experienced young ladies helped you to finish the day with a flourish, what was wrong with that? It was specified that the child was born in 1969. He was sixty then. It was just prior to the purchase of Citrus Fresh, the shower gel that gave you zest on sleepy mornings. One of their finest deals. He thinks hard. In 1969, their San Antonio factory hadn't yet opened, there would have been no reason to go to Texas, even less to Houston. This woman was talking nonsense.

He felt a splitting headache coming on, and tried to reassure himself. But of course, the Star Blonde shampoos, it was after them. The dates collided in his memory, and yet he'd always been great with numbers. He could see again the wide, deserted avenues of heat, the arid red landscapes, and those idiot Texans in their Stetsons and pointed boots. Migraine had set in. Did he have it off with some cute chicks? Yes. Professional girls? Yes. A lot? It was so long ago. This woman was crazy. She was after his money, like the others. He tried slapping the name Michelle onto a pert little ass. It rang no bells whatsoever. He used to ask them their names as a nicety, but instantly forgot them.

He saw himself once more in the nightclubs, in the hotel bars, how he'd follow their wiggling butts along the carpeted corridors, from the elevator to the bedroom. Things went well, it was simple, mostly, he had nothing to do but sit back in a deep armchair. The girls would make themselves comfortable, grab a cushion to avoid sore knees. Sometimes, rarely, he would lie them down on the bed.

He wasn't one of those men who were in search of their mom, maybe because he'd been deeply in love with his wife and, indeed, very paternal. He had enjoyed starting a family. He was a serious man, responsible, which is why he'd never have taken the risk of having a bastard son or daughter. The girls always had condoms on them, had even introduced him to the things.

The name of the attorney was unknown to him, but the

typography on the headed paper was really pretentious. The migraine was now skewering him. He must close the curtains, the light was sawing into his eyes. He must close the curtains and call Henry. Henry would know how to take care of it, avoid a scandal. Buy the broad's silence, and then? One check more or less in his bank account wouldn't change his children's inheritance. Felicity had asked him, "What would you really like, Daddy, for your birthday?" He'd been incapable of answering her. Oh, how his head was hurting!

Michelle. Houston. He had travelled a lot. One room with a red satin bedspread, another with green drapes, reddish hair, and the shadows dancing on the walls. He wasn't keen on leaving the lights on. At night, outside, the headlamps of the cars just passing by, and his virile pleasure. A simple, raw pleasure. Most of the time, he didn't even have to pull out his wallet, it was the client's gift.

He remembered one particular time—actually, wasn't it in Texas? Yes, most probably, it was coming back to him, the girl had wanted to keep the TV on. There was no doubt she was a professional, she'd seemed skilled and focused on her work, but before starting, she'd asked him: "Which channel d'you want to watch?" He'd found that strange. He'd chosen a political talk-show, and the two activities hadn't been incompatible. He'd even rather enjoyed being sucked off while important men debated impending laws and jurisprudence. For a long time, the two activities had been superimposed in his mind. Perhaps it was because of that novelty that he remembered her, rather than some other girl. And he remembered an actress, too, quite famous in her day, voluptuous, but not on the bed, in the armchair, nice and snug. Could it have been that time?

He could still see the neon lights of a restaurant flashing. He'd refused to sign a contract, the guy had been put out, but kept up appearances until dinner. A research engineer who thought he'd cracked an alcohol-free deodorant. But he hadn't bought into it. The dinner had ended early, he wasn't leaving until the following day. He'd returned to his hotel and asked that reception find him a girl. His sadness at that time came back to him. Reception had sent him Michelle. Was she really called Michelle? Or Samantha? Was it that very girl? In any case, it was in Texas, of that he was certain. Because of the restaurant's neon lights, which were attached in his memory to the façade of the hotel. A fine Houston hotel. The rooms had high ceilings, and the TV, placed on a low table, seemed all the smaller. Now he felt as if two screwdrivers were penetrating behind his eyes.

Tranquility. Henry would sort everything out, that was his role. He must ring Henry and not give it another thought. Isidore was known to be a man who was swift to act, yet didn't get carried away. A measured man. But this morning, a muted rage was making his hands shake. He was being accused of being a man who hadn't acknowledged his child? The finger was being pointed at him? He was being cornered? There was proof and he'd be forced to admit to an offence he hadn't committed? Suddenly, he felt the urge to vomit and broke out in a sweat. His clenched fist went slack and the letter slid onto the carpet. A dog, a rabid hound, was sinking its teeth into his heart.

The precise sensation, of jaws gripping his poor, swelling ribcage, was horrendous. He must stand up. He hoisted himself using the arms of the chair and his entire body instantly caught fire. Maybe not his legs, but his lungs for sure. The pain made him reel. He must reach the door, call Mrs. Valeras, who was always there to serve him. He realized that he was standing upright, imagined his calves, firm as a statue's. But when it came to walking, everything shattered inside him; he was the idol with feet of clay, he was the volcano erupting with pain.

He was in such agony that he collapsed onto the nearest table, bringing down, as he fell, the crystal ashtray, his Christmas present from the children last year, a useless present, he'd quit smoking years ago, even cigars. The carpet cushioned the impact, and the ashtray landed softly, with a muffled sound. From kneeling, he tried to stand up. As a little boy, he'd learnt how to roll with the punches, hadn't he. The breath escaping from his chest felt like it was ablaze. He expected to throw out flames, but everything around him remained still and unchanged. He let out the moan of a small child and curled up on his side.

It was just then that Mrs. Valeras walked in. A shrill squeak, as from a mouse. Mrs. Valeras doing a fine impression of one.

"Sir! Sir! Sir!"

With a tragedian's fervor, she cried out, "Help! Please help!", when there were just the two of them in the apartment. Motionless and dying, he watched her flapping her arms about. Finally, she ran out of the room.

When she returned, Death was there, he could feel it lodged like a lump at the back of his throat. He stared at the ceiling and realized with amazement that he was still feeling angry. Two men and a woman, seeming sure of themselves, had entered the study. The old man watched their swift, precise gestures; they had a strange calm about them.

"Sir? Sir, can you hear me?"

Mrs. Valeras had joined her hands in prayer, she was weeping, she was red in the face. The nurse lifted the wrinkled eyelid of the collapsed old man and flooded his eye with a beam of light. Death, wise and patient, was rubbing its hands.

"We're going to give him a shot of adrenaline. Move back."

They prodded his arm, he could tell a tourniquet was being applied.

"Sir! Sir! Can you hear me?"

The needle went in and the shock was atrocious; he bounced up, yet he hadn't moved a muscle.

"Sir! Sir! Can you hear me?"

8

It was June 29 and, across Catholic Austria, the feast day of Saints Peter and Paul. Despite the war, the music from the bandstand in Vienna's Stadtpark set the blossoming groves dancing. This, the first public holiday of summer, was a real day to feel happy. Martha was proudly holding her little boy's hand. He was seven years old, and never before had they visited the capital city together like this. For the occasion, she had tied a large blue bow around his neck, a kind of floppy necktie like the children of the rich wore. She had bought the ribbon from the peddler in Loebendorf. The collar of the shirt was starched, the trousers short and the socks pulled up, while the puffed sleeves stuck out from the slightly too tight jacket. Isidore wasn't allowed to run around, but he knew how to behave anyway.

They had got up at dawn. The sky was a silky blue and the air already sweet. They had walked to Leobendorf's railway station. Martha was smiling at the thought of how thrilled the child would be to climb onto that spluttering, steaming, iron machine. People were crowding onto the platform and Isidore gripped his mother's hand as tight as he could when the whistling sound rang out. Never would she forget the amazement in her little boy's eyes.

The journey to Vienna took a good hour. The countryside flashed by. Fragrant meadows waved their wild grasses and, in the distance, the crests of the dark forests seemed to sway on the horizon. Martha had brought a sandwich, wrapped in a handkerchief. Tomorrow, Isidore would tell his friends how lucky he'd been, setting off on an adventure with a big blue bow tied around his neck.

It was two years since Austria had declared war on Serbia. Franz Ferdinand, the nephew of the old emperor, Franz Joseph, and heir apparent to the Austro-Hungarian throne, had been assassinated in Sarajevo in June 1914. His imperial uncle had thought a punitive offensive would suffice to restore order. He had summoned his troops and they had marched off, singing. Things had then snowballed and, with wild and compelling momentum, all the nations of Europe had wanted to get involved. Jubilant, the young recruits had headed off with gusto; two years later, the life of Austrians was rationed, a card for bread, a card for meat, there wasn't even any real coffee anymore.

But Vienna was far from the combat zones and bombardments. Vienna remained, radiant and carefree. Along its avenues strolled ladies dressed in white on the arm of officers who bought them posies of violets. These freshly shaven servicemen in spotless uniforms banished the reality of the bearded, bedraggled soldiers fighting on the frontline.

In the spring of 1915, a major Austro-German offensive had broken through Russian lines in Tarnów and taken Galicia and Poland in a single concentric advance. The Viennese newspapers had peddled the usual lies and printed grand statements about the unyielding will to win, the minimal losses of Austrian troops and huge losses of their enemy counterparts. Martha had heard all about it, but Martha wasn't interested in the war; her battle was for her son.

The Feast of Saints Peter and Paul was a splendid ceremony, and the large St. Stephen's Cathedral, with its lozenge-patterned roof, was certainly the most impressive thing that Isidore had ever seen. The Viennese had flocked there to pray for the death of the enemy, and their singing had soared with fervor. Martha had lit a few candles in Stephansdom in the past, but that was before Isidore's birth and today, it all seemed new to her.

For six years, she and her son hadn't left the little town of Leobendorf. Summer, autumn, winter, spring, day had followed day in a chain dance of tiredness, and she had held out. Getting up, getting dressed, getting the child ready, working, working to pay the rent on the room, to pay the baker and grocer, to feed the little one, going to the wash house, to Mass, to bed, and then starting all over again. But today, it was a holiday.

As they left the church, she turned to Isidore and told him she was going to take him to an extraordinary place. "I hope you'll always remember it." And the son was discovering a different, unsuspected mother, who knew how to take the train and find her way through the huge city's maze of streets, a woman who wanted to create joyous memories for him. That mother was the most fantastic mother in the world.

They passed fountains adorned with golden statues, store windows sparkled in the sun and fine motorcars gleamed; Isidore would remember all that, too. The gentlemen in their boaters and the ladies in their voluminous hats dazzled him. They turned at the corner of Strauchgasse, and Martha pushed open the double door of the Café Central.

"If you would care to follow me."

The waiter led them to their table. Maybe the factory girl in her Sunday best wasn't quite as at ease as she wanted to seem, but her child emboldened her. She fleetingly wondered whether Isidore, with his blue bow, could pass as a little aristocrat, with her as his nanny, but it was too obvious that they didn't belong in this world. The child's eyes were popping out of his head and his mouth was agape.

They sat at the red-marble pedestal table assigned to them. Above their heads were dozens of elaborate lamps, suspended from the imposing vaulted ceiling. At a time of shortages, this place seemed like an isle of plenty, there were even pastries displayed on a huge counter near the entrance. All this magnificence came at a price. Martha tried to sound as relaxed as possible when another waiter approached them.

"We would like two hot chocolates, please."

Mother and son waited patiently. Isidore gazed at the friezes of small white stars on blue marble that embellished the columns. The porcelain cups arrived, along with the pot of chocolate and two little dishes of cream. Martha poured the chocolate, brown, thick, piping hot. Then demonstrated how you should scoop a little whipped cream with the silver spoon and dip it into the chocolate.

Isidore conveyed this treat to his lips, eyes sparkling with pleasure. The first sensation to hit him was how hot it really was, and the metallic taste of the spoon seemed unreal to him, then came the unctuousness of the cream melting on his palate, and the sweetness mingling with the bitterness. If he'd dared, he would have laughed with delectation, but the moment was so solemn, and he was scared of spilling some and staining his blue bow. The very air above his cup seemed lighter to him. The spoon scooped up another little pitted cloud, more delicate than a feather, before sinking into the dark, glossy lake that awaited it. As a wonderful, sweet mud slipped down his throat, a general impression of time having stopped became imprinted within him, the tinkling of glasses and cups all around, the vague murmur of patrons from their tables, and his mother's gaze full of tenderness, so different to that of ordinary days, when she looked like a tired woman to him. Martha was watching her son with all her soul, wanting to store this moment of pure delight in the vast edifice of her memories, as one might a kiss, a chocolate kiss and a longing to lick one's fingers.

When not a single drop remained, the waiter cleared away the cups. They wouldn't have felt fuller after a feast. They still had a little time before catching the train back to Leobendorf.

And then the day would disappear, and Martha felt nostalgic in advance.

"Come, we're going for a stroll. You know, I worked in Vienna before you were born, I know this neighborhood well."

Martha was thinking of Franz Brombeere. She didn't know that he hadn't fought in the war. The asthma he'd suffered from since childhood had excused him of his military obligations. Already, upon finishing his studies, the draft board had certified him unfit for service. This had made him very happy, he who'd always been gentle as a lamb. Indeed, heroism hardly suited Franz's nature. At mobilization, to safeguard the Brombeeres' honor, his father had found him a position at the military archives. There was no glory in it, but Franz would have gladly filed documents for twelve hours a day if it meant avoiding having to stick a bayonet into the belly of a Russian peasant.

Was Martha hoping to come across him? Hoping that fate would make them bump into each other on the sidewalk? The young mother knew how to suppress her dreams. She'd never had any illusions when it came to Franz. She had merely shared the bed of the person whose servant she was. But she remembered, too, how she would press her ear to the chest of the young man while he read poems to her, she remembered the paleness of his skin and his particular way of breathing, the vibrations that reached her ear and her heart, and the book in a foreign language that he held close to his face. Lautréamont was the name of the poet, Isidore Graf von Lautréamont. It was her secret. Franz was gentle, he was different from other men. She had said to her son: "Your father was a good man, but he died before you were born." In Isidore's class, there were two boys whose fathers had died in the war, as heroes, the lucky things. Martha took her child's little hand in hers. Was that why she'd decked him out in a blue bow? Just in case?

Maybe the hot chocolate had quenched his thirst for adventure, but the boy already seemed less impressed by the wide avenues than when they had first alighted from the train. Vienna was rolling out its cobblestones under the horses' trotting. They landed on the corner of Graben and Bräunerstraße. Had Martha knowingly gravitated to this street, as if on a secret pilgrimage? (When she would think about again, at night in her bed, she would deny it, sincerely.) The Galerie Miethke was one of the most famous, if not the most famous, gallery in Vienna, Franz had brought her there three times, and she had found the place magnificent. But if Isidore and Martha had walked past it, that was merely where their perambulations happened to take them.

The high windows facing the street were all of a piece. Through them, one could see paintings exhibited on bare walls. Matha gripped her child's hand a bit tighter because she had just caught sight of something. Without thinking, she entered the gallery and headed straight for the wall at the back.

The painting wasn't very big, but the resemblance was astonishing. And it took the little boy mere seconds before he, too, got the shock.

9

Isidore knew what he still had to do. Taking his beautiful banknotes, he went to Madison Avenue and bought himself a pair of those shoes he'd so often polished. Convinced that a man's quality is judged by the shine on his leather, he was smiling. He had one more purchase to make. He strode back up the avenue. A triumphal march of the new, stiff derbies that promised their happy owner painful blisters that very evening, but Isidore didn't fear suffering now that he was rich.

He walked exactly two-and-a-half miles, which was a good thing since footwear that looked too new would have betrayed him. He kept repeating his lies in his head. He arrived in front of the window of Brooks Brothers, purveyor of shirts to Abraham Lincoln himself. He went in. When he came back out of the store, he was ready.

He headed for Fifth Avenue and bought a huge bouquet of pink roses, which wasn't the done thing, but how could he have known? The stalks risked soaking his fine trousers, so he stretched his arms out like some frightened, love-sick fool. He couldn't simply walk anymore, he bounded forward at each step, wanting to shout his own name into the October wind. When had he ever felt this happy? On the sidewalk, he saw that a man had hung a sign on his car saying:

"For sale—100 dollars—I lost everything on the stock market."

Isidore didn't know how to drive, but he'd won, he had. He was rolling in it, he was! Proud and ridiculous, he was Hope making its debut. A young peacock turning its head and discovering, with amazement, its fanned tail.

When he arrived in front of the enormous building and presented himself to the porter, for the first time since the start of that day, the soles of his feet were burning.

No, he wasn't expected. Yes, it would be too kind of him to inform Mr. and Mrs. Hoffmann. No, he didn't have a visiting card on him, unfortunately. The porter scowled, but the bouquet of flowers reassured him and, as already mentioned, those who met Isidore found him likeable. Mr. Hoffmann was at home. Isidore bowed and followed the attendant into the elevator.

A servant with a white lace frill on her chignon made him wait in an entrance hall gleaming with marble. On a console table stood a large vase of magnificent blooms. Isidore compared his grotesque bouquet; he should never have come here. He recoiled when Lotte's father appeared. It was too late to run away.

"What may I do for you, young man?"

Isidore's pulse quickened.

"Sir, I've come to pay my respects to Mrs. Hoffmann."

The father raised an eyebrow, he wasn't a man to waste his time. On Tuesdays, late afternoon, he'd come home to change before heading to his club for his weekly game of billiards.

"Mrs. Hoffmann is out. And I was on the point of leaving, myself."

"Oh! Excuse me, sir, I didn't realize, I mean, in which case . . . I had also come to see you, but I will return . . ."

The serious formality with which the young man expressed himself made him seem comic. He was still holding his flowers out, and swaying from foot to foot. Lotte's father felt sorry for him. He shouted:

"Maria!"

The lace-coiffed servant immediately returned.

"Relieve the gentleman of his bouquet."

Then, addressing Isidore:

"You say you'd also come to see me?"

"Yes, sir, I came to ask your permission to take your daughter Lotte to the movies."

The father smiled, so that's what this was about. He looked more closely at Isidore. From the young man's way of pronouncing Lotte's name, he had instantly picked up his German accent.

"*Sind Sie Deutscher?*"

"*Nein, mein Herr, ich bin Österreicher.*"

"*Österreicher? Wießt Lotte, dass Sie mit ihr ins Kino gehen wollen?*"

"*Ach! Ja, mein Herr!*"

Isidore regretted answering so enthusiastically; he rectified that immediately.

"*Wir sind ja gute Freunde.*"[8]

This made the father's hackles rise.

Isidore mustn't say too much. Since yesterday, he'd been coming up with all kinds of crazy plans, one of which consisted of asking for Lotte's hand in marriage as soon as he had suitable shoes, but, all things considered, permission to go to the movies would already be a victory. He'd had time to prepare several lies. What was crucial was for his story to match what he'd said and written to Lotte over the past months. Truth and lies are like water and oil, you think you can combine them, but the oil always ends up rising to the surface. A good lie would act like white vinegar, able to change the taste of the water without changing the color.

His first brainwave was to say the he'd been brought up by a harmless old couple, Mr. and Mrs. Gruber. Why had the name Gruber come to him? He hadn't the slightest idea. A

[8] "Are you German?" - "No, sir, Austrian." - "Austrian? Well, well, and does Lotte know you'd like to take her to the movies?" - "Oh! Yes, sir! . . . We're good friends."

storekeeping couple, his uncle and aunt on his mother's side. He'd decided to make his mother die in childbirth, his birth, and his father at war, and the Grubers, they'd have sold hats in Vienna. They'd have believed in him, and wished him a fair wind by giving him their savings so he could make the great voyage and live his American dream. That was important, the old folks' blessings. Which was why he'd written to them regularly, to give them his news, but unfortunately, the two had died in quick succession last year. Or then, only the husband? Isidore couldn't decide—on the one hand, making them both die rid him of them once and for all; on the other, it was a lot of deaths for just one story. When he'd arrived in New York, he'd become a salesman in a shoe store, and thanks to hard work and discipline, had put enough money aside to open his own store.

He suddenly felt exhausted. It was Lotte's mother he'd really hoped to meet, imagining her gentle and soothing, whereas a one-to-one with the father would soon seem more like an interrogation.

"Please, do sit down. Would you like a lemon soda?"

The father had reverted to English to indicate that there would be no familiarity between them.

"No, sir, thank you."

"So, Austrian, and you were born in New York?"

"No, sir, I was born in Vienna, I arrived in New York four years ago now."

"You came over alone? Forgive me, but how old are you?"

"Twenty, sir."

"Ah! Your parents sent you here to pursue your studies? The best universities in the world are American, they chose well. Personally, I studied engineering at Heidelberg University."

He had said this with false modesty. Since Isidore said nothing, he added:

"Indeed, I remember it very fondly."

Isidore felt as if his heart were about to explode.

"And you, young man, what are you studying?"

He must play a tight game. Not lie, not tell the truth.

"I'm interested in finance."

"Finance? Well, things aren't too hot for financiers these days! And we men of industry will pay a high price for the speculators' games."

Speculators were the great culprits of this whole fiasco. But Isidore decided it would be best to admit that he was one, rather than venturing into university territory.

"'Speculation' is a dirty word, you're right, but if one seriously tried to understand the overall tendencies of the stock market, one could have anticipated what has happened and invested in the right way."

"Oh, you're not a student anymore? You work in a bank?"

"Yes, well, no, not at all, but I'm one of those speculators, as you call them, I don't hide from that."

To Isidore, the air seemed charged with electricity. Anything rather than say he was a sales assistant in a shoe store (false) and a former shoeshine boy (true).

"Well, if you're a speculator, I imagine you've had to eat your hat these past few days."

His tone was mildly sarcastic.

"And if you want the humble opinion of a man who's interested in the economy rather than in finance, I think this crisis will leave no one unscathed."

Isidore didn't want to mouth off; he came from a world where respect was knocked into small boys with a stick. Lotte's father was an important businessman, Lotte's father had everything, authority, money, and Isidore was but a tightrope walker, dancing on the wire of hope; at the slightest puff from the father, his fall would be terrible.

He looked around him, noted the grand piano at the other end of the drawing room, the dressers and pedestal tables loaded with ornaments and photographs in their silver frames.

The place breathed order and affluence. Those who lived in such an apartment knew who they were, were as much in their right place as the furniture filling it.

In his wide-armed chair, the boss of the Chlorodon factory stretched his legs out a little. Would the conversation take an interesting turn?

Isidore sensed that he needed to respond intelligently, and prayed to the Holy Eels to come to his aid.

"You're right, this crisis will doubtless be awful and spread, but it's like with everything, one has to see the bigger picture. I, for example—and I wasn't the only one, of course—I thought the market would be bearish, and I acted to turn that to my advantage."

"You mean to say you bet on a fall?"

"Yes, sir."

"How long ago?"

"Just over a week, sir . . ."

Isidore could see the dot, dot, dot between the man's eyebrows.

"That's impressive, young man, you had a good hunch."

Isidore beamed, showing all the teeth he'd brushed hard that very morning with the "fresh-tasting" toothpaste.

"And do you think, young man, that a self-respecting father would allow a speculator to take his daughter to the movies?"

"Oh, sir! If you asked me to, for Lotte, I'd never see another broker for the rest of my life!"

Isidore had said this with such conviction that the father burst out laughing, yet couldn't help but admire the young man's pureness of heart.

"In that case, you have my permission to take her to the movies on Saturday evening."

10

In his class, children were collapsing onto their desks, unable to fight the first symptoms. Influenza had arrived in Leobendorf, just like everywhere else in Europe. The newspapers weren't mentioning it—in this time of war, military censorship demanded that people die exclusively in combat.[9] Having at first thought it was a strain of plague or cholera, so devastating was its effect, doctors in hospitals and dispensaries were reduced to signing death certificates, powerless in the face of an epidemic that felled your healthy youngsters in less than forty-eight hours.

Isidore had been sent home by the teacher, and his mother had put him to bed, shivering with fever. Martha had been dipping into her savings, in the secret hiding place at the back of the wardrobe, those for exceptional expenses, like the time they'd gone to drink hot chocolate in Vienna, what madness; and now she regretted it because her savings had melted away. She had gone out to fetch the doctor, who had prescribed aspirin without even glancing at her, without bothering to come to the bedside of the little patient. Aspirin was all the doctors had at their disposal to bring down 40-degree fevers, and overdosages were killing as often as the illness they were fighting.

When she got home, the child's waxen complexion alarmed her. She gave him the medicine and prepared cold water

[9] Indeed, the name "Spanish flu" derived from the fact that, since Spain wasn't at war, its newspapers had been allowed to write about the epidemic.

compresses, which she applied to his forehead, groin, and neck, then tried to get him to drink a few spoonfuls of a weak broth, but the child seemed too exhausted to swallow anything at all. She didn't imagine losing him because Isidore was a robust child, and childhood illnesses hadn't affected him. She watched over him all night and, in the early hours of the morning, now drained, saw with relief that his temperature had fallen. So she lay down beside him and fell fast asleep.

"Mommy? Mommy, I'm thirsty!"

Isidore still felt very weak, he buried his head in the familiar scent of his mother's mane of hair.

"Mommy?"

Martha struggled to surface, her head ached. She got up, almost staggering, and went to fetch a glass of water for the child. She was cold. She hoped she hadn't caught this wretched flu, too, and lay back down.

"Sleep, my darling, you need to sleep to get better."

The fever gripped her within a few hours, and her entire being began to fight the burning demon bearing down on her. There was no aspirin left, and she didn't even think of it, unable to move, suffocating, each breath producing a rattle. The child watched the change in his mother with fear. But he reassured himself, she'd soon get better, just like he had. She would say things to him, but so quietly that he couldn't understand, and didn't dare ask her to repeat them for fear of tiring her more.

"Yes, Mommy, okay, Mommy, rest, it'll get better."

She finally fell back to sleep and he snuggled up to her. Mother and son had always slept in the same bed. But his big mommy's teeth were chattering now, scaring him.

In the middle of the night, Isidore woke up. The sheets were drenched. He wondered if he'd wet the bed, but when he touched his mother's nightdress, realized that it was she who was bathed in sweat, with her eyes wide open. This time, he panicked.

"What can I do, Mommy? Tell me, what can I do?"

Martha was looking at her son with the greatest pain in the world.

"Give me your little hand."

Isidore had neither brother, nor sister, nor grandparents. She remembered her own loneliness as a child. When she'd been placed with those two wicked people who beat her like in the fairy tales. Forced her to do the household chores, but that didn't bother her, quite the opposite: dirty things, scouring the grime from the floor and the grease from pans, that didn't cause her suffering. Suffering is for those who think they have a right to joy.

She remembered Isidore's birth. How scared she'd been, seeing that red water running between her legs, but never would she have abandoned her child. How scared she'd been when Hermine Brombeere had sent her packing. She saw again the woman's shining helmet of blond hair, her silk dress, and her thin, white fingers. "Leave now! Filthy little slut!" How scared she'd been, pregnant, alone in the streets of Vienna with a little one in her belly she'd have to protect, when she didn't even know how to protect herself. Today, her son was nine years old and had only her in the world, she couldn't die. She sat up with a shudder and gripped her child's hand as hard as she could.

"I have a secret, an important secret."

Isidore moved his ear closer because his mother was barely whispering.

"Your father isn't dead but he doesn't know you exist . . . Your father is alive . . . He has a big house . . . very beautiful . . . overlooking the Stadtpark . . . a house in Vienna . . . He's called Franz Brombeere . . . that's his name, you must remember it . . . Repeat his name."

The little boy repeated:

"Franz Brombeere."

"Promise me you'll never forget it."

The child promised, swore.

"Franz Brombeere, he lives in a big house in Vienna on Johannesgasse . . . right in front of the park."

Isidore didn't know what Johannesgasse was, but he would remember that, too.

"Franz Brombeere."

She had closed her eyes; her breathing sounded like a sheet of paper being torn.

Isidore had always known that his father was alive, or rather, had never believed that he was dead, strange as that may seem. He also knew that the day he would see it, his father's face wouldn't be unknown to him, as if it had been graven within him and was just waiting to be unveiled.

"Do you forgive your Mommy?"

Isidore wasn't sure what he was supposed to forgive her for, but he smiled at her.

"Yes, Mommy."

Martha gazed at her son.

"Isi, if ever you're unhappy, to feel brave . . . think of me . . . but if you do think of me, do so with your best smile . . . because you have such a good smile. You've never cried, you know . . . not even on the day you were born. Promise me . . ."

"Yes, Mommy."

Through the window, stars may have been shining, and Isidore thought he heard a cry in the distance piercing the quiet of the night; he felt terribly small and useless, but he kept on smiling, showing all his teeth.

"D'you want me to go see the lady next door?"

"Gegeget ththe neigheighborrr."

She had muttered so quietly, he'd strained to hear. Maybe his mother didn't want him to, maybe she did. He had to do something anyway. He didn't bother to get dressed, and in his too-big socks and nightshirt down to his calves, he looked like a little ghost. On his face gaunt from illness, shadows like sodden violets circled his blue eyes. He got to the landing and knocked on the door, but no one came. Anxiety gripped his throat. He must find help. He went down one floor and started hammering with all his might, as if raving mad:

"Open up! Open up!"

Finally, a woman appeared.

"What on earth's going on, who's banging like that?"

Isidore didn't know her. They'd moved too often, he and his mother. To avoid bringing trouble on themselves. They remained discreet, "keep your head down, Isi," Martha would say to him, "keep your head down and don't talk to strangers."

"My mother's sick, she needs treatment, quick!"

"And who might you be?

"I'm Isidore. My mother's sick! Help me!"

The neighbor crossed her arms on her chest with a look of defiance. She'd heard all about this flu, folks were dropping like flies. An invisible hand was hovering and would usher young and old into oblivion; she'd seen the cart crisscrossing the streets of Leobendorf to collect the corpses to be flung into the pit. Only yesterday, the grocer had told her that at the town's dispensary, they barely had time to remove the dead from the beds to make room for the dying.

"And where have you sprung from, like this? Which floor do you live on?"

"The fifth, are you coming?"

"Where's your father?"

"He's dead."

Isidore had said those words so often that the fact he was alive made no difference. The neighbor looked disgusted.

"He died in the war."

Isidore was right to think that would reassure her, and felt it best to add:

"My father was a hero."

She indicated to him to scarper.

"Go back home, I'll be along."

"My mother's sick, you must help us."

"Yes, yes, right you are, I'll be along, now be off with you!"

The boy's eyes were bulging.

"We live on the fifth."

In his nightmares, he would revisit this scene thousands of times, his socks and nightshirt too big for him, how he'd gripped the sticky banister in the darkness of that dump, a small specter of a child whose candle projected his flickering shadow as he climbed back up the stairs. What time was it? Would he have to go to school tomorrow?

He lay back down against his mother, who wasn't shaking anymore. To get better you need to sleep. The dead woman's body was still warm and damp. So, wrapping his little arms around her, he whispered:

"The neighbor's coming, Mommy, she'll help us."

And he gave her his best smile, to show her how brave he was.

11

A blood clot had deprived his heart of oxygen. Since then, a stent had been inserted and recommendations made: physical exercise, no alcohol, no cigarettes, and the famous "rainbow diet." "Food that's varied in color and full of flavor," the doctor had said, handing him the book written by one of his colleagues. "Fill half of every plate with vegetables of different colors, because colors are a feast for the eyes, making the food more appetizing!" Lean meat, skinless poultry, and insipid fish cooked without butter, or lard, or salt. And no more fried food. Poor old Mrs. Valeras had had to change her ways. Two white tablets every day at breakfast would complete his recovery, as long as he avoided any excitement, of course.

It was thanks to the coronary that Henry Hogan had been able to curtail the media storm and scandal that the other attorney had been hoping and praying for. This had suited Michelle Alvez fine, as she preferred to remain discreet, conditioned by her line of work, perhaps.

The big boss of the Chloros group wasn't a man to run away: he'd held out his arm for a sample of his blood to be taken, and the result had been indisputable: Pearl really was his daughter.

Once the fact had been established, a figure had to be agreed on, and Henry had taken care of that. Henry dealt with everything. Isidore had only been obliged to exchange a glance with that Michelle on the day the check was signed. He had found her hideously vulgar. The case had set a legal precedent; now, if a mother wanted to request that an alleged father take a DNA test, he could no longer get out of it.

At seventy-nine, discovering that you have a twenty-year-old daughter was annoying, to say the least. Thank goodness that Lotte was long dead. Henry had insisted that the children be told, after all, they weren't children anymore. This kind of secret always ended up being revealed, and they would have, inevitably, held it against their father. Whereas if Isidore owned up, they'd have no choice but to accept it.

He hadn't remarried after Lotte's death, and for all these years, had derived a certain pride from his status of inconsolable widower. But he was only flesh and blood. He'd sighed and come round to Henry's point of view. The doctor had said he mustn't carry heavy things anymore; a secret illegitimate daughter would have weighed on him too much.

He had tried to understand the reason for his initial anger. He had thought, with bitterness, how sadness had punctuated his entire life, and that, sometimes, anger had come as reinforcement, to bolster him, to stop grief taking over the last, as yet unconquered, corner. Anger and disgust, too, when he'd seen that woman. He did remember it, yes, he'd had sex with her, one evening in Texas. The tow-colored hair, the greasy skin, such a contrast to Lotte! How could he have got this hooker pregnant? He had hoped she'd got it wrong, being a client for just one night meant nothing, and then the DNA had spoken. More than 99.9% reliable.

He had dined out with Henry that evening. Silently, the big boss had chewed a filet steak, without sauce, which had then sat on his stomach. He'd spent his life whitewashing himself, making people believe that he belonged to a world that wasn't his own, and he'd almost succeeded until that woman had dragged him back to his true origins: the gutter and bastardy.

"Don't worry, sir, we've begun negotiations. The other side will be easy to convince, they're only after your money."

Henry Hogan knew how to be reassuring.

"And the young girl?"

"Yes, sir?"

"She didn't ask to see me?"

"No. But thanks to you, she'll pay off her loan before her little friends do."

Isidore hadn't fancied a dessert. Anyhow, he wasn't allowed one.

The next day, he'd called Hogan and simply said to him: "I'd like you to organize a meeting with Pearl for me." He'd paused a moment, then specified: "At my place, whenever suits her."

It was agreeable working with Henry, you could request anything from him, he would always answer, *Very well.*

So, the following week, Henry had asked his boss:

"Would Tuesday suit you? At teatime?"

Henry was British. Pearl didn't drink tea, Isidore didn't either, but that didn't matter. Mrs. Valeras would bake *mantecados*, little lemon- and cinnamon-flavored Spanish cookies, which she would arrange prettily on an immaculate porcelain plate.

Isidore had insisted that the meeting take place at his home. It was only on the morning itself, a few hours before she was due to arrive, that the similarity with his own story had suddenly struck him and he'd felt the ground sway. With the difference that he had really wanted to meet his father, but Pearl hadn't.

He was imagining the scene. He saw her entering his building and being as impressed as he would have been, as he had been. She wouldn't be talkative.

"Are you happy at Columbia?"

"Yes, very."

"You're studying law?"

"Yes."

He had planned to tell her that he hadn't done this intentionally, that he was a responsible man, that if he'd known, he would have contributed financially much sooner. Was that why he wanted this meeting? To persuade an unknown girl that he wasn't a scoundrel? He was keen to avoid talking to her about himself, about his coronary, his children, and wondered which mask he'd make himself wear this time. He'd only ever be an imposter. He regretted that Hogan hadn't dissuaded him from getting her to come. This meeting would be nothing but going through the motions, it was bound to be.

He heard the bell ring and then Mrs. Valeras' steps as she went to the door. The young girl would have undoubtedly preferred some public place, a tree in Central Park or a banquette at the back of some café.

When a space is associated with power, it becomes a territory. In his padded armchair, the industrial magnate's heart was racing as if before a tryst. The familiar sound of the latch unlatching. Mrs. Valeras' high-pitched voice welcoming the stranger in, the shrill sounds of their conversation—they were too far away for him to catch their words. *Come in, he's expecting you. Thanks. Can I take anything? Do give me your coat. Yes, thanks.* That kind of introduction.

Mrs. Valeras was standing at the drawing-room door.

"Your daughter is here, sir."

Pearl felt sick. She'd never consider this man her father. You don't call a stranger *Daddy* when you're over eighteen. The very word seemed the most absurd thing in the world to her, and the two syllables had, invariably, caught in her throat since childhood. And anyhow, he was too old. If pushed, she wouldn't have minded a grandfather, but a father, no thanks, it was too late; she'd built herself up without one and, contrary to what people thought, she was tough. If she'd accepted to meet him, it was more out of curiosity. Of course, she knew what he looked like, that photo cut out of a magazine had had pride of place on the sideboard since she was four. But she was curious to see the man on glossy paper come to life, to hear the sound of his voice.

She hadn't expected to be shocked by the luxuriousness of the apartment. As she was following the servant, she remembered the low-ceilinged sitting room she'd grown up in, too small for the huge TV and their bulky, dirty-white leatherette sofa.

She found him much older than on the magazine photo. An old man. She loathed the contrived scenario, the smugness of the man posing in his own décor. It was easy to intimidate her, she was unarmed. She'd sensed that from her very first day at Columbia University. She'd felt ashamed of her image, her hick pointed boots, her acid-wash jeans, and her rather nasal Southern accent. Ever since, she'd tried to emulate the New York girls' style, opened her mouth wider and drawled her "i"s less.

Pearl had always been a good pupil, classrooms were where she felt most at ease, most herself, and in that respect, Columbia was paradise; the lectures were great and the professors wonderful. She'd enrolled for law but had discovered a whole load of unsuspected subjects, and she got up every morning thinking how lucky she was. Lucky to have a father come out of the blue to pay for her studies and give her a carefree student life. Of course, she'd accepted that money, but really didn't feel indebted, really couldn't care less about it.

And when she had stood in front of him, before they had even exchanged a word, she had felt the balance of power shifting. No one could have said that Pearl unsettled people. She was neither tall, nor charismatic, nor very beautiful, and she dressed in an ordinary way. That particular day, she had tied her hair up into a kind of slightly messy bun, there was no attempt to be stylish, nothing that sought to attract attention.

He had found it highly impolite, Mrs. Valeras daring to announce it in that way, out loud. He had no secrets from the woman who'd been in his service for nearly forty years, but all the same. *Your daughter is here.* He had only one daughter, she was called Felicity and was the spitting image of her mother, Lotte, an exquisite woman he'd loved with all his heart, and not a whore with troweled-on makeup.

But when Pearl appeared, it took a few seconds for the shock to hit him. At the door of his drawing room, in jeans and a baggy checked shirt, stood a vision that had returned from hell, a vision from a very distant past, a young dark-haired woman with blue eyes and rosy cheeks. And this memory was tinged with an immense sadness. So, whether as an automatic reflex, or simply because it was what She had told him to do, Isidore cracked his best smile.

12

Isidore had taken Lotte to watch *Lucky Star*, a silent movie by Frank Borzage lasting an hour and forty minutes. The story of an impoverished farm girl named Mary who met a certain Tim just before he left to fight in Europe with the battalions of the First World War. Unfortunately, Tim was wounded and lost the use of his legs. Once he was back home, the attraction between the two young people remained very strong but, because of his disability, Tim didn't dare declare his love. And that was before reckoning with Martin, a lumbering oaf and Tim's former sergeant, who had also set his sights on Mary. A turbulent romance then, featuring war and male rivalry, and ending well, thankfully, proving that love could transform people and allow them to overcome poverty, disability, and the harshness of the world in general, which allowed Isidore to identify with Mary one minute and Tim the next, and almost moved him to tears, although crying in front of Lotte was unthinkable.

Lotte was moved, too, but not for the same reasons. It was the first time a boy was taking her to the movies and, although the story was gripping, for an hour and forty minutes Lotte had leant her shoulder against Isidore's shoulder, and he hadn't tried anything. And yet, in the darkness, she had felt the warmth of the boy's body through the cotton of his shirt—he'd taken off his jacket so as not to crease it—and sensed each rise of his ribcage.

She had imagined herself leaning over to kiss him on the

neck, but hadn't dared. Particularly at the emotional moments, when Mary and Tim seemed doomed to an impossible love, Lotte had leant a bit more heavily on Isidore, and, in response, he, too, had leant with all his weight against her, to meld even more in sedentary symbiosis. The tension was so high.

Of course, at that moment, the two sweethearts longed for something else, they were burning with desire; they also knew that the memory of this forbidden contact would remain forever imprinted on their hearts. If one day they finally had the right to be husband and wife, since neither Isidore nor Lotte hid this desire, they wanted to get married, feel at ease together, and for her to carry his child in her belly, but none of all that would be worth this hour and forty minutes spent resisting and relishing, protected by the dampening contact of the layers of fabric separating them.

They emerged from the dimly lit theater, both ardent and glowing from within. He accompanied her home. It wasn't late, the air was mellow.

In the darkness, under the street lamps' orangey light, the two sweethearts were virtually floating. They walked fast, as if to use up a surplus of energy. They chatted about the film and other things, often interrupting each other; Lotte was an exuberant young girl. For once, Isidore wasn't suffering. Maybe that's what love was, a release removing you from time and space by making you experience the absolute in the present moment. He wanted to hold her hand, but she refused. And yet that wasn't for propriety's sake (people didn't hold hands in the street in New York in 1929); Lotte's reactions were as disordered and unconsidered as her sweetheart's.

After this episode, Isidore behaved as appropriately as he could. Sometimes he got it right, sometimes he just improvised, which was his trademark; the Holy Eels out there helped him to duck and dive, and generally dance around the truth. Lotte's father had to like him, that was his main aim.

The economic crisis was ongoing, with those speculators ruined by the markets soon joined by hordes of out-of-work men. As the stock-market crash became a banking crash, the whole system collapsed, businesses went bankrupt, factories shut up shop, nothing could survive anymore. On the promise of a free coffee and doughnut, Americans would line up for hours.

In March, Isidore watched, dumbfounded, as 350,000 people waving placards descended on Manhattan because they were hungry. Like everyone else, Lotte's father was affected, but being a good administrator, he was financially resilient and, fortunately, lots of people continued to brush their teeth.

For someone with a wad of lovely banknotes hidden under his pillow, there were bargains to be had. The young man knew it, but he'd decided not to buy a shoe shop; that dream wasn't big enough for him, and he didn't want to grovel at anyone's feet anymore. He explained this to Lotte. She replied that he must talk to Daddy about it.

Since their first movie night, Isidore had been allowed to pick her up once a week to take her somewhere in town for two hours, for a stroll, a milkshake, or to watch another movie. Each time he would encounter either the father or the mother, or both, and would give them his best smile.

"My word," the father would say, "he's most charming, this boy!" The mother, a shrewd woman, had gauged that he wasn't from the same social milieu as them, but since Isidore always turned up with a big bouquet of flowers, their stems dripping onto his trousers, and presented them to her with utmost solemnity, she had allowed herself to soften slightly towards him. And she liked his being Austrian, blood always tells.

Isidore would talk stocks and finance with the father. He'd think three times before saying anything, scared to say something stupid. "My word," the father would think, "he's very level-headed, this boy." So all was going pretty well, but Isidore knew that time was short, he needed to embark on some business or other, but which one?

For Lotte, there was no problem that her daddy couldn't solve.

"I'd rather not involve your father in all this."

"And whyever not?"

Isidore's actual skills remained vague, particularly since he still hadn't been invited to dine with the Hoffmanns, and thus undergo the inevitable interrogation. Lotte hadn't mentioned that he worked in a shoe store; as long as her parents presumed that the young man was a student, she would neither confirm nor contradict their presumption. Isidore had accepted that Lotte let out that he was an orphan, but he'd stressed that he'd been a happy and cherished orphan, he didn't want anyone's pity. In short, everyone was on the alert and lost in supposition. Isidore sensed that the moment when he'd have to present himself officially was approaching, and he'd need to find something a bit glorious or impressive to do with his life between now and then. But what?

Lotte had her own idea. Mr. Frederick Hoffmann might be tough in business, but he always gave in to his daughter.

Craftily, she'd picked her moment. One Sunday when her mother was out, she sought out her father in the calm of his study.

"Daddy darling, I have something to ask you. It's about Isidore, but you must promise to keep a secret."

The father blanched but remained stoical, helped by his starched collar; he put his newspaper down firmly. It suddenly struck him how very naïve and candid his daughter was, and he feared she was about to confess the unthinkable to him.

"Please, don't tell Mommy this."

"Of course, sweetheart, just tell me."

"Isidore isn't a student."

The father was flabbergasted; it was less bad than the worst, but serious all the same.

"But he told me that . . ."

"No, Daddy, Isi never said a thing. But you taught me that a lie by omission is also a lie. And this morning at church, I did a lot of thinking, and . . . I never want to lie to you."

And as she said that, she put her arms around his neck like she did as a child, seemingly to soften him up, but with a more pernicious aim since she knew her father was a man made uncomfortable by any physical contact.

He stiffened, while searching his memory for the name of a university.

"Daddy, I love him."

Oh dear, this time the worst wasn't far away.

"Isidore is very intelligent and very capable. Would you just give him a chance?"

"A chance? What do you mean by that?"

"A chance at your factory!"

Instinctively, the father found the idea displeasing. Letting this boy into his factory would be to make official something he didn't wish to make official. He was ready to close his eyes on a bit of flirting, but for years now, he'd intended Lotte to make a fine and grand marriage, with the eldest son of a wealthy American family. *Oh, the young these days, you allow them to go to the movies, and then the sky's the limit!*

"But Lotte, he isn't an engineer, you want me to employ him as a factory hand? If he hasn't done any studies, what do you want me to ask of him? And anyhow, what's he doing today? I mean, what does he spend his days doing?"

Suddenly, the father feared that Isidore might be a crook, he'd said that he speculated, but where did he get the money from, to play for a fall? His daughter! With a gangster? He looked at her, she was so beautiful, he'd promised her a radiant future and now here she was, dallying with a scumbag. "Lotte could push Frederick through the eye of a needle!" the mother would say.

"Darling Daddy, I beg you, do that for me."

The father sighed. After all, if the young man was working for him, he could keep an eye on him.

"Alright, alright, that's enough. I'll see what I can find for him."

And that's how Isidore started to work in the accounts department of the Chlorodon factories, where the fresh-tasting toothpaste was made. And that was already a total overestimation of the abilities of someone who had no idea what an accountant's assistant had to do. "Manage payment of suppliers, get hold of invoices, send payments, process pay slips, watch stock levels . . ." he'd been told. Isidore had tried to put on a calm front.

The most important thing was for the accounts to be accurate. His written English might be ropey, at best, but he'd always been good with numbers. He knew how to count, and importantly, knew how to recount, because not being cocky can spare you many errors.

Deeply moved by this helping hand from Lotte's father, Isidore was determined not to miss this opportunity. The factory was in Brooklyn, so he'd moved in order to be the first to arrive and last to leave. He wanted to learn, to make progress, he'd bought a notebook to write down his mistakes and memorize them. He might not be one of those superior men who impress with their intelligence, charisma or strength, but he was scared. Scared since his mother, in a sweat-drenched nightdress, had died one night in a shabby furnished room in Leobendorf. Scared of the other boys at the orphanage, scared in the big city of Vienna, scared on the boat that had delivered him to Ellis Island, scared in the streets of New York with his tin of polish in his hand, scared of ending up like a dog.

And today he was scared of losing Lotte because he thought he didn't deserve such happiness.

Fear had gripped his belly and knotted his guts for years, but all fear is pegged to a hope, that of pulling through.

13

There are those who want to understand the world, and those who want to change it. There are those who ask *why*? And those who answer *because*!

Isidore had no desire, at first, to change anything whatsoever, he simply wanted to find his place, even thinking he was prepared to sit wherever he was told to sit. But for boys such as him, society barely left the jump seats; if it was a comfortable armchair he was after, like that famous padded leather one, it was up to him to make it for himself.

Although toothpaste wasn't yet an essential product in 1930, and despite the terrible crisis that was devastating the country, the Chlorodon factory kept going. Lotte's father was obsessed with innovation, convinced that they stood at the dawn of a new world.

"Soon, even children will brush their teeth!"

They must innovate, but how?

From time to time, Mr. Hoffmann would summon Isidore to his office to get him to taste a cinnamon-flavored toothpaste with *spicy freshness*, or a salty one with *sea-breeze freshness*.

"So? What do you think of it?"

"I don't know, it's unusual, but I think I prefer the fresh-tasting Chlorodon."

With his good smile, the new accountant's assistant could almost have been used for advertising. Unsurprisingly, everyone liked him. Serious, polite, good-humored, and discreet with it, since he'd made very sure not to tell his colleagues that he was dallying with the boss's daughter. As for the father, he preferred not to think about it. He pretended to himself that his new accountant's assistant was merely a good recruit—"Never have the account books been so well kept"—and that some other boy, whom he barely knew, was taking his daughter to the movies. "She's playing the love-sick girl, but she's young, she'll get over it." He had divided his head into two compartments.

Banks continued to go under, and Isidore kept his lovely money inside an old sock. He didn't want to deposit it in any safe.

Since he'd been working for her father, Isidore seemed even more timid to Lotte. It was almost always she who took the initiative. If they went to drink a Coca-Cola and she reached for his hand under the table, he turned crimson. Time dragged for the girl dreaming of an engagement ring, but she remained convinced that Isidore was the one, the man that fate had sent to her one sunny Sunday, the purest boy she knew. She sensed that he was a mass of contradictions, at once joyful and very anxious, innocent and capable of violence. One moment she felt like mothering him, the next like running away with him. Maybe it was simply because Isidore was the first thing she was being denied?

Objectively, Mr. Hoffmann couldn't reproach him for anything, the young man was doing his best to be adopted, but he would never be the one he'd dreamt of for his daughter. When Lotte had shaken her long, curly blond locks, wanting to have them cut off, into a fashionable urchin style, her father and Isidore had stared wide-eyed in horror at the very idea, so she hadn't dwelt on it. She congratulated herself for maneuvering so successfully for the two of them to see each other every day.

"How's it going at work, darling Daddy?"

"Very well indeed, Lotte."

"You've nothing to tell me about?"

"No, nothing. Since when have you been interested in business, sweetheart?"

"You know very well."

"No, I don't know."

"Are you pleased with Isidore?"

These conversations were painful for the father. His daughter was driving him into a corner, one in which the accountant's assistant and the future son-in-law became one and the same person; and once again, he clung to his vision of a large property in the Hamptons with white shutters, a yacht, and Lotte on the arm of a young man, just back from playing polo or cricket, with a cable sweater slung over his shoulders.

"Do you speak German or English together?"

"We speak English, of course."

That wasn't strictly true. Mr. Hoffmann did indeed address Isidore in English in front of the other employees, but when it was just the two of them, he would sometimes drop in one or two words in his native tongue, and he was grateful to Isidore for not exploiting this linguistic complicity.

Lately, his "dear Germany," as he called it, was in a terrible state. The economic crisis plaguing the United States was as nothing compared with the post-war plight of the former Empire. Having dreamt of exporting his toothpaste across the Atlantic, he'd had to go back to the drawing board, refocus on the American market, protect his workers. Frederick Hoffmann knew when to be prudent, but he had a weakness for technical advances, and many years later, when he saw that famous striped toothpaste squirting out of a competitor's tube, he would be furious not to have thought of it himself. Yes, they must innovate, but how?

Isidore wasn't that interested in which formula would achieve the whitest teeth possible. What fascinated him was the factory itself, the machines that filled the tubes to a regular beat. Bang! Bang! Bang! The workers with grimy hands who greased the sheets of tin before shoving them into the grinding machine. The production-line work. Bang! Bang! The sound of the welding machine, the men's concentration, the repetitive movements, that perfect mechanical ballet.

One day, he learnt of the imminent bankruptcy of the Williamson Barber Father & Son factories, a small manufacturer specializing in shaving cream, located three blocks away from Chlorodon. Two workers, fearing that their boss would soon shut up shop, had turned up at Chlorodon in search of work, and Isidore had instinctively known that this was the opportunity he'd been waiting for.

He went to find Lotte's father early one morning, and presented his proposal to him. Mr. Hoffmann listened to him distractedly, and interrupted him mid-sentence.

"Williamson Barber might well be an opportunity, as you say. But if the factory is closing, it's because it's in difficulty, and we don't need any additional difficulties in the current climate. And anyhow, shaving cream? Seriously? Nothing will ever replace good old shaving soap."

Isidore took a moment.

"Mr. Hoffmann, with all due respect to you, I did take a look around at Williamson's."

The boss threw the young assistant accountant a look that combined astonishment and disdain.

"That factory opened three years ago, their machines are more modern than ours, but the same machines all the same. In my opinion, what's of interest to us at Williamson's isn't the shaving cream, it's the tubes."

"The tubes?"

"Yes, sir, the shaving cream is packaged in tubes, and we, too, manufacture tubes, and it seems to me that tubes are the future for hygiene products, and even the future for cosmetics."

The father went quiet. He'd pictured the shaving cream in

round metal tins, like the Nivea-cream ones. The young man had clearly sniffed out a golden opportunity.

"Isidore, I can't hide anything from you, you're our assistant accountant and, consequently, you know my company's finances almost as well as I do. We're surviving, but we're walking a tightrope. Even if this buy-out actually was a good idea for Chlorodon, we wouldn't have sufficient funds. Need I remind you that, over the past six months in this country, an average of a bank a day has gone under? No one will lend me any money."

"That's the thing . . . I have a little money."

How much?, the father wondered to himself.

Isidore was standing quite still, and had lowered his eyes.

"I have a little money and I could lend it to you, you'd give me an IOU, and when business picks up, I mean when the economy gets going again, as we're all convinced it will, you can pay me back."

"You have enough money to buy the Williamson factories?"

Isidore smiled.

"We'd have to go and negotiate, but I believe they're in dire straits. They got into debt for all those machines, some are almost new, they were over-ambitious."

"And why are you proposing a simple loan to me when you could ask me to . . ."

The father was struggling to find the right word; that of "partner" stuck in his throat. Isidore had foreseen that.

"I'm eternally grateful to you for allowing me to work for you. Every day I learn a lot. I simply wish to continue learning. That money isn't being used by me, and I believe that . . . it would be a real shame if Chlorodon missed out on this opportunity."

"Is that all?"

Isidore went bright red. The two men eyed each other in silence.

"And who knows? Maybe shaving cream isn't such a bad idea? More and more women are shaving."

The father couldn't help thinking of his daughter. A frank and manly conversation should already have been had, once and for all. Did this loan change things? Perhaps. At any rate, the young man had been astute enough not to take advantage of the situation openly and suggest throwing Lotte into the balance. Was that implicit? He wondered. Would he owe him anything at all, apart from what was on that IOU? No. Would it put them on a more equal footing? Yes. Where had he got that money from? From speculating? Solely? It seemed unlikely. The gangster thought crossed his mind again. *How dreadful*! Isidore seemed so honest, the head accountant had spoken of his "exemplary probity." Should he be wary?

"We could change the name, too! Williamson and Chlorodon don't go together. And we'd have to change their label so it resembles ours, and people will be pleased to buy the two tubes as . . . as a kind of complete kit for the groomed man, do you see?"

Mr. Hoffmann couldn't quite believe it. Maybe Lotte was right after all.

Isidore saw a flicker of interest in his boss's eyes. Without understanding why, he remembered an occasion at the orphanage when some boys had beaten him until his ears bled. He saw himself, curled up on the cold flagstones of the refectory, and could still feel the warmth of the red liquid trickling down his neck.

14

First there was the noise, like that of an orchestra tuning up in the pit. The noise of bodies arriving and banging into desks and sliding onto benches, the sound of coats being removed, zips opening bags and pencil cases, the clatter of the great unpacking of textbooks, notepads, pens, and all the chatter. They had to settle in and it was almost ceremonial. While they took possession of the place and scattered into clusters, there was whispering, a burst of laughter, there were those who were already ready, those lingering on something else, there was the dishy guy in the back row indicating to his best girlfriend that there was still a seat beside him, and the girl who could barely conceal how happy this made her.

Pearl, on the alert, noticed all such attempts to approach or get closer. She, too, garnered a few surreptitious glances, but struggled to interpret them. She didn't feel equal to this. To bolster herself, she thought: *They don't know that I'm the daughter of the boss of Chloros.* But she was also the daughter of Michelle.

"Is this seat free?"

"Yeah."

Pearl had been working on her "yeahs" since her arrival, her accent was her greatest preoccupation, she had to erase this linguistic stigma. She would observe the other girls, the length of their hair, their jewelry, their bags. Winter was fast approaching and it was cold, hell, it was cold! Soon, she'd need some fur-lined boots and a thick coat. She didn't want to be the bumpkin of the lecture hall, didn't want to look like that twit of a girl who'd just arrived from the South.

"Hi, I'm Adrian."

Pearl gave him the once over: khaki trousers, navy shirt, horn-rimmed glasses that gave him the amiable-intellectual look.

"Hi."

"What's your name?"

"Pearl."

"You see my friend, over there? The guy with a yellow T-shirt and a moronic smile?"

She turned round and saw a boy who looked furious.

"The one in a yellow tee? He's not exactly smiling . . ."

"Yeah, well, anyhow, he thinks you're really cute and would like to go out with you."

The boy had clearly understood what his pal was up to, and indicated that he'd kill him when he got the chance. Pearl had to laugh. A lover was always a good idea, although she'd have preferred a girl as a friend. One who wouldn't be like her, a New Yorker friend, with style.

All that she knew of life was what she'd read in books, classics from the 19th and early 20th centuries that her English-literature teachers had recommended to her. She applied those codes of behavior to the lecture hall and, with a knot in her stomach, wondered how not to stick out. She'd never been a popular girl, never had a serious boyfriend. Adrian, as it transpired, would become her great friend; not the boy in the yellow T-shirt, with whom she'd go for a slice of pizza and find perfectly nice, but nothing more.

"Where are you from?"

"Vermont, and you?"

"Texas."

"Cool."

Pearl pouted dubiously; she was forever apologizing for herself.

"No, honestly, I find it cool, it's cowboy country."

It turned out that Adrian found everything cool, life in general and studying at Columbia in particular. He was also the offspring of an unmarried mother, he was also lower middle class but, unlike Pearl, didn't think that his admission to the prestigious university had been based on a misunderstanding, or owed anything at all to luck.

Pearl's approach to friendship was passive, to say the least. Never would she have gone up to a girl to ask: "Would you like to be my friend?" But if a move was made towards her, she was ready to give her all, from the very first second. She knew that she waited to be chosen; even more than that, she waited to be recognized. And, paradoxically, anyone would have been acceptable. Literature was full of soulmates and exemplary friendships. As soon as love came into play, you had to find your other half. And hence the poets had decided to ignore all those who'd make do with the first to show up, without agonizing over it. Because rare were the jars that found their lid, the one that fitted them perfectly in size and shape. In most cases, a square of tinfoil and a little good will sufficed. The semblance of a lid, molded and folded around the edges. You just had to be careful not to tear yourself, if you decided to swap jars. All tinfoil squares knew that.

"Are you doing business law?"

"Yes."

"Cool! Me, too."

Business law and taxation, the department of sharks. Not the international law of those who wanted to work at the UN and change the world; not the intellectual-property law for those who wanted to be on the side of Art. Pearl had picked her camp, that of money, the one in which she'd no longer be her mother's daughter. She had naively thought that, 1,600 miles away from her native city, she'd no longer feel ashamed of her origins, but the opposite had occurred. Never had she felt so alone and pointed at.

As for her father, should she call him her father? Her genitor? Isidore? The old man? She was wary and remained on her guard. For the rest of her life, she would remember their first meeting, and Mrs. Valeras' lemon and cinnamon cookies, and their bitter taste.

"Are you happy at Columbia?"

"Yes, very."

"You have a room on campus?"

They had carefully avoided any subject that touched on Isidore's children or Pearl's mother. The old man was uncomfortable with the thought of Pearl knowing that he'd been with prostitutes, not realizing that, for her, it was the most natural thing in the world.

"Had you visited New York before?"

"No."

The conversation had progressed normally, without too many bumps: what did Pearl think of New York? Had she been to MoMA? No? She must! Pearl had visited Houston's Museum of Fine Arts with her 8th grade class, and also the Museum of Natural Science with their biology teacher, Mr. Bouliet. But since arriving in New York, apart from strolling, eyes up, between the skyscrapers, and mooching around smart neighborhoods to try to capture the atmosphere in those streets with the wrought-iron balconies, she hadn't set foot in any cultural venue.

"I would be delighted to accompany you there."

He must have regretted saying that. Whether prompted by spontaneous enthusiasm or a polite reflex, the fact was, they were stuck with it now.

"Let's make a date."

"Okay."

"Next Saturday?"

"Yes, fine."

And that's how things had started, due to overeagerness. Isidore would never have admitted to himself that he wanted to see this young girl again because she was the splitting image of the one who had died in a fever-soaked nightdress.

* * *

Sitting on the steps of the grand stairway outside the library, Pearl and Adrian were eating a chicken sandwich. Adrian was chewing conscientiously, which made his glasses move. The two friends were never apart now.

"I'm going to MoMA tomorrow, with Isidore."

"Cool! Does he do business law, too?"

For a moment, Pearl continued to contemplate the mayonnaise oozing between the bread.

"No, he's my father . . . well, my genitor, if you prefer."

Adrian preferred nothing at all, but Pearl had suffered a great deal during her childhood from having to keep silent about her origins, from not being able to admit that she was, as her mother said, "a condom slip-up," the fruit of the ancillary union of a toothpaste magnate and a prostitute. She knew better than anyone how a secret could taint her relationship with the outside world. So she decided just to tell Adrian the story without holding back. And amazingly, Adrian thought it was *super* cool. The Chloros empire was quite something, Pearl would have no problem finding her first business-law internship.

"I prefer to do my own thing."

"Yeah, but it's awesome, all the same."

Pearl liked it that Adrian said exactly what he thought, and indeed, his thoughts were never nasty.

* * *

The entrance hall at MoMA, with its tall windows, made her

feel like she was walking into a cathedral. Isidore was waiting for her. He was wearing a three-piece suit, extremely elegant, old-Europe style, or at least, Americans' idea of old Europe.

"Hello, Pearl! You're right on time!"

She didn't tell him that she'd arrived twenty minutes early and had milled around the neighborhood, annoyed with herself for agreeing to spend her Saturday afternoon with an old stranger.

"Come, we'll take the elevator. I thought we should begin at the beginning. We'll never have time to see everything anyway. And it's my favorite section, personally, the stuff that's too modern . . . you know . . . Do you like modern art?"

She wondered if he wasn't the most uncomfortable out of the two of them. He walked in front of her, at a pace she felt was too energetic for the occasion. Pearl knew nothing about contemporary art, but, ever the diligent pupil, had perused the catalogue of MoMA's permanent collection at the campus library the previous day.

"I like Andy Warhol."

"Ah yes, Andy Warhol, of course . . . of course."

The elevator took them up to the fifth floor, there were lots of tourists around, cameras slung around their necks. Pearl felt oppressed, Isidore never stopped talking: "Do you know this painting?" "And him?" "And do you like it?" Not a moment of quiet contemplation in his approach. And he smiled too much. She found him ridiculous, and yet she, too, smiled, and felt annoyed with herself for being *nice* to the man who had screwed her mother one lonely evening. The harm was irreparable; Van Gogh's and Picasso's paintings could flaunt their colors and brushstrokes all they liked.

"And Cézanne, do you know Cézanne?"

Pearl needed some air. She was tough, she didn't need a father, never had needed one. So he could pay for her studies and leave her in peace. She had a vision of herself as a great attorney, she'd pay him back every cent, she saw herself in front of a pile of gold coins, she wanted to owe him nothing.

"The colors in this one are marvelous, aren't they?"

She didn't reply, just kept advancing randomly among the static works. She was split between the calm of her movements and the frenzied pounding of blood in her throat. She so regretted coming here, but she could no longer leave. Not out of politeness, no. Since childhood, she'd had a desire to please at all costs. This flaw guided her actions and reactions, she was prepared to deny herself simply to be liked.

She stopped in front of a painting depicting a pregnant woman draped in red, with the title *Hope, II*, and couldn't help but notice the irony of the situation. The woman's head was bowed, her eyes closed as though in prayer. Her breasts were magnificent, full, their pink nipples outlined against pale skin that was almost blue in its transparency. There were three women at her feet, among the folds of her cloak, three women with their eyes closed, their bearing suggesting chasteness. The artist had balanced a skull on the rounded belly. The painting's background seemed to have been sprinkled with specks of gold and silver, and the red cloak itself was highly decorated. Pearl sensed Isidore's presence behind her.

"That's beautiful."

"Yes, I think so, too."

She let out a deep sigh.

"You like it?"

"Yes, a lot."

"It's an allegory."

Pearl thought of her mother, did she know the word 'allegory'? Suddenly, she felt like crying.

"There's a peacefulness about it."

"Peaceful and sad, I'd say, no?"

Maybe people who explain paintings are always trying to explain themselves.

"It's a painting by an Austrian artist."

"Oh, really?"

Isidore put on a cheery voice to mask his disquiet.

"Yes, an extraordinary painter, and I'm not saying that because he's Austrian."

Pearl peered at the small label on the wall and read it out loud.

"Gustav Klimt? I don't know him."

Isidore remained silent for a moment, lost in thought.

"Yes, he painted landscapes and . . . some very fine portraits."

15

And that's how, on November 24, 1930, the Chlorodon "fresh-tasting" toothpaste factories acquired the Williamson Barber Father & Son "no water or brush needed" shaving-cream factories, marking the start of the development of the Chloros empire.[10]

Mr. Hoffmann had given an IOU to Isidore. Three years later, Isidore would be appointed financial director, and, more importantly, would marry Miss Lotte Hoffmann in grand style, as befitted "the young son from a good family who had sadly lost his parents" that he was, according to the version adopted by the Hoffmanns, who decided not to question Isidore on his origins so they wouldn't have to cover them up, but, aided by their daughter, posited a story that their son-in-law was careful not to contradict. Sometimes, not telling the truth is enough.

"Chloros is, first and foremost, a family business."

On that evening of July 1952, the patriarch would be conferred the Bronze Medallion of New York City, because the backstory of this captain of industry was exemplary. The mayor in person, Mr. Vincent Impellitteri, would present it to him.

Mr. Frederick Hoffmann had been working on his speech for weeks. He could have begun it like this: "The great Chloros

[10] In 2022, Chloros was the third largest cosmetic and hygiene products group in the world. The business owned 250 subsidiaries, was present in 60 countries, had products marketed in more than 175 countries and capitalization of 429,779 million dollars.

adventure took off on the day I acquired Williamson, and that wouldn't have been possible without my dear son-in-law." But he had preferred to tell the tale slightly differently. Sometimes, several truths coexist.

The Grand Ballroom of the Waldorf Astoria hotel was buzzing with men in tuxedos and women in white satin evening gloves. Amidst the cigarette smoke, Frederick Hoffmann had been asked to come up onto the dais and speak straight into the microphones, because tomorrow, in the newspaper, they would recount how lovely the gathering was and how successful the evening.

"Even if shaving cream took a certain time to—if you'll pardon the pun—*penetrate* the market . . ."

Laughter in the ballroom.

Of course, they had occasionally misfired. That tube of shoe polish, for example. Thanks to his son-in-law's obsession with putting everything into tubes. It was actually one of the rare occasions when Isidore had dug his heels in, and had even wanted to meddle with the composition of the product, despite knowing nothing about chemistry, proposing that they add beetroot juice to the final formula. A preposterous idea, to say the least, in the eyes of the father-in-law, which had wasted them both time and money, but it had served as a good lesson to them. Particularly to Isidore, who, after the event, had promised himself to stay as far away as possible from his former life. He had secretly dreamt of a "success story," in which the former shoeshine boy took his revenge and became the biggest purveyor of polish in the United States; but what's the point of a story when you've got no one to tell it to? Even Lotte didn't know that he used to charge 10 cents to kneel down and spit.

There had also been the tube of deodorant cream, then the new magnesium-hydroxide toothpaste. When Isidore's and Lotte's first son, Peter, was born, they had moved to aluminum tubes. Substantial investment had been required, and a complete overhaul of their factories. But that particular choice had been a watershed. As a general rule, Isidore could sense the direction of the winds of progress, and Frederick Hoffmann had soon found that he could trust him. So close were the father-in-law and son-in-law that they were often taken for father and son.

"When Peter, my grandson, got his first milk tooth, we created Chlorokids, the first toothpaste for children! That was an extraordinary adventure, and it's one of the things I'm proudest of today."

That evening, Lotte looked resplendent. She was wearing a dress of blue silk and a river of diamonds. She had finally got her hair cut into a bob, on her fortieth birthday. She had greatly contributed to the success of Chlorokids thanks to her idea of putting a drawing of a kindly fairy on the label, the Tooth Fairy, who wore a blue dress and was blond, strangely resembling Lotte, in fact; maybe the illustrator had been inspired by her. The drawing was so popular, they'd had postcards printed of it: "A free card for every tube purchased." And so hundreds of thousands of little Americans had pinned the fairy above their beds in the hope that she would protect their little teeth and give them a coin when one of them fell out, and most importantly, they no longer forgot to brush their teeth before bed. Once adult, they wouldn't be able to do without. This marketing exercise had run alongside a campaign aimed at dentists—"Fluorine will make your teeth shine!"—and the mass recruitment of demonstrators. But Isidore's stroke of genius had been to persuade his father-in-law to advertise directly in the classrooms of the nation's elementary schools.

Frederick belonged to the very select Metropolitan Club. Thanks to his contacts, they had been able to meet some members of government and had found themselves lobbying for oral hygiene, and for their own interests. In the meantime, they had bought a toothbrush factory and the grandfather had decreed that a second size of brush must be designed.

"You must admit, there's nothing cuter than a miniature toothbrush!"

Smiles all around.

Having dipped a toe into lobbying, the father- and son-in-law had become friends with an undersecretary of state who would prove very useful a few years later, when the US entered the war. Sixteen million recruits would serve in the American armed forces until 1945. Sixteen million men who would need to be equipped with the famous GI pack, and slipped into every toiletry bag there would have to be, among other things, a toothbrush, a tube of toothpaste, and even a tube of shaving cream.

"I can definitely say that the confidence the Secretary of Defense showed in me was a turning point in the life of my business, and in my own life."

Applause.

Frederick Hoffmann had decided not to dwell on the misgivings his name had prompted: *they surely weren't going to ask a German to supply the American army*! He'd sent his son-in-law to negotiate for the company, and Isidore H. Ferguson had succeeded in being persuasive, as always.

The Chloros tubes had thus landed in France under the bombs, and the intrigued Europeans had discovered how advanced the GIs were, compared with them, when it came to toiletry bags. At the end of the war, the production capacity of the business had quintupled, and Frederick didn't hold back from flooding his dear old continent with the progressive items he was producing across the pond. Then their French, Italian and German subsidiaries had sprung up, all wanting their share of those "ultrabright" Hollywood smiles—Chloros had been the first brand, just after the war, to get movie stars to promote it in ads; once again, it was Isidore whom the father-in-law had sent to persuade them.

What a life Isidore had had! What good fortune he had had!

He owed everything to the Hoffmanns. Under the grand chandelier of the Waldorf Astoria hotel, he gazed at his children. Peter was nineteen and Felicity seventeen. Their youngest, Thomas, wasn't there that evening because he'd been sent to a summer camp to play tennis. Isidore admired the way Lotte had brought up their children. He had let her get on with it, she knew all the codes.

Isidore was crazy about his last son. Thomas was a gentle child with blue eyes, extremely likeable. When people met him, they would exclaim: "What a charming little chap, that one!" There was a great complicity between the father and his youngest; he tried not to make it too obvious in front of the two older children, but he couldn't help it. Isidore was proud that Thomas played tennis like the children from good families. He'd never played it, had obviously never even tried to learn.

Still today, despite being the No. 2 of the Chloros group and thus respected by all—because he had the reputation of being a workaholic, and nothing like a son-in-law parachuted into a post he didn't deserve—despite that, then, whenever he went to the Metropolitan Club, he remained terrified at the thought of one of those pushy young men, born with a silver spoon in their mouth, suggesting, "A little tennis on Sunday?". "I'd love to but, sadly, I've work to do," he would reply, putting on his best smile. "Even on Sunday?" the rich kids would mutter, but in the end, this would merely increase their admiration for him. *My son Thomas will never feel shame. A tennis match? With pleasure! And he'll beat the lot of them. My son won't live in fear.*

Peter, his eldest, was a young man who, like his mother, loved to read, had secured a place at Harvard, and as soon as he graduated, would join the family business without a second thought. Felicity was more artistic; at least, it was towards painting and drawing that she'd been steered. Isidore had noticed that she tended to be a little too fond of cream buns at teatime, but she had a pretty face and her parents were very rich, they'd have no problem marrying her off.

"Yes, I believe in plastic, plastic's going to change everything! We're going to create 1,257 jobs! And I'm proud to open the new factory, bringing together all that technology does best today, in the north of this city that I love so much and owe so much to, because I may be fortunate enough to be American by adoption, but I'm a New Yorker at heart."

Renewed applause.

It was this giant factory that had brought Frederick Hoffmann the medallion he was receiving tonight. It was time to drop aluminum, time for radical LDPE and HDPE, or radical low- and high-density polyethylenes. Low density for the soft tubes, high for the rigid bottles. The number of products needing to be tubed had rocketed: skincare creams, shampoos, gels of all description. Since the group had turned towards the female market, their prospects for growth were brilliant.

Frederick Hoffmann looked towards his loved ones; his wife had filled out a lot, it gave her a certain reassuring softness. She smiled at him. "Bravo, my darling, you were perfect!", "Daddy, that was great!" "We're so proud of you, Granddad!" What a fine family they made.

Hugging and kissing, flashbulbs flashing.

A few hours later, Isidore and Lotte held hands at the back of the chauffeur-driven car. "That was a lovely evening," Lotte said. Tired and a little tipsy after all that champagne, she leant her head on her husband's shoulder. They knew each other so well. She, too, must have revisited part of her life during her father's speech. What a distance they'd come since those Italian ices they'd eat in Coney Island while eyeing each other hungrily, and those little notes they'd secretly exchange with racing hearts!

Lotte remembered their first kiss, the first night they'd slept in the same bed, the birth of their first child.

We easily recall first times in life, but what's awful about last times is that they don't introduce themselves as such.

Carefree, sinking into the soft comfort of the large sedan's seats, Lotte didn't know that that evening at the Waldorf Astoria was the last on which they would be happy.

Part Two

Over nocturnal dark floods
I sing my sad songs,
Songs that bleed like wounds.
However, no heart carries them to me again
Through the darkness.
—From "Night Song" by Georg Trakl

1

Tommy and Charlie liked to introduce themselves by saying, "We've been best friends since we were born!". And indeed, with their mothers themselves being friends and giving birth a week apart, they had, as it were, put them into the same cradle, then the same park, the same nursery school, and so on. Today, Tommy and Charlie were at junior high and there wasn't a memory they didn't share. They were inseparable, to the extent that if one liked a particular sport, it would have been unthinkable for the other not to try it, too, and life had worked out well because they both loved playing tennis.

Thomas was the third child of Lotte and Isidore Hoffmann Ferguson. His mother wanted him to read books, like Peter, his big brother, the idol, who would be starting at Harvard in September. When Peter was thirteen, he had already read all of Dickens, all of Walter Scott, all of Goethe, and he wrote poems and was top at math. Peter was perfect, except that, at nineteen, he couldn't catch a ball. Tommy wasn't bad in class, but the lessons bored him. His father would say to his mother, "Leave him be, he isn't mature yet, he's just as intelligent as Peter, don't you worry." His father called him "my champion" or just "champion," and his mother would mock.

"Oh, the darling champignon!"

"I'm right, you'll see, he'll become a champion of something, that one . . . He's exceptional, our Tommy."

And Lotte would make big eyes at him because she thought

it best not to heap too much praise on children, for fear of making them conceited.

When Tommy would win a match and crow about it, his mother would rebuke him: "Be humble, Thomas, please." But if his eyes met his father's at that moment, he saw all the pride in the world in them.

Girls didn't interest him, he felt very different to them. Apart from Felicity, his big sister, but a sister didn't count as a real girl. Their complicity had been built around a whole series of secret codes and linguistic games. The latest of the latter consisted of making the other one say "Yeah" to then complete a word.

"Want some more cake?"

"Yeah!"

"Low!"

Or:

"Are you pleased?"

"Yeah!"

"Ti!"

Needless to say, this kind of puerile behavior totally exasperated Peter.

It was Lotte who had found the summer camp. "At Camp Hooray, we play tennis everyday!" She had immediately told Charles's mother about it, the two boys would share a room, everything had worked out splendidly. A month of intensive tennis coaching in Vermont, Charlie and Tommy were thrilled.

As for a room, it was actually a cabin for eight boys who talked loud and fast, and never stopped playing silly practical jokes, soon to be aimed at the puniest in the group.

For those who weren't being targeted, the atmosphere was great. When not playing tennis, they were taught how to make torches with paraffin, tie different knots, and recognize edible plants, a bit like Scouts. Every morning they would make their beds, sweep the floor, and even take turns to do the dishes.

Charlie sulked a bit because he'd never made his bed in his life, let alone swept the floor; Tommy hadn't either, but he was more adaptable, and since they were the two youngest in the cabin, they kept a low profile.

Tommy had never ejaculated. He knew what it meant because Charlie had started puberty a little earlier and had immediately told him about the pleasures of erotic orgasm. Tommy did have erections, most often during English classes, even though his teacher wasn't particularly pretty. In general, his erections were, to say the least, unpredictable.

So, the first group jerk-off, involving four boys from their cabin, that Charlie and Tommy had watched had proved highly informative. Tommy had expected it to look like mayonnaise, as that's how Charlie had described it to him, but the semen had been a murky white and far more liquid and slimy than anticipated. Mainly, the speed at which the semen spurted out had fascinated him. The four jerk-off kings did it in public, then, but most evenings, the other boys masturbated in their beds, not showing anything to anyone. Many of them had spent the past year falling in love, a love as passionate as it was short-lived. Not Tommy, he preferred tennis matches. At junior high, love created silences and tensions, and then there was the torment of your first braces and the trial of acne. Tommy was lucky, he had a peachy complexion.

There were three hundred-and-twenty adolescents spread out in forty cabins, not including those housing supervisors and management. Morning saw the raising of the colors and the singing of the Camp Hooray anthem.

Hip hip Hooray!
We learn every day
We grow every day
At Camp Hooray
Hip Hip Hooray!
Men we'll be one day

Hip hip hooray!

Which Tommy had promptly turned into:

Hip hip Hooray!
We sweep every day
We scrub every day
At Camp Hooray
Hip hip hooray!
Little fags we'll be one day
Hip hip hooray!

This version had gone down a storm, and even if Tommy hadn't joined the group jerk-off on the first night, it had given him the reputation of being a rebel and he'd had no difficulty making friends.

Thomas might well have mocked their stupid anthem, but if they hadn't become men during their month-long camp, they had certainly grown up.

He'd started to write letters during the hour-long break after lunch, and had discovered how agreeable and liberating the activity was. It was the first time he could imagine becoming a journalist, or even better, a special correspondent. He pictured himself covering conflicts in mega dangerous warzones on the other side of the world, and smiled at the thought of his mother, who was forever fearful of something happening to him.

To his parents, he wrote quite formal letters, in which he would talk about what he was reading, mainly to please his mother. At school, they'd been asked to read *A Tale of Two Cities* during the vacation, and the novel bored him to tears, he was frank about that and mocked Dickens' style of writing. Lotte was a very loving mother, but she demanded perfection from her children. If Tommy had known how rebellious she'd been, and about all her scheming to marry his father, he would have been flabbergasted. His postscripts were aimed at his father. *I beat Charlie 6-2, 6-1 yesterday, he was furious!*

To Felicity, he sent letters that were far more tender. His big sister was the only person in the world to whom he could admit his feelings. His admiration for his father was boundless and he deeply respected his mother, but he never would have dared to write to them that he was longing to be back with them and missing them, apart from Peter. Indeed, Thomas hadn't written to Peter, who would have just pointed out his grammar mistakes. This big brother, who was six years older than him, had always put up barriers to prevent the baby of the family from identifying with him.

The last day of camp finally arrived, and a ceremony was organized for that evening, with prizes given and applause for the best tennis players, the best servers, the best volleyers, in both singles and doubles, but also for all those who had won something during the camp: darts and archery contests, sack races, a medal was even awarded to the best campmate. Everyone had been assigned a particular role, and Charlie and Tommy were in the team that would set off the fireworks.

"Are you asleep?"

"Well, no, dork. You can see my eyes are open."

"Shall we go for a walk?"

They slipped out without making a sound.

It must have been a little past five in the morning, and Tommy found it wonderful to be up in the expectant silence of dawn breaking. It was one of those mornings when the freshness of the air is divine. The day was set to be a scorcher.

The two boys felt as if they were entering a tale in which the fairies had put everyone in a castle to sleep, and they alone would be able to move forward among those for whom time had stopped.

They were in their pajamas, barefoot. They crossed the large lawn, where the cabins were lined up, as if in a dream. The sun glinting on the oil-like water of the lake was breathtakingly beautiful.

"Shall we have a swim?"

"Come on, let's do it!"

Grinning, the two boys pulled off their pjs. These four weeks of tennis had left their mark: pale shoulders, chests and thighs, tanned forearms and calves. They did hesitate briefly, conscious of the solemnity of the moment, almost ashamed at the thought of disturbing the calm of the water.

The shore of the lake was sandy and cool, not an unpleasant sensation under the toes. Charlie was first to enter the water, slowly, and then faster, to show he wasn't scared or cold.

Tommy felt the sensual swell of the water. A feeling that couldn't be shared, he and Charlie were alone, each overcome by the ice-cold liquid's caress on their young bodies, a sensation that was gentle and violent all at once. The sparkling of the sun's rays on the surface of the water made him screw up his eyes. He dived in to feel even more immersed and alive, then started to swim, with swift, even strokes.

"Tommy, wait for me!"

Charlie was determined to catch up with him, but wasn't as good a swimmer as his friend. Tommy stopped. They were now just a few yards away from each other.

Tommy might have grimaced or looked strange, but his best friend could see only the nape of his neck above the surface. The two boys were flooded with silver reflections. On the shore, the weeping willows' branches were bowed and perfectly still. Suddenly, Thomas had disappeared under the water. He hadn't dived in, had made no effort; he'd allowed himself to be engulfed in slow motion. It was to play a trick on him. Tommy would suddenly emerge and grab hold of his leg, like some slimy fish. How long before Charlie would start calling out to him?

"Tommy! Tommy?"

To scream.

"Tommy! Tommmyyy!!!"

Maybe Tommy was a champion underwater swimmer and had never told him. It was the best trick in the world, he must have swum over to the other shore, over there, near the weeping willows, and popped out of the water without Charlie seeing him, to give him the fright of his life.

"Tommy! Stop it! Where are you?"

There was no point shouting, one can't hear at the bottom of the abyss. And Charlie knew, despite hope distorting his reason, he knew that the image of Tommy's inclined nape, of the slow submersion of his hair, that that image would come back a thousand times to haunt him.

Tommy was swimming, Tommy had stopped swimming, and, without a backward glance, in a stunned spasm, Tommy had experienced a tiny moment of absence. In front of his best friend, Tommy had drowned without making the slightest splash.

2

This was kids' stuff. In the darkness of his rage, Isidore had searched for someone to blame, unable to admit to himself that no one was to blame. Who could have foreseen what had happened? Tommy was a strong swimmer, he was athletic, he was in perfect health and had never had an epileptic fit before. The lake was so calm, not a fish that could have bitten his toes. Had the sparkling surface of the water triggered the fit? The neurologists had come up with the hypothesis of juvenile myoclonic epilepsy. And so? What did that change? The boys should have been supervised! The camp's staff had failed. Oh, they were so sorry, so very sorry, what an appalling tragedy, but it had all happened so fast. Two young boys had taken a dip in the lake early in the morning, they had meant no harm. It was Charlie's fault. Whose idea had it been to go for a swim? Who had said, come on, let's do it?

Before the accident, they had been stable, relying on their four feet and their three children. Grief always involves a subtraction. Three minus one, two. They had two children left. Isidore had always found refuge in numbers.

There's the person we are, and the person we dream of being, and the two so rarely coincide that the latter always prevents the former from enjoying being that person. It was in that gap between the life of an orphaned shoeshine boy and his dreams of marrying the daughter of a rich industrialist that Isidore's freedom was to be found. His freedom and his anxiety. His life had surpassed his expectations, in misfortunes and in joys, but this misfortune was too much. A great ordinary misfortune, the kind that makes you raise your eyes to heaven asking, why me?

The causal chain was useless. There was no point going back in time to try to seize and grip onto something concrete, an anchor on the border between before and after, that moment of which he could say, I was happy until I could never be happy again. It wasn't when the child had died, but when the phone had rung and Lotte, in her pink dressing gown, had picked up the receiver. The morning after that great celebratory event, an entire evening of sitting comfortably, and then waking up to the strident dring-dring of the phone, and Lotte standing, then feeling the ground give way beneath her feet. She had cried out. Or maybe she'd remained silent, Isidore could no longer remember because he had wrecked that memory by replaying it so many times. Through telling it, he had distorted it, and now the moment the news had been received lay like a broken, useless toy, its truth erased, because memory will always prefer an orderly account to a vague impression. But Isidore had known immediately, of that he was certain. He had known that it was about Tommy, and that Tommy was dead.

And yet, after the loss, Isidore and Lotte had been determined to live. The time following the tragedy had been nothing but slowness. Isidore had learnt to tolerate his pain. Well-meaning people, their friends, those who had never been through such a tragedy, would tell them: "You mustn't let yourself go, you must live, you have two fine children! Just look, Peter is wonderful! And Felicity, isn't she a ray of sunshine?" Isidore had the right to feel sorry for himself, but not to give up the ghost. He had to sign contracts, buy factories, champion oral hygiene, sit at the table, carry his fork to his lips, and say thank you for the dinner. He had to protect his wife, who was suffering far more because she was a mother and mothers felt the death of a child to their very core.

And then Isidore's grief had finally got lost, buried under

the layers of the years. He hadn't even been able to be sad when Lotte had, in turn, died. The vulture had already gnawed all his sadness away.

Certain philosophers see life as a pendulum that swings from right to left, between joy and sadness, suffering and recovery, excitement and boredom. In this way, it's reassuring to think that if things are going badly, there's a strong chance that they'll go better, and then inevitably go badly again, but then better once again, and so on, indefinitely.

This back and forth was unknown to Isidore, having seen himself tip right over too many times. Tip over irredeemably. He'd tipped over into joy when he'd said to Lotte, "And I'm Werther"; when he'd bet on the fall of General Electric; when those two workers had told him about the bankruptcy of the Williamson Barber Father & Son factories; and even when they'd bought the Star Blonde shampoos. But too often, he had tipped over into the arms of sorrow. After Tommy, even if Isidore had remained standing, he had never really walked again.

For his parents, Thomas had continued to be printed in the negative. Tommy hadn't gone back to school, hadn't won the club cup, hadn't had the beginnings of a beard needing to be shaved, hadn't filled in forms for a place at university, hadn't passed his driving test, hadn't left home. But the more time passed, the less painful were these visions, because Tommy had stopped growing up at thirteen and imagining him in a soldier's uniform seemed absurd.

Lotte and Charlie's mother had become distant, but unlike her husband, Lotte hadn't held a grudge against the young boy. Charlie had also suffered greatly from the death of his best friend. Lotte had happened to cross paths with him, once at the wheel of a car, another time with a pretty girl in a polka-dot dress on his arm. They had been invited to the young man's wedding. When she had received the ivory invitation card, with its thick, velvety paper and elegant script, Lotte hadn't been able to stop her hands from shaking. On another occasion, at the tennis club, because the two families still moved in the same circles, Isidore and Lotte had noticed that one of the rooms was reserved for the fortieth birthday party of Mr. Charles Bratwood, and the ground had seemed to give way under their feet. Forty years old, that was a big deal! The life of their child had suddenly appeared to them in its vacuum, a puff of smoke, a series of images that were intangible, transparent, alienated, which they had superposed as time had passed to turn their grief into sediment; and the elderly parents had found themselves aghast, unable to of make the link between the boy of thirteen and the man blowing out his candles in a private room. And then they had gone home and managed not to think about it anymore.

3

Pearl and Isidore had returned to the museum, and not only to MoMA, but also to the Met, the Guggenheim, the Frick . . .

Isidore had soon realized that Pearl didn't like his way of commenting on the works, his habit of asking her questions about her preferences and tastes.

When it came to taste,[11] Pearl didn't really have any. Or any particular sensitivity towards these rows of paintings, sculptures, or flashing neon-light installations. It was beautiful, it was interesting, it was well done. But she remained at the level of the dilettante, who praises the resemblance and raves about the technique, the virtuosity of the artist's depiction of tousled hair, the softness of the velvet jacket, the folds of a drape. So, 19th century portraits garnered her admiration, but when faced with stripes or splotches, abstract, or even worse, conceptual art, Pearl thought, deep down, that she could have done it herself. It couldn't be that hard to chuck pots of paint over a canvas. As for whether a bicycle wheel stuck on a stool could be art, she would readily accept that it could, ashamed to belong in the camp of those who didn't get it. And yet she had made an effort and read some art manifestos. "Art has moved from representation to presentation." She'd seen this statement as a kind of key. In the olden days, artists would represent—battles, horses,

[11] "Taste is fine for wine lovers and cooks. Art has nothing to do with taste," a certain Gustav Klimt said.

women, orchards—and then in modern times, they'd been content merely to present—slashed canvases, broken violins, bits of old iron, and upside-down bidets.

Pearl would have liked to have something intelligent to say, would have loved to have impressions worthy of exchanging with this man who just wanted to get a dialogue going, but, appalled at her own banality, she kept quiet.

She had noticed that the two of them didn't move at the same pace, which had nothing to do with Isidore's age because he was a very sprightly octogenarian; a form of arrythmia, of desynchronization between their ways of advancing, stopping, moving from room to room, losing themselves, or not, in contemplation before a painting, kept them at a distance from each other. This discrepancy was deeply symbolic: father and daughter didn't know how to be together. Paintings prompted a strange need for solitude in her. Out of the corner of her eye, she would see Isidore veering away, accelerating, sometimes even charging towards works of art; she found it almost embarrassing. And yet, when he would suggest meeting again to see a new exhibition, she was incapable of refusing. And so they had ended up learning how to wander around together separately.

She wasn't that familiar with elderly people, their simultaneous slowness and impatience. Isidore was elusive, Pearl found him puerile and strict in turn. Sometimes there was a certain entitlement about him, that of the man with bags of money who was never denied anything he desired. Sometimes he seemed like a dreamer to her, lost in his thoughts, and then he would smile at her with a tenderness that she found painful.

For her birthday, he had given her a red coat, very beautiful, very expensive.

Pearl hadn't told her mother about these artistic excursions, proof that she felt guilty about swanning around with the enemy like this. She didn't want to hurt anyone. It was inevitable that mother and daughter would end up seeing each other very rarely and only exchanging vague news around Christmas and birthdays. Things would have been different if, once elderly, Michelle had needed money, if she'd depended on her daughter financially. The brilliant attorney would have acted like the model daughter. But after the legal case, Michelle had received her own check, so Pearl's support had become unnecessary.

The university had asked students to find themselves an internship for the end of the year. Pearl had told Isidore about this, and he'd offered her New York's three biggest law firms on a silver platter. "You can just tell me which one interests you, I have very good friends at all of them." The young woman still had misgivings, and had confided in Adrian, who told her that she was tying herself in knots with her "ridiculous scruples."

Father and daughter had agreed to meet at the Museum of Natural History, where dinosaur skeletons towered over collections of coleopterous and lepidopterous insects. They had both pretended to admire the classifications of rocks and granites, and then, for a change and because it was spring, they left to have lunch at an Italian restaurant on the corner of Columbus Avenue and Seventy-Fifth Street. As the year had progressed, their relationship had become gentler, less rocky, and this lunch on the terrace was almost enjoyable. Isidore took great interest in Pearl and liked to make her talk. She told him that she hadn't yet decided about the internship.

"Accept to be helped."

"I'm scared of not being good enough."

"I do understand. When I was offered my first job at Chlorodon, I was terrified at the thought of making a mistake, I re-counted everything ten times. I was in love with the boss's daughter and it was she who'd got me the position."

"Was that your wife?"

"Yes, that was Lotte, she became my wife after that. There's no harm in accepting little leg-ups. Seize this opportunity, Pearl, of course you could find a law firm on your own, but what's the point? If you go to Barnett, for example, it'll be a fantastic internship, and anyhow, sometimes it's good to have wires pulled for one, one tries even harder to show one deserves it, I'm sure you'll be perfect."

"Will you tell them who I am?"

Isidore sighed. This was hard for the man who had lied all his life.

"I intended to say that you're my illegitimate daughter, attorneys are familiar with the term, but if you prefer, I can say that you're the daughter of a lady friend, does it bother you?"

"What?"

"My saying that you're my daughter?"

"No, and anyhow."

"Anyhow what?"

"I'm not . . . well, not really . . ."

He was looking her straight in the eye.

"I know, Pearl, I know it all the more because I, too . . ."

His sentence was left dangling. Isidore had never told this story, not to anyone. Neither to his children, nor even to Lotte, and he realized that he wouldn't be able to tell it to Pearl. He had erased the story from his personal mythology, it belonged to another Isidore whom he would have hardly known, barely come across. He found that astonishing, and merely smiled.

"Oh, really?"

Pearl had noticed that Isidore spoke very little about himself, his childhood, his life in Austria. He always began his story in 1929, on the day of the crash.

"I will never be your father and I know what I'm talking about."

She felt a knot in her stomach.

"But you could see me as a kind of . . . Father Christmas."

She burst out laughing.

"A guardian angel, if you prefer, who will protect you when you need it. A shoulder, an old, slightly hunched shoulder, but money can provide some fine, firm shoulder pads, believe me. Pearl, you have your life in front of you, a guardian angel can't be turned down. I won't have seen your first steps, won't have heard your little girl's voice, won't have taught you to ride a bike, but if it's any consolation to you, I never taught any of my children to ride a bike, either. I wasn't a very present father . . . more the kind who comes home late from the office, or is always between two flights and . . . anyhow, enough about that."

Isidore saw himself again in the apartment with everyone asleep, when he'd get back from his business dinners; he regretted nothing. Then he thought of little Tommy, racket in hand, how many of his son's matches had he watched? Pearl wouldn't replace the child he had lost.

"I know I don't have many years left to live, and they're bound not be the best years, but we can get to know each other, we can share things, and then . . . I'd like to make your life easier than it was expected to be."

They paid the bill and left the restaurant. When it was time to part, he took her in his arms to say goodbye. Pearl found it so simple, and yet she'd made such a mountain out of it.

4

Monday morning, the files were piling up and Pearl was already tired. She took a deep breath, stretched out her legs, and rubbed her eyes. The entire management committee of the Keller company would be there at 10 A.M. She had barely forty minutes left to check everything again. "I'm counting on you, Pearl, it's a very big deal," Jules Barnett had told her.

Pearl deserved their trust. Just as Isidore had predicted eight years previously, she had worked harder than any other associate at the prestigious law firm and a splendid career awaited her, particularly if she managed to play a good game with the Kellers. A case that was, to say the least, convoluted, and on which, for six months, at seventy hours a week, she'd been wracking her brain to come up with stratagems she could turn into legal evidence. She wasn't there yet.

Her phone rang.

"It's me."

"Oh, Adri! All well?"

"Yes, I've just read something incredible . . ."

"Great timing, I've got the Kellers coming this morning and I'm drowning in cross-border taxation. Didn't you tell me about an arbitration deal with Honduras?"

"With Nicaragua, you mean?"

"Oh . . . yes, well never mind."

She automatically ran her hand across her thighs to try to smooth the creases on her skirt.

"Pearl, I'm calling because I've just read something in *The Guardian*."

"Oh yes?"

It was a navy blue skirt that made her look quite strict. She hadn't had time to iron it that morning and regretted it. She would have liked her appearance to be impeccable.

"Do you get that paper?"

"Yes, probably, I think so . . ."

Maybe Nicaragua and Honduras have similar legislation, she mused. She checked her watch.

"You must read the article on page 16."

"Oh . . . okay . . . okay . . . Why?"

"You won't believe your eyes. You did say to me that your father's Austrian, didn't you?"

"Yes . . . Sorry? Why?"

"Fine, you're not listening to me. I'll keep the article for you anyway. Are we seeing each other soon? Can you do lunch?"

"Um . . . yes . . . okay, well, no, I'm afraid, not right now, but yes, I'll read the *Guardian* article. Gotta leave you now, wish me good luck!"

She hung up before Adrian could wish her anything at all. She counted her files again, big red binder files, and lined up her yellow Stabilo pens like a small army on the defensive ridge of her mahogany desk. The assistant entered without knocking.

"I've done the photocopies you asked for."

"Thanks, Claire. Leave them there."

She ran her finger over the card binding of the folders.

"Is Mr. Barnett in his office?"

"Yes."

"I'd better go."

She stood up. Never mind about Honduras. She put on an appropriate smile. No one knew the Keller case as well as she did, not even Barnett, not even Arnold Keller. She thought of Adrian again, who had opted for arbitration. Occasionally, they would dream and promise themselves that, one day, they'd set up their own law firm together. Their friendship had merely strengthened over the years. They were so close that they'd wondered if they shouldn't date, but then they'd laughed and never mentioned it again. Pearl's love life was pretty chaotic because she devoted all her energy to her work. As for Adrian, he went from one amorous disaster to the next. Pearl played the part of the great comforter, handing him tissues and promising him he'd end up finding his soulmate.

As was to be expected, the meeting with the Keller management committee was hard going. These people seemed to measure their power by their ability to change their line of defense without their interlocutor ever showing the slightest sign of weariness or exasperation. You had to smile at them, show selflessness. Pearl knew how to do that.

One of the green-tied gray suits implied that he had new information that would inevitably change their line of attack. They'd have to go right back to the beginning again. Pearl knew how to do that, too. She was a tough cookie.

During the meeting, Barnett had observed her out of the corner of his eye. Pearl had very rarely been invited to express her opinion, that was the game. She took care of the preparatory work, Barnett did the sales pitch and reaped all the praise. But if there was the slightest error, all the blame would fall back on her. She wasn't overly shocked by this, Barnett knew how to recognize good work and reward worthy associates.

They had accompanied all the Kellers back to the elevator, and Barnett had turned to Pearl with a smile that she'd found hard to interpret. Was he pleased with her? Had the meeting gone well? She'd asked the assistant to go and get her a sandwich. She had to get back on the job immediately and draw up a list of their priorities, and she also had to ask the certified public accountant if there was any chance of circumventing section 43, an idea she'd had during the meeting but wanted to check before mentioning it, and there was something else, but what?

"Do we get *The Guardian*?"

"No."

"Could you pick one up for me at the kiosk? And no onion in the tuna sandwich! Thanks so much!"

She had waited, staring vacantly at the creases in her navy blue skirt. This fabric really was poor quality, to think how much she'd paid.

She went to make herself a cup of tea. She needed to clarify her thoughts. What a total shambles this Keller case was! Of course they'd evaded taxation, and with a vengeance. She thought what a strange line of work she'd chosen. She hadn't become an attorney to defend widows and orphans, but she hadn't imagined herself licking the boots of such nudniks, either. Indeed, one of them had been blatantly eyeing her up for the entire meeting. Pearl wasn't what she appeared to be: a pretty young woman with a pale complexion and sad eyes who'd just finished her studies. She'd never be thrown by a lecherous leer, she'd heard her mother mocking men's desires too often. "If they only knew," she'd say to herself. And that gave her mettle. For a long time, she'd seen her origins as a defect, but today she realized, particularly since being around young women from more conventional backgrounds, how little she quaked in front of men.

The assistant returned with a bad sandwich and the newspaper. Pearl had forgotten the page number Adrian had told her, wasn't even sure anymore what she was looking for. An article on Austria? She turned the pages, scanning headlines and columns. The merger of Nynex and Bell Atlantic, the allocation of 8 billion dollars to the construction of new prisons, the preparations for the Olympic Games in Atlanta, the release of the movie *Jerry Maguire*, and finally she arrived at page 16 and it took her a few seconds to absorb the shock. She read the article, but too fast.

She answered her phone.

"Adri?"

"So? Did it go well with the Kellers?"

"I read the *Guardian* piece."

"Did you see? Pretty cool, isn't it?"

"You mean she looks like me?"

"Well, she sure does look like you! Pearl, she's your double!"

"You're exaggerating, there's a likeness . . ."

"And the beauty spot? Below the eye? If I'm not mistaken, haven't you got exactly the same one, in exactly the same place?"

Pearl smiled at the thought of Adrian knowing this detail. People attached great importance to a beauty spot when genetics were concerned. A beauty spot was like a marker, a stamp, something irrefutable, the proof was in the spot.

"Yes, that's true."

"And then the fact that it's an Austrian artist. It could be a portrait of your grandmother! Well, maybe not your grandmother, but an aunt or someone from your family! They say the original portrait was painted in 1910. The model must have been born during the 1890s. How old's your father?"

"Eighty-eight."

"Hold on, let me work it out . . . He's never mentioned it to you?"

"No."

"You should show it to him!"

"Hey, don't get carried away, it's just a blue-eyed brunette with a beauty spot."

Adrian paused for a moment.

"Pearl, are you kidding me? She's your double!"

"Alright, alright, I'll talk to Isidore about it. Gotta leave you now, gotta go."

Pearl loved Adrian's enthusiasm. She looked closely at the

color photo that took up around a quarter of the page. She reread the article more calmly.

In 1910, Gustav Klimt painted the portrait of a very young woman, in three-quarter view, hair loose, wearing a large brown hat, a fur stole around her neck, and with her shoulders seemingly bare. This painting, titled Backfisch (Damsel *in English) was exhibited at the Galerie Miethke in Vienna in 1916 and bought by an unknown person, of whom no trace can be found in the records of the time. In 1917, a year before Klimt's death, and for an unknown reason, the painting was altered by the artist: the hat and stole were removed, the shoulders covered in a white, floral-patterned shawl, and the hair tied back in a demure chignon. In 1925, the Galleria Ricci Oddi purchased* Portrait of a Lady, *unaware that it was an altered version of* Damsel. *It wasn't until eighty years later that, last week, a student at Piacenza University, Claudia Maga, felt intuitively that these weren't two different paintings, of which the first had been lost, but one and the same painting, if radically reworked. When the painting was X-rayed, this young art history student was proved right. And this would be a big first since, to date, no other such reworking is known of within the great artist's oeuvre . . . Who was this young woman? Why did Klimt decide to change her appearance? The mystery remains.*

5

Hello, Chadi, is Mr. Isidore at home?"

Mrs. Valeras had retired some time ago. She had been replaced by a slim, almost angular, man with a prominent Adam's apple and an extreme approach to politeness. This refined butler contrasted all the more with an aging Isidore who had become increasingly irascible, one moment full of the joys of spring, the next gloomy, verging on cantankerous. His love for Pearl had grown over the years.

Although his son Peter had replaced him at the head of the Chloros group and contributed to the family business with exemplary application, Isidore could only see him as a conceited rich kid. As for his daughter Felicity, she had turned into a sweet, smiley woman, if slightly depressive and unsure whether to kill herself with cream buns or glasses of gin. Isidore had confided in Pearl that he couldn't fathom how one could be born with such good fortune, her mother's beauty, her father's bank account, and just waste one's life like that. Showing that there's a plus side to being illegitimate. To obtain something, nothing's more of a spur than having been deprived of it.

"Yes, madam, he's in his study, he's expecting you."

"Has he been out today?"

"No."

"How do you find him?"

"A little tired, madam."

Pearl took off her jacket. She had learnt to love this apartment. A familiar calm pervaded it. The entrance hall walls lined in salmon-pink fabric, the beige carpet, the broad consoles dotted with ornaments that Chadi would dust meticulously every day, an apartment that seemed to be suspended in time.

"Would you like me to bring you some refreshment?"

"No thanks, Chadi, I'm fine."

She walked towards the study.

Isidore was sitting in the big armchair she'd first seen him in, ten years back. How young she'd been then. Never would she have suspected that they'd end up being so close.

"Hello, Pearl."

"Hello, Isidore."

She went over and kissed him on the temple with sincere affection. He smiled at her with every one of his wrinkles.

"How are you doing?"

"Fine, fine, but I didn't have a good night thanks to my cough returning, it wakes me up and then I can't get back to sleep, I've slept badly for so many years, you know . . ."

Asking an elderly person how they're doing was bound to send you down a tunnel. She decided to cut it short.

"There's a new development in the Keller case."

"Aha! Tell me all. What have those crooks wangled yet again?"

Pearl laughed, the only thing that still really amused Isidore was the world of business. Of course, she'd come to talk to him about the painting, that strange portrait that had obsessed her all week. She'd even gone to a store to buy a book on Gustav Klimt. Unfortunately, *Portrait of a Lady* wasn't among its illustrations, or even mentioned in the text. From this she had concluded that, until now, it hadn't been one of the artist's well-known works. She'd had lunch with Adrian, and they had fired each other up. With his usual enthusiasm, Adri had convinced his friend that the portrait was of her grandmother, it couldn't be otherwise. It was just surprising that Isidore had never mentioned it, after all those afternoons striding around museums, or maybe Isidore was unaware of its existence; this required clarification. As for Pearl, she hadn't paid much attention to the whole repainting business, and anyhow, was it that important that the young woman had been depicted with and then without a hat?

After beating around the bush with Isidore on the rain, the weather generally, the Kellers, and Isidore's rheumatism, Pearl took the plunge.

"Do you remember my friend Adrian?"

"The one who was at the Dietrichs' on New Year's Eve?"

"Oh yes, that's true (what a tedious evening, now she thought about it.) Well, Adrian showed me an article in *The Guardian* about a painting by Gustav Klimt."

Isidore didn't react.

"Adrian thinks I look a lot like the model."

Isidore said nothing, but Pearl could feel a kind of electricity in the air. She started to rummage in her bag.

"You'll see, I've brought it along for you . . ."

She searched too nervously for the piece of paper, and yet she had folded it carefully.

"I slipped it into my diary . . ."

She sat down, put her bag on her knees and started emptying it of its entire contents. Isidore watched her doing so, in silence.

"I'm sure I . . . Ah! Here it is!"

She handed the article to Isidore, who took it in an almost affected way.

He barely looked at it and gave it straight back to her.

"Yes, it's true that you resemble her."

Pearl wasn't expecting so little reaction. Maybe the resemblance wasn't that striking. She felt uncomfortable. Was she imagining things?

"Adrian says I'm her double."

Isidore merely smiled.

"That's going a bit far, no?"

"We thought that, since Klimt is an Austrian painter and you're Austrian . . . that . . . maybe it was someone from your family . . ."

Now Isidore's expression hardened.

"Did you know this portrait?"

"No."

The old man's tone was categorical. Pearl was disappointed, but she wasn't yet ready to give up.

"Do you think it might be possible?"

"Everything is possible, but an oil painting doesn't have a DNA . . ."

She didn't like him referring to that episode. Pearl knew that Isidore had suffered a heart attack on the day he'd received the attorney's letter. She knew him well now, this man hated to have his hand forced, but she found his using the DNA argument to close the conversation appalling. It was a bit like him saying to her, "you caught me out once, but you won't a second time."

He stood up from his armchair and walked a few steps.

"So you don't think it could be . . . an aunt or . . . a grandmother?"

"Chadi!"

The butler appeared at the door as if by magic.

"Yes, sir?"

"We're ready for coffee. You'd like a coffee, Pearl?"

"Yes, love one."

"Thank you, Chadi."

Isidore came to sit on the sofa beside Pearl, and patted the back of her hand kindly, as if wanting to console her.

"A grandmother . . . perhaps, but you know, I barely knew my family and when I left Vienna, I was so young!"

"How old were you?"

"I was sixteen."

"When did you last go back there?"

"Never."

Pearl was really surprised.

"You mean to say that, all this time, with your many business trips around Europe, you never returned to Austria?"

"Never."

"Oh, that's crazy, I didn't know that."

Isidore remained pensive.

"Would you like to go with me?"

"Where?"

"To Vienna. Would you like us to go there together?"

Pearl's eyes lit up.

"Me? I'd love us to!"

Unlike many of her friends, who had backpacked across the old continent after graduation, Pearl had started working at the law firm straight away. She had travelled very little, just once to Mexico and around Argentina.

"We could go to Vienna and see this portrait."

"Ah, but it isn't in Vienna, it's in Italy."

"Then we could go to Vienna and then on to Italy, and even . . . spend a night in Paris. What do you think?"

"Barnett would have to let me be away for at least a week."

"Ten days, that would be better. In Vienna, I'll take you to drink the best hot chocolate of your life!"

The old man had found his smile again.

" . . . and then we'll stroll around the Ring, and I'll show you my father's house on Johannesgasse. What a house that was! A real little palace, it looked over the Stadtpark!"

"Stadtpark?"

"Yes, all the aristocrats of Vienna owned mansions along that stretch of Johannesgasse. And the Brombeeres were . . ."

Pearl was staring wide-eyed, Isidore had never told her that they belonged to the aristocracy.

"Who are the Brombeeres?"

Isidore's burst of enthusiasm was cut short. A ghostly image of the Brombeeres' mansion loomed before him. Why had he uttered their name?

"They were my father's parents."

"Oh, really? But you don't have the same name as them?"

"I . . . I changed name when I lost my mother."

Isidore's eyes had misted over; not wanting to seem indiscreet, she remained silent, waiting for what would follow.

Just then, Chadi walked in. He placed the tray with the two cups of coffee on the occasional table without making a sound. This man was quite something.

"Don't worry, I'll take care of Barnett."

"No, I'm perfectly able to ask him myself."

She leant forward to pop a sugar cube into her cup and two into Isidore's. A warm feeling rose in her chest, Europe was a dream for Pearl. Strangely, the first image that came to her wasn't the Eiffel Tower, but the Tower of Pisa. She liked imagining them, her in a super chic outfit, him in a white linen suit, with the tower leaning over their heads.

"And when could we set off?"

"This summer?"

"It's very hot in Italy over the summer, maybe that's not a good idea. But how about September?"

"And that would give me time to wrap up the Kellers."

"I'll ask Henry to come up with a good itinerary for us."

He paused, took the cup she was handing him. Pearl noticed that the old man's hands were shaking a little. Then, with heart-rending tenderness, he said to her:

"How lucky I am to have a daughter like you!"

6

Summer had gone by and the Kellers had won. Pearl had worked doggedly so that those crooks would emerge with heads held high, and Barnett had complimented her, she was skilled. New Yorkers kept complaining about the scorching weather, but like a good Texan girl, Pearl loved to see the sunshine flooding the Manhattan sidewalks and making the mirrored cladding of the skyscrapers sparkle.

Indulging her natural tendency to gather information, study, and make notes on everything, she had bought three guidebooks to Austria, plus the Lonely Planet guide to Vienna and its pocket version for a long weekend, and the one on *The Italian Lakes*, and *The Green Guide to Italy*, and then *Walks in Paris*, and *The Ultimate Guide to Paris*, and *Secret and Unusual Paris*, and finally, two splendid art books, one on the Louvre, the other on the Musée d'Orsay.

In glossy magazines, European women all seemed beautiful and refined, and as for *Parisiennes*, my god, they wore dainty pumps, split skirts, and chiffon blouses. Pearl had got increasingly carried away buying increasingly uncomfortable garments, and was perplexed to see her suitcase turning into a disaster area. An eclectic pile of unwearable and ill-assorted clothes that were bound to see her labelled "the overdressed American."

Adrian had taken her to see the movie *Ridicule*. It was set in the 18th century, at the court of Louis XVI. It didn't help her with her suitcase packing, but did convince her that French women were unfaithful seductresses, and French men peerless in their refinement. She liked to imagine herself meeting a subtle, eloquent and dangerous man. Then Adrian suggested an evening watching *Roman Holiday*, with Audrey Hepburn and Gregory Peck. The movie had come out in 1953 and was somewhat removed from the Italy of 1996, but this time Pearl dreamt of herself in love, on the back of a Vespa, clinging to a handsome Italian.

These love-sick shopgirl fantasies that she allowed herself as a guilty pleasure were a perfect contrast to her actual love life, which was, to say the least, cynical and mundane. Pearl put her career before everything, and her career certainly paid her back in spades. Of course, she wouldn't ride around on a Vespa with Isidore, who was now eighty-eight. Even if the old man hadn't stopped jumping for joy since they'd first planned this trip, Pearl knew she'd be leaving him at the hotel to trek around on her own most of the time. They talked about the trip a lot. He'd planned an entire itinerary, particularly for Vienna. He beamed at the thought of seeing that city again. He hadn't mentioned his childhood again to her, and Pearl sensed a kind of awkwardness as soon as she brought the subject up. Keen for him to reveal that part of his life to her, she hoped the trip would ignite that spark.

This great journey would be Isidore's last, and father and daughter contemplated it with all the solemnity a pilgrimage demanded. It was a journey through time, and Pearl sensed that afterwards, she and Isidore would have a story to share, a story she could make her own; she felt ready. Being the result of a condom slip-up, being a weird mix, the fruit of the fixed-price fornication of a prostitute mother and an oral hygiene-multimillionaire father wasn't enough for her anymore. At twenty-eight, it was time to build a different family mythology for herself.

Pearl wasn't big on interior decoration, and on the eve of their departure, her apartment was in total chaos. She sighed in front of the various piles of clothes accumulating on her bed.

It was clear she wouldn't be able to travel light. A smart, red-wheeled suitcase, a gift from her father, subtly indicated the capacity she mustn't exceed. Their plane left at dawn the following day. Isidore had said that the chauffeur would pick her up at 4:30 A.M. She had to get the job done this evening. She poured herself a glass of wine and called Adrian to buck herself up.

Adri thought it wonderful that she was heading to Europe with her father. He was still really intrigued by the portrait story, but he'd understood that, for Pearl, the stakes had changed.

"Did you tell your mother about the trip?"

"No. Well, I told her I was going to Paris for ten days, but not that I was going with Isidore."

"And?"

"And you know my mother . . . She didn't ask me a single question, but did ask me to bring her back some perfume and a scarf."

She let out a small sigh.

"Pearl, why are you calling me?"

"Because I don't know what to put in my suitcase."

She was supposed to get to bed early, but was going round in circles. She started on her toiletry bag, went to the kitchen, wondered if she should take her vitamins, too, went back to her bedroom, should she take a swimsuit? No. And yet, a swimsuit didn't take up much room, rolled into a ball . . .

The hours had flown by, her suitcase was just about done. She made herself a sachet of freeze-dried noodles in some Chinese broth. She bought the sachets in packs of ten from Chinatown. They were quick. You just had to boil water and mix in a bowl. The spice burnt the lips. How lucky she was to be traveling so far! She brushed her teeth, washed her hair, dithered a lot over the hairdryer, let's hope Viennese hotels have hairdryers. Isidore had booked them into the Hotel Imperial, she imagined chandeliers and marble, and in this case, imagined correctly. She set her alarm for 4:00 A.M. It was a nine-and-a-half-hour flight, after all. She'd opted for jeans, a flowery blouse, and a long woolen cardigan that was very cozy—she could almost wrap herself up in it.

She got into bed but was far too excited to sleep, switched the TV on, went to fish her weekend guide to Vienna out of her bag, thought it better to keep the surprise, put the book back. She was pleased to be taking a break and leaving the brown carpet at Barnett's behind. She went through all the associates and colleagues in her head. She had to fight, prove that she had her place there, deserved to be entrusted with the big cases. One of her friends from Columbia had joined a prestigious law firm and, after much insistence, had finally given in to the advances of her boss. She no longer really knew whether it was a good idea or a terrible mistake to sleep with him. Now she was in a tight corner. And yet, when she spoke to Pearl about it, she described him as an attractive man. Pearl had no such concern with Barnett, or any of the other associates. At least that was something. She tried to relax. Suddenly, she was in a cold sweat. Her passport! Had she put it safely into her bag? She tossed and turned on the pillow, confusing piles of files and visions of picturesque European lanes.

It was only when her alarm clock rang that she realized that she had finally dropped off. It said 4:00 in glowing red digits. She leapt out of bed, zapped the alarm. It took her a while to understand that another, more distant, bell was ringing in the apartment. It wasn't her alarm but the phone. She headed for the kitchen. It must be Isidore reassuring himself that she was actually up and about, and she smiled at this thoughtfulness. She picked up.

"Hello?"

"Miss Pearl?"

She recognized the gentle, polite voice of the butler.

"Chadi?"

"Miss Pearl, I . . . Something has happened."

Her blood froze. She pressed the receiver to her ear as if that could prevent some misunderstanding, as if to ensure that she wouldn't hear anything bad. Chadi's voice was choked.

"It's sir. He's dead."

7

The explanations that followed had reached her in a fog. Upon rising, Chadi had discovered that his master was cold, sir wasn't moving anymore, he'd immediately called emergency services, quick, quick, but it was too late. On arrival, they'd concluded, without the shadow of a doubt, he'd died of a heart attack.

Once she'd got over the shock of the news, Pearl realized, with surprise, that the death of her father left her indifferent. It is astonishing how certain deaths leave us like gaping wounds, while others stitch that wound up themselves. The void left by Isidore wasn't as big a void as all that. Perhaps because she'd always known her father as old. And yet, very soon after their first meeting, when she'd glimpsed the possibility of this love, she'd realized with horror that we can only miss what we know. She'd had to be reasonable, stifle those fancies of a stolen childhood and an idyllic adolescence. As had Isidore. They'd accepted that their relationship couldn't be built on regrets. Ten years was enough to create some good memories. They knew that their time was precious.

He'd told her one day to see him as a Father Christmas. The reading of the will would show quite how that Father Christmas had provided for everything.

Things had been arranged with the agreement of Peter, the eldest son, because management of the Chloros empire was down to him. Isidore may have thought Peter conceited, but he knew his son to be an upright man, a workaholic, and that he could trust him. Chloros was Peter's and Felicity's inheritance because that fortune would never have been made without their maternal grandfather. The sums of money at stake were so colossal, they could almost be considered burdens. The patriarch had asked Peter to watch over Felicity, not let her stuff herself too much, try to find a meaning to her life, at past sixty, place her at the head of some foundation where she'd feel useful, for abandoned dogs or something, because Felicity loved dogs with all her heart.

For Peter and Felicity, the announcement of Pearl's arrival in the family had seriously shaken the image of their parents as an ideal couple, but the siblings had just had to swallow this affront. They were grateful to their father for at least keeping things separate. Not once in the last ten years had Isidore indulged in the farce of a reconstituted-family birthday, Christmas or Thanksgiving. He spent such holidays with Peter and Felicity, as he always had. With Pearl, he'd go to the museum, have lunch, supper, coffee.

On the rare occasions that Peter had come across Pearl, he hadn't been particularly cordial, and yet he'd thought her very pretty and, more than anything, saw what a brilliant and serious young woman she was, both qualities he respected. As for Felicity, she had found it harder to control her emotions. She went over the top, overdid the sympathy, became almost cloying, and ended up making Pearl—and herself—feel uncomfortable.

For the reading of the part of the will that concerned her, they had put Pearl at the end of the large glass table, in the seat of honor. With Peter and the lawyer to her left, Felicity, eyes red from weeping, to her right. Pearl knew Isidore to be generous, but she hadn't expected to receive 100 million dollars. She tried to hide her alarm when the sum was announced. She pretended to herself that she was in a meeting room at Barnett's and they were dealing with some mundane case, in which she was simply one of the intermediaries. Isidore had told her to trust Peter.

"Peter isn't like us, money is his language, he's spoken it since birth." During the hour that it took to sign the various documents, she realized that everything had been settled for some time; Isidore had clearly discussed it with his son.

"How much do you want to leave her?"

"A hundred million. What do you think?"

"I think nothing, Dad, it's your money. But yes, 100 million is a sizeable sum. Having said that, it's far from being a third of your fortune, even taking away Mom's share that we obviously get, so, if ever Pearl decided to take us to court . . ."

"Pearl would never do that, she isn't like you."

Pearl smiled at this imagined riposte; Isidore could be cutting, but had he really had such a high opinion of her? Had he preferred her? She looked from Peter, in his tight gray suit, to blond Felicity, squeezed into a brown dress that made her look like a barrel. They were her half-brother and half-sister, and she, Pearl, would only ever be Isidore's half-daughter. One hundred million dollars. She would entrust this money to Peter, so he could manage it. She had no idea what change it would make. She fancied buying some new boots in a swish store, but she was hardly going to buy herself 100 million dollars' worth of boots! She promised herself not to talk about this money to anyone.

A few days later, she had phoned her mother.

"Isidore has died."

"Isidore the genitor?"

It was Michelle's joke. In a Texan accent, she would make *Isidor* and *genitor* rhyme.

"Yes."

"Right, and how was Paris?"

"I didn't go. But I am going to take a short break, I'll come and see you."

"Oh, right. When?"

"Next week.

"Okay."

She sounded a little disappointed.

"I'll find you a scarf here. There are beautiful scarves to be had in New York, you know."

"You're kind. Makes me happy."

Pearl didn't know how to spoil her mother without harming her. Would this woman be happy with a million in her bank account, or would it cause problems for her? Did her mother have enough discernment to defend herself from the swarms of shameless profiteers?

She decided not to think about it anymore. Lurking deep inside her was the notion that this money wasn't hers, that she should manage without it. And a sum like that would soon turn your head. Her work would be her salvation. So she kept piling up her files with the diligence of a beginner and made sure her life continued as normal, as if nothing had changed.

Adrian had asked her whether she missed her father, and she'd looked at him with such sincere astonishment that it had thrown her friend. Did she have no heart? Isidore had died, and once she'd got over the shock, and the disappointment of not doing that trip to Europe with him, she had reverted to the time when her father was but a photo from a magazine, framed and placed on the sideboard in the sitting room, and when that was enough for her.

* * *

"Hello, Pearl, Peter here."

"Hello, Peter."

"I'm just calling because I'm with Felicity and we were wondering if you'd like to keep some memento of Daddy."

Daddy. She couldn't grasp the meaning of this question, too surprised at Peter calling her.

"A memento?"

"Yes, we're at the apartment, preparing for the sale with the auctioneer, and we wanted to check if you'd like something."

The tone was friendly. Pearl thought of the old-master paintings, the 18th century chests of drawers, the items hunted for in antique stores. She saw once more the salmon-pink walls, the ornaments, the clocks, the Chinese vases, and all the other treasures the apartment was crammed with. But it was all so well arranged, everything so perfectly in its place, that she struggled to imagine the items separately. She remained silent.

"You don't need to give me your answer now, of course, take your time. And maybe you'd like to come by the apartment to see what you might like. Anyhow . . . let me know."

Pearl's voice had gone. She who spent her days arguing for and against, whose job it was to have an answer to everything, was mute. Was she sad? Sad over losing her daddy? But she'd never had a daddy! She was strong, she was tough, she had built herself up without fatherly love, she was invulnerable. She remembered Isidore in museums, when he'd literally dive on paintings, and how it annoyed her. She couldn't help but smile, her heart contracting. Ten years, that was enough to create some good memories. And then it came back to her.

"Peter?"

"Yes."

"I . . . Yes . . . There is something I'd like, but I don't know if it has any value, anyhow, you'll tell me, and obviously, you don't have to agree to it."

"Tell me."

"I'd really like the armchair that was in his study."

Peter burst out laughing.

"You mean his old chair? That bulky padded-leather thing?"

"Yes."

"No problem, I think we'd have donated it anyhow, but seriously, is there anything else?"

"No, no, his armchair would be lovely, and thanks so much, Peter, for thinking of calling me, I'm touched."

"Don't mention it, it's the least we could do. I'll get the chair delivered to your place this week."

"Thanks."

She didn't have the strength to say anything else. She quickly hung up and dissolved into tears.

8

When she'd introduced Jonathan to Adrian, Pearl had sensed that her friend was having to force himself. She knew him too well not to know that his "Cool! Awesome!" sounded false. She'd wanted to believe that this was totally predictable. Jonathan and Adrian were opposites in every way.

Adrian was brilliant, but with his face and hair and horn-rimmed glasses, he looked like an eternal student. His new suits and ties, and the five-zero arbitration deals that went with them, did nothing to change this. Compared with Jonathan, and his suave "Call me Johnny," Adrian just didn't measure up. In truth, no one did, because Jonathan was handsome as few men are, with his turquoise-blue eyes, square jaw, and Greek statue body; Jonathan was rare.

Pearl had met him at a private viewing that Peter and his wife had invited her to. She rarely saw her half-brother, but he would kindly invite her, from time to time, usually to events organized by the Foundation his wife presided over. The couple hadn't had children. Over time, and with her father-in-law's millions, Peter's wife had become an influential philanthropist, and the soirées she organized were lavish. That evening, Manhattan's finest had raced to write a check for a reception center for the homeless. Pearl had asked Barnett to accompany her—these events were like fishponds for hooking new clients. Barnett, the master strategist, had soon realized that the illegitimate daughter of the late Isidore Hoffmann Ferguson was their best recruit of recent years. Pearl was going on thirty, he'd soon propose that she buy shares in the law firm and become a partner.

Jonathan had cleaved his way through the crowd, glass of champagne in hand. Pearl was wearing a dress with flounces that gave her a slightly old-fashioned look; she preferred to call it classic. She might deny it, but the new balance in her bank account had given her more confidence. She'd immediately clocked Jonathan, and felt really flattered when he'd sidled up to her.

"Pretty dress."

"Thank you."

"I'd like to see it tossed in a ball at the foot of my bed."

What a cheek! It had given her goosebumps. She suspected it wasn't the first time the boy was using that chat-up line. She had described the scene to Adrian. Her friend had rolled his eyes, "What a trashy guy!". The truth being that, if *he* had said such a thing to a girl, she'd have burst out laughing, at best. And Adrian hadn't realized that Pearl had fallen for it, until he'd met Jonathan and he'd said to him, "Call me Johnny," with those dumb turquoise eyes of his. It had been pretty obvious to Pearl that the two of them didn't hit it off.

Pearl and Jonathan had started going out together. She'd made an effort not to work too late in the evening and to work less at the weekend. She liked the way people turned to look at them in the street, or rather, to look at Johnny; she wasn't a fool, she was in love.

The young man had big ambitions. He behaved like a businessman without, strictly speaking, having a business. He and his partner—a certain Jake, a rich kid fond of lie-ins—had plenty of ideas. Lately, the two wanted to set up a chain of fruit-themed restaurants: fruit juices, fruit salads, fruit soups, sautéed fruit, ground fruit, puréed fruit. Johnny was looking for investors, was really busy, loved to say, "Can't today, I've got one meeting after another." At that game, Pearl beat him hands down; if he rang her at the office in the middle of the day, she never gave him more than five minutes. When she slept at his place, which happened increasingly frequently, she'd be up at 6:00 A.M. She'd leave the apartment, smartly dressed, while he was still asleep. She'd close the door as gently as she could, put on her shoes on the landing, then scurry off into the early morning like the serious, hardworking mouse that she was. Deep down, her heart was telling her that she and Johnny lived in different worlds, but she silenced the voice that called the young man lazy. He just needed to find some investors and squeeze some fruit.

For Valentine's Day, he had a heart-shaped box of chocolates delivered to her office. Adrian had commented: "Wow, how original!" Pearl had granted him that. But that evening, Johnny had invited her to spend the following weekend with some friends in the Hamptons.

"D'you know the Hamptons in winter?"

This implied that she knew them in summer, she hadn't replied.

"You'll see, no one's around, it's magical."

It was one more milestone. The dreaded introduction to the gang of buddies. Ten to one, they'd belong to the jeunesse dorée, or in this case, more like platinum. Pearl ticked a certain number of boxes because she'd studied at Columbia, because she worked at a big law firm, and because, even if it went unmentioned, no one was unaware that she was "the illegitimate daughter of." But she'd only lived that life on the late, and feared committing some faux pas. Which is why she remained on her guard, a cautious observer.

She knew they would consider her one of them at first sight, particularly since Pearl wasn't beautiful like some girls who were parachuted in thanks to their long legs, those notorious supermodels who blow-dried their way into society. But Pearl was being smuggled in, a stowaway. She could be unmasked at the first gaffe, the first incongruous childhood memory, a coming-out ball, a sailing course, anything. She was all the happier to be Johnny's girlfriend because he belonged to the inner circle. She felt proud when she slept in his room, and when he held her hand in front of everyone as they walked in the snow.

It was one of those weekends when the main activities consisted of doing some sport (a little), drinking cocktails (a lot), and bad-mouthing those who hadn't been invited.

"Remember when Kat threw up in Marc's grandmother's bed?"

"God, we were young!"

"But wasn't it at that party that Lucy stepped out with Ben?"

"Ben Frankel?"

Pearl barely knew their clique. To seem laidback, she leafed distractedly through a pile of magazines and newspapers she'd bought specially. She was three years older than Johnny, but she sensed how much she had missed out on a youth.

"Who fancies an eggnog?"

"Ooh, I *love* eggnog!"

"You know it's my specialty?"

"D'you use whiskey?"

Pearl felt totally out of sync. She could try to reassure herself, tell herself that she was just as good as them, these greenhorns who knocked back eggnog at teatime, *they can hold their liquor, even if they can't hold a pen*, but her heart was in her boots, she so wanted to make a good impression.

"You're nuts! I use rum."

The young woman burst into laughter. They were four perfect little white couples. The girls with their manicured nails, the boys with sweaters tied around their shoulders. A fire roared in the hearth. To Pearl's right, Lisa and Karen were talking about that tramp Stacy, who'd gone out with Lisa's brother, despite

Lisa expressly forbidding her from doing so. Pearl sank deeper into the down-filled sofa and pretended to be engrossed in her reading.

"Pearl, would you like one?"

"Sorry?"

"Would you like an eggnog?"

Johnny was there, smiling at her. Pearl felt a pang, this man was almost the ideal. Could Lisa and Karen see it, too? Were they suddenly going to realize that something wasn't quite right, that Pearl shouldn't have been on that sofa with a gorgeous man who was asking her if she'd like an eggnog? A man who was her boyfriend. She smiled inanely.

"Yes, sure, but not too strong for me."

Jonathan went back to the kitchen. Someone suggested a card game that Pearl didn't know. Karen and Lisa weren't talking about Stacy anymore, but a certain Rhonda who'd slept with a university professor.

"Let's be honest, who hasn't fantasized about a prof?"

They both chuckled. Pearl wondered whether it was an invitation for her to join their conversation.

Outside, gray snowflakes were falling from a sky white as a dream. Pearl imagined that this house was hers, theirs, that she and Johnny were married and were hosting their friends one winter afternoon. That she didn't work so much, that she no longer had anything to prove and was one of those lucky ladies-of-leisure who went to the spa.

Milk, cream, sugar, egg yolk, nutmeg, cinnamon, rum. The eggnog was delicious and piping hot. With every sip, she relaxed into that blissful feeling of being warm and cozy when it's cold outdoors. The rum's vapors felt like a caress, and the two girls jabbering on the sofa didn't seem so loud. She was turning the pages of her magazine when it hit her. A picture she knew. But at first, she didn't quite understand and her eyes flitted to the next page. She read, but couldn't think straight.

Then she sat up. Her portrait. It was written in capital letters: *THEFT OF KLIMT PAINTING IN PIACENZA, ITALY*. And choking with surprise, she spat out her eggnog over the beige sofa's lovely cushions.

9

In the art world, several species and subspecies of thief exist. From the mere amateur to the powerful mafia, from art dealer to trafficker, there's sometimes just a single step. But there are also the smooth talkers, the liars, the small-time junk merchants who swindle old ladies by persuading them that the portrait of their grandfather isn't worth the nail it's hanging on. They're doing them a favor, ridding them of that elongated face with barely symmetrical, almond-shaped eyes, and they'll carry off the Modigliani, whistling as they go. There are the antiquarians with a smart store out front, who wheel and deal in the backyard. There are the pirates, the adventurers, the treasure-hunters, the grave robbers. There are the forgers, both artists and fanatics. There's the fabled gentleman burglar, who steals with style. There are the DIY-ers, those who slip under the covers of historic buildings being restored and attack the gargoyles and angels on facades with a chisel. Among museum attendants, there are those who will close their eyes and supplement their income, and among senior officials, those who will carry the suitcases of banknotes.

It's rare for it take place under everyone's nose, most disappearances are carried out in utmost secrecy. Hidden in safes, warehouses, and free ports, millions of treasures patiently wait. When a museum displays hundreds of works to the public, its storerooms harbor thousands. Not to mention the official buildings of countries with a glorious past, how great the temptation then for employees to help themselves in passing!

But when a theft makes the headlines in the international press, it's something quite different.

One month after the director of the targeted museum had discovered that the portrait of the girl with the carmine lips had been stolen, he had been contacted by a customs officer in Ventimiglia who thought he had intercepted the painting. Unfortunately, it turned out to be a forgery.[12] This was symptomatic. Once the theft was announced, the vultures would have called each other up to know who had pulled it off.

And in this kind of case, there's always a smart-ass ready to jump at the chance and get a portrait knocked up pronto by a forger friend, and then call the vultures back. "I've got it!—It was you? How much?" Unscrupulous buyers, used to fencing stolen goods, jostle for it. Take it or leave it! What does the smart-ass risk? Not much. Selling a fine forgery as if it were the real thing to someone prepared to buy a stolen painting under the table, that's fair game.

In the case of *Portrait of a Lady*, the sucker was Bettino Craxi, a former prime minister drenched in corruption and tainted by scandal. The police went no further with the investigation. The man had escaped to Tunisia to avoid twenty-seven years in prison. One charge more or less on his record would have made no difference. With the biter for once being bit, customs officers wouldn't waste their time pursuing crooks who swindled each other. End of story.

"*As for the real missing painting, police are still looking for it.*" So ended the article that Pearl was reading with the greatest interest.

She'd shown it to Jonathan, who'd raised his eyebrows and promised to read it later. He wasn't convinced by the resemblance between Pearl and the young woman in the portrait.

[12] The theft was discovered on the morning of February 22, 1997, and the forgery was intercepted on April 1, 1997.

She'd said, "Yeah, you may be right, she doesn't look that much like me, apart from the beauty spot." And they'd talked about something else.

Pearl and Jonathan had met in winter, so the spring of their love affair was a season out. It is said that the early days of a relationship are when the loved one is beyond compare, that the person who falls in love can see only qualities in the other person. This isn't quite true. Even those most blinded by love will notice the niggles, those small things that aren't quite right and annoy them from the start. But they want to believe that they'll gradually fade, that the two of them are sure to find common ground, a compromise. Being in love doesn't exclude being lucid, because noticing the other's flaws doesn't necessarily mean you're adding them up.

So right now, in early April, Johnny's defects didn't count. Pearl knew that he was a lazy rich kid who loved nothing but sailing and playing golf, but that was a minor setback since Johnny looked handsome when the sea breeze ruffled his hair, and when he hit the golf ball, with an almost perfect swing, his body arced and he looked like a Greek statue.

Pearl was naturally suspicious and wary, particularly with men. "Never trust!" her mother would say. Johnny was always short of cash, but he never wore the same sweater twice and led a charmed life. She would see him getting caught up in his petty lies and scheming, his excuses that were far-fetched, to say the least. "Darling, so sorry, I'm snowed under."

"What d'you feel like doing today?"

"Don't know, we could brunch at Emilios', I think Benji and Lisa, and maybe Karen, will be there."

She didn't respond.

"Did you know they were an item?"

"Who?"

"Benji and Lisa."

No, she didn't know and couldn't care less. Going to eat scrambled eggs at an absurdly expensive place, drinking endless mimosas from 10:30 in the morning, just to leave the table four hours later, fit only to sleep on a sofa, wasn't really her idea of fun. Pearl might have succeeded in being accepted by Jonathan's clique, but she really struggled to appreciate their company. In fact, the effort she'd made to be liked by these people was inversely proportional to that she'd made to appreciate them. Pearl would never like sailing or golf. She knew that things would only get worse. Her narcissistic tendency didn't prevent her from being clear-sighted. "But darling, you just don't know how to get the most out of life."

She and Jonathan would make love, drink cocktails at trendy bars, go to parties where they always bumped into the same people and talked about the previous party, especially if some of those people hadn't been invited, wonder whether to go to the next party, and end up going because they just had to.

Pearl worked unreasonable hours, and after leaving the office really late, she always had to meet Johnny somewhere. When she'd say to him, "I'm going home, I'm tired," he'd sigh, "But darling . . ."

Above all, even above Johnny, Pearl wanted to become a partner at Barnett & Barnett. When she didn't spend her weekends at the office, she'd take her files home with her. Johnny found that sexy, the attorney who even read her papers in bed. It made them look like a cute couple in some rom-com. But recently, they'd dine out, come home, make love, and then she'd prop up her pillows and get down to work, while he'd set off again for more mojitos. He'd given up on his idea of squeezing fruit for the senior execs of Manhattan; one of his friends was in real estate and they were onto something big.

"You wouldn't like us to visit a museum?"

"A museum? Oh no, please, you sound like my mother.

She was forever dragging us around museums as kids, it was *so* boring!"

Pearl sighed and thought of Isidore. She missed the old man more than she'd have imagined. Would Johnny have appealed to her father? She knew the answer, no point dwelling on it.

The phone rang.

"Adri?"

"Yes, I know I haven't called for ages, but I've had to work like crazy and today's the first Saturday I can breathe a bit, and we were supposed to . . . I was supposed to . . ."

Pearl could tell that her friend's voice wasn't his happy voice.

"Are you okay?"

"Well, Alice has left me."

"Ouch."

"Well, it was predictable, we never saw each other . . . but anyhow. I was just wondering whether by any chance you were free this afternoon, we could go see the Byzantium show at the Met, it's supposed to be amazing."

"Absolutely!"

She loved the thought of seeing her friend again and avoiding brunch with those half-wits. She instantly felt bad for calling them half-wits. *We just don't have the same interests, that's all.*

She had a ready-made excuse.

"In the end, I'll have to see Adri this afternoon, he's in a bad way."

Jonathan muttered something, but didn't seem to want to know more. All the same, Pearl added:

"Alice has left him . . ."

Johnny raised an eyebrow.

"Doesn't surprise me, that guy's *so* boring!"

She didn't even tell him that they were meeting at the museum. Johnny was barely interested in Pearl's life in general. *Am I interested in his*?

Pearl was early, that was her trademark, she bought two tickets for The Glory of Byzantium and looked through the catalogue, which promised 350 works of art from 25 countries, and a breathtaking array of mosaics, murals, enamels, silks, jewelry, and illuminated books.

Adrian arrived, his hair was a mess, but he didn't look as downcast as she'd imagined he would. The two friends hadn't seen each other in a long time and were happy to be reunited. Almost as soon as they'd entered the exhibition, Adrian started to find everything cool because it was the first time the fabulous icons and illuminated manuscripts from Saint Catherine's Monastery of Sinai, hidden in the sands of the Egyptian desert for one thousand five hundred years, were being displayed.

"Two monks from Saint Catherine's of Sinai are here permanently to watch over the treasures, can you imagine?"

Pearl wondered if she was the only person who needed some quiet contemplation in museums. But she'd ended up accepting Isidore's chatter, and her friend's running commentary reminded her of him, in a way. Adrian had launched straight into the Byzantine legacy within the conflicts tearing the Balkans apart, then on to the former USSR, and had even tackled issues between Turkey and Greece.

"Have you read Samuel Huntington?"

"No."

"*The Clash of Civilizations*. It was published last year. How did you manage to miss that book?"

"I work a lot . . ."

"I work a lot, too. Huntington has sussed it all out, I'm going to give you a copy."

Pearl wasn't familiar with sacred art. It wasn't that easy to go into raptures in front of crucifixes, reliquaries, patens, and other talismans, or in front of the subtle but obsessional variations of the same liturgical motifs. She felt a bit lost and wondered whether she'd ever rid herself of her Texan-bumpkin boots.

They arrived in front of the Novgorod archangel with the golden hair.

"He looks like your Jonathan!"

Pearl laughed.

"I won't allow you to sneer!"

She moved closer and read the label: Unknown artist, 12th century. Loan from the Russian Museum of Saint Petersburg. "*What remains are those huge and haunted eyes that don't so much look as reflect the Eternal. The richness of the applied golds produces the light that is the soul of the icon.*"

"You see likenesses everywhere, you do!"

At that moment, Pearl thought she saw a certain tenderness in Adrian's eyes, which unsettled her.

"That Klimt portrait really *is* you, Pearl."

She shrugged her shoulders to hide her disquiet.

"Anyhow, it's been stolen!"

"Oh yes, you've heard, it's crazy! Did you read the article?"

He'd returned to his normal tone of voice, that of an enthusiastic commentator.

"Yes. It's an unbelievable story."

She looked at the archangel and thought of Johnny. It was true that he had golden hair. Adrian was standing back a little. He was in baggy jeans and his same old Columbia student's sweatshirt. She added:

"Farcical, even."

"I didn't realize you knew about it, I'd saved the article for you."

He always saved articles for her, he was so very thoughtful.

10

Pearl had moved. She now lived in a grand building with two porters and two elevator assistants, one for daytime, one for nighttime. She even had a cleaning lady, who would make her bed and tidy her crazy mess as best she could. She and Pearl almost never crossed paths. Had Pearl's mother paid her a visit, she'd have been very impressed. Pearl had some new clothes, more expensive clothes, and wore heels, higher heels. Barnett increasingly let her have her say at meetings, she wasn't far from being the woman she'd have wanted to be, if it weren't for Jonathan, who was too handsome for her.

They'd had their first argument, nothing serious, but he'd left her place slamming the door and hadn't called her for two days. With a sinking feeling, Pearl realized how attached she was to him. When she'd finally decided to ring him, he'd acted as if nothing had happened, and she'd felt enormously relieved. Jonathan could sometimes be a bit quick-tempered. Pearl liked to think he was passionate.

They were meeting up that very evening, at a party being thrown by one of his friends whom Pearl was supposed to have encountered several times but couldn't remember at all. She'd made the effort to pop into Macy's during her lunch break, and had bought a lilac-blue silk dress that flattered her figure and gave her a melancholy look, when she'd wanted to appear triumphant.

"Triumphant?" the sales assistant had queried, raising her eyebrows. "In that case, you should take these pumps."

She had handed Pearl a pair of vivid-red stilettos.

"Red? Are you sure? It won't clash with the blue?"

"Not at all, quite the opposite, and you need the matching croc clutch, too."

The sales assistant knew how to convince, she was paid on commission. Pearl had bought dress, stilettos, and clutch, and returned to Barnett & Barnett with her heart racing. She saw herself again, arriving at Columbia ten years earlier, in her cowboy boots . . . had she really moved on since then?

At the entrance to the large reception room, she could tell it was the kind of do where Jonathan would be totally in his element and she'd have to show she was worthy of him. The guy hosting it was a one-man reception committee and thought he was high-class. She told him her name and he smiled knowingly, even though he barely knew her and wouldn't have recognized her if he'd passed her on the street.

"I'm Johnny's friend," she clarified.

"Yes! Of course! He arrived earlier, should be over there, with Benji. Do grab yourself a glass of champagne!"

Standing proud, on a round table, was one of those pyramids, with champagne cascading from the glass at the top and filling all the glasses down to the bottom. Pearl had never actually understood how it didn't end up flooding everywhere. A waiter handed her a pre-filled glass from a tray, like that no one risked ruining the magical crystal-fountain effect.

She downed it in one and put the glass back on the tray. She'd had a tough day at the office but was feeling upbeat and wanted to make the most of this party. She asked the waiter where the guests' restroom was, and took another glass of champagne.

"To the left, after the second reception room, miss."

The restroom was decorated in 18th century-boudoir style, all marble and pink and gold. She placed her glass of champagne on a spotlit dressing table. Sitting and chatting on a bergère sofa were two women, a tall brunette with very short hair and a blonde as fashionably skinny as a model. They kept saying, "Oh my god! That's insane!". Pearl sat down and looked for her lipstick in her new croc clutch, but she must have left it at the office. The two girls headed off, and with a final "But that's totally insane!", the door closed.

Now alone, Pearl felt her enthusiasm waning. Was this world really her world? Did she want it to be? She adjusted her chignon and decided to go find Johnny among the guests; the apartment extended over two stories and a 10,000 square-foot terrace (*My god! Insane, indeed*!). She bumped into two or three acquaintances, but didn't linger.

"Hi!"

"Have you seen Johnny?"

"Yes, he's over there!"

Big smiles and a minimum of small talk, that she did know how to do.

"Oh, you're here!"

"We really must have lunch one of these days!"

"Yes, give me a ring . . ."

She could feel her cheeks burning slightly, one of the worst feelings. Was it because she feared being found out? But found out for what? Suddenly, she was face to face with Lisa.

"Hello!"

Lisa's expression was strange, her eyes bulging. Pearl wondered if she was drunk or had taken drugs, and yet it was still early. Lisa about-turned in a way that was, to say the least, aggressive, but Pearl decided to pay no attention. Everyone was now heading towards the terrace and, finding herself against the tide, she took refuge in a wide corridor with several closed doors. No doubt the bedrooms of the host and his family. The one-man welcoming committee was far too young to own an apartment like this just for himself.

Halfway down the corridor, leaning between two doors, was a man in a white-linen suit whom she instantly identified as a silver fox. It was a mixed-generation party, but most guests were in their thirties, like her. He stared at Pearl and waited for their eyes to meet, then smiled at her. A reveler emerged from one room clutching a magnum of champagne by the neck, and headed in the direction of the terrace. As he passed in front of them, he knocked over a vase of artificial flowers. He burst into laughter and a young Asian woman in a staff uniform rushed to right the miraculously unbroken vase. The man in the linen suit looked appalled as he watched her doing so.

"Don't tell me you're leaving already!"

His voice was smooth. Pearl was slightly taken aback by the question.

"No, I'm looking for a friend."

"A friend or a boyfriend?"

He'd said that with a twinkle in his eye. Pearl thought him a bit old to be flirting with her, but she didn't mind escaping the throng with a friendly stranger.

"A boyfriend."

"Aha, let me guess, to be with a young woman like you, he can only be very handsome and seductive."

Pearl blushed.

"Yes, he is very handsome . . ."

"But is that enough?"

The man had edged forward and now placed a hand on Pearl's shoulder. He leant towards her ear but spoke so quietly, she couldn't make out what he was saying. At that precise moment, she saw Johnny coming out of the first room with that slut Rhonda, who was adjusting the straps of her dress and wiggling her ass.

Pearl was dumbstruck. Johnny and Rhonda hadn't seen her.

They'd swung right, heading for the terrace like everyone else. *Johnny and Rhonda*? Rhonda who had quite obviously just had a quickie with Johnny. Rhonda who was giggling as she adjusted her straps. Johnny, walking fast like someone who's just committed a crime, but so sure of himself in the way he swung his shoulders while keeping his back ramrod straight.

Pearl turned to the man in the white suit.

"No, it isn't enough."

Although frozen in horror, she still managed to forge a path through the women in all their bling, advancing, head down. *What a damn fool I am*! She weaved between tinkling glasses and bursts of laughter, gripping her wretched croc clutch, digging her stiletto heels in to stop herself from running. Get away from this place, quick, quick.

Johnny and Rhonda, what a damn fool I am!

Outside, the spring freshness of April felt like a slap to her. She wanted to burst into tears, but was too numb for that. She hailed a cab. It was only once the car door was shut that she felt the talons of a vulture tearing into her gut.

The night porter greeted her. He was a sturdy, mustachioed man of fifty-eight who'd probably served in the military because he readily stood to attention.

"Good evening, Miss Pearl."

"Good evening, Leonard."

"A package for you was delivered today. Shall I get it brought up to you?"

Pearl tried to put on a normal face.

"No, no, give it to me now."

"It's just that . . . it's very bulky and . . . heavy."

"Very heavy?"

"If you've got a moment, I'll go get it."

He went off to the storeroom, clattering his keys. She checked her watch, it was past nine. She thought of Johnny, was he still at the party? Was he looking for her? Had people said to him, "Pearl was here just a minute ago"? Did he suspect that she'd seen the two of them? The porter came back out with a wooden crate similar to those used for wine, but much bigger and flatter. She had no idea what it could be.

"Are you sure that's for me, Leonard?"

She couldn't see any kind of label or markings to indicate where it was from or to whom addressed.

"Yes, Miss Pearl, absolutely sure, my colleague was positive. I'll come up with you."

In the elevator, the man could barely wedge the crate under his arm. They arrived at the eighteenth floor, *Johnny and Rhonda writhing around.* Pearl suddenly felt nauseous. She opened the door and Leonard carefully put the crate down in her entrance hall.

"Thanks, Leonard."

"At your service, Miss Pearl."

Now alone, she took a closer look at the mysterious object. She didn't even have a tool to open it with. Go back down to ask Leonard to lend her a nail-puller, or some thingy she didn't know the name of? There were nails all around the edge. She went to fetch a bread knife from the kitchen. A splinter was inevitable. She knelt down and kicked off her cursed pointed pumps. Could it be a practical joke? She thought of Johnny. A making-up present he'd have sent her that afternoon perhaps? *Cheating bastard.* To her great surprise, when she slid the blade into the gap, the two panels separated with ease and the cover lifted.

11

A fine new fabric, spotless-white and padded, was protecting a flat, lightweight object. Pearl's heart began to pound. With great care, she unfolded it, and as soon as that first corner of green paint was revealed, she knew. Before her stood the portrait of a woman, in three-quarter view, with a chignon and a beauty spot under one eye, exactly where Pearl, too, had a beauty spot.

The painting vibrated with beauty. It took Pearl's breath away as she drowned in those sky-blue, green-flecked eyes. Was she really the double of this woman? The line of the eyebrow, very pronounced, the faintly prominent nose, the well-defined carmine lips, and those cheeks . . . The artist had succeeded in creating the illusion of a blushing young woman. In its translucency, blood seemed to flow under the model's skin.

Yes, that's me alright, she thought. Whenever she was out of breath or embarrassed, hot red patches would inevitably appear on her face and even her neck. There was also that distinctive hairline, she noticed it now, two arcs that met in a point, mid-forehead. A narrow forehead, quite high, rather lovely. It was like looking at herself in an embellishing mirror. But the real difference between Pearl and the young woman in the portrait lay in the gentleness that emanated from the painting. She stood up and looked at herself in the mirror above the console in her entrance hall. The expression in her eyes was closed and sad. And hard.

There was a knock on the door.

"Who is it?"

"It's me."

Jonathan. She felt sick. *The portrait*! She must hide it immediately.

"Johnny?"

"Well, yes."

"Two seconds, I'm coming!"

Her own voice surprised her, all sweetness and light when, ten minutes ago, she wasn't sure whether to scream with hatred or weep with despair. She didn't dwell on this, quickly carrying the painting, still half-wrapped in the fabric, into her bedroom. On top of the wardrobe? Too high. Under the bed.

She went back into the hall. The crate was still there, wide open, in the middle of the floor. Johnny wasn't the curious type, but he was still likely to ask what it had contained. She picked up the back and the cover, but they both escaped from her grip and the corner of the crate landed on her little toe. She couldn't stifle a cry of pain.

"Everything okay?"

The two-timer! *As if he cared about me*!

"Yeah, yeah, sure, just coming!"

She grabbed everything and rushed into the kitchen, and without time to think, balanced the crate and cover on top of the fridge. It struck her that her place was far too tidy since having a cleaning lady. *It sticks out a mile.* If Johnny asked her the slightest question, she'd have to come up with something, but anyhow, it wasn't as if he'd be spending the night at hers, was it?

With her heart still racing and her mind totally confused (Good god, who on earth could have sent her that painting? Were Johnny and Rhonda in that room for an entirely different, perfectly innocent reason? Did she risk ending up in prison? Receiving stolen art . . . Should she tell Barnett about it? Had Johnny realized his mistake and that he loved her more than anything? Was he going to ask her to marry him?), she opened the door.

"Hi!"

"Hi!"

Finding him handsome, she was instantly annoyed with herself. *This guy's an asshole.*

"Can I come in?"

"Yes, of course!"

She'd tried to sound as neutral as possible, was she really going to let him get away with it? *What a damn fool, what a damn fool I am*! She looked at him and wondered if he knew that she knew. Going by his cheerful demeanor, she suspected that was unlikely.

"You okay?"

"Yes."

"What were you doing?"

"Nothing, tidying stuff away."

He raised his eyebrows. The fact that he wasn't generally interested in what Pearl did could have its advantages. He went to the sitting room and sprawled on the sofa like the man of the house. She'd noticed that Johnny was the sort who was at ease everywhere, and that this was common among those who'd been raised in a world of opulence and good manners. These folks took others liking them for granted, couldn't imagine not being welcomed into a new environment, with the result that they almost always were.

"Why d'you leave the party?"

She looked him straight in the eye. Hesitated. And, in spite of herself, heard herself answering him:

"I didn't feel well."

"Oh really?"

He had the tenderest turquoise gaze in the world. He gestured for her to come sit beside him, which she did, feeling her heart pounding in her throat. He took her in his arms.

"You should've come and found me, we'd have left together!"

He planted a gentle kiss on her forehead. Red patches starting burning her cheeks.

"I couldn't find you, there was such a crowd, and I wanted you to make the most of the party."

"You're too sweet."

He placed his thumb under her chin and drew it forward to kiss it, Johnny did that so very well, with him, it was always like a kiss in the movies.

"Johnny?"

"Yes?"

She must tell him. *Be strong*. Tell him about Rhonda or about the painting?

"You shouldn't kiss me . . . I think I'm ill . . ."

"D'you have a fever?"

"No, but really, I . . ."

She pulled away; she wouldn't be able to think if she stayed in his arms.

"Really, I don't feel well. But it's nice of you to come."

It's nice of you to come? *What a damn fool*! She reassured herself by telling herself that if she refrained from telling him what she really thought of him, it was to protect the painting, but deep down, she knew she was being a coward.

What was she hoping? That things could still work out? She saw Rhonda again, giggling in the corridor. Was it really that shocking? Was her negative view of infidelity down to her mother? One could separate the act from any motive, see it as a kind of tautology. Johnny had fucked Rhonda simply to fuck Rhonda, with no link at all to the fact that he was Pearl's boyfriend. *A tautology, no but, seriously*? She kept smiling at him, all the same. He suddenly seemed uncomfortable.

"Right, then I'll be off."

She'd seen a documentary on TV about how, if you placed

a starfish on the sand and it was encircled with water, meaning the water was equidistant from each of its five arms, it would remain immobile, not knowing if it should move to the right or the left, or up or down, and would just let itself die.

I'm a starfish, she thought. And yet being indecisive wasn't really like her.

"Okay."

He gave her a peck on the cheek. She didn't go with him to the door, which closed with a thud.

The silence that followed felt deadening. Slowly, she walked to the kitchen and opened the cupboard where she kept a bottle of whiskey for guests. She poured herself a glass and downed it in one, burning her esophagus. She didn't want to think about Rhonda, or Johnny, or how she'd behaved like a beaten dog who forgives its master everything. She poured herself a second glass and went to her bedroom.

Good god, what to do? She got down on all fours and pulled the painting out from under the bed. How beautiful it was! The young woman's skin almost glowed, *what softness*, Pearl was all stirred up inside. She must act rationally, ask the questions in the right order. She got up and went back to the kitchen to pour herself a third glass. This time, she put it on the coffee table in the sitting room and went to fetch the painting. It was light. She cleared some space on a shelf, removing a vase and two candlesticks, and propped the painting there. She daren't handle it too much, hadn't removed the fabric protecting its back and still three of its corners. She curled up on the sofa, glass in hand. She must draw up a list.

Who had stolen this painting?

Who was behind the theft of this painting?

Who had sent it to her?

Was it the same person?

Why had it been sent to her in particular?

Just because she was her double?

Because she and this woman were related?

If Pearl and the unknown woman in the portrait were related, it must be through Isidore, that was quite obvious. Was Isidore capable of getting the work stolen before dying? It seemed pretty unlikely, particularly since they were about to embark on a journey to see it.

Someone who knew Isidore? Someone who knew Pearl? Adri?

She burst out laughing, imagining Adrian commissioning a theft from New York. Adrian and the Italian mafia? No chance.

She went back to the kitchen to fetch the crate she'd put on top of the fridge, pouring herself another glass on the way. The simplest thing, of course, would have been to inform the police. Go to the police station, give back the painting, say, it's nothing to do with me, end of story.

The more she looked at the portrait, the more fascinated she became. She moved closer to it, felt like touching it, but sensed what sacrilege that would be. Her eyes followed the curve of the lips, it was as if the young woman's mouth could come alive by Pearl looking at it, the parted lips seemed just about to whisper something to her. *Her mouth is full of flowers*, she thought. She moved even closer; now almost touching, the two of them played that Cyclops game, their eyes getting bigger, realigning, superposing, and it made Pearl quite dizzy. The skin of the unknown beauty glimmered like a moon reflected in water.

No, not the police. But what if someone knew! *Who had delivered it*? She must ask Tad, the day porter, who had delivered the crate, but without arousing suspicion . . . Oh, her glass was empty again! She drank straight from the bottle. Could she have seen the Johnny and Rhonda thing coming? Was it the first time it had happened? As far as she knew, the two never saw each thutherr . . . She took a big swig . . . Other. The taste of smoked hay.

She must hide it. Get rid of the crate and hide the canvas somewhere. She took hold of it as carefully as she could, but the whiskey made her clumsy. She folded the white quilted fabric back over the corners as if tucking in a baby, tenderly. She could have done with being tucked in, too. *But where to put it*? The best place was in her wardrobe. The canvas was no bigger than a skirt. Except that her skirts were on hangers. *A coat cover*? *Yes, good idea*. Was she drunk? There was surely a way she could reorganize her dressing room. She felt full of energy. She sent sweaters and slacks flying . . . *But no*! *The winter duvet*! She fetched the stepladder and climbed up to reach the top of the cupboard, where she stored her two big suitcases and that duvet. She gave a big tug, almost came crashing down, spread the duvet on her bed like a picnic tablecloth. It was white, which was perfect.

She placed the wrapped canvas at the center of the duvet. She was tempted to gaze at it one last time, but a feeling of urgency drove her on. She folded over the comforter's edges with all the application of a schoolgirl, this side, that side, into a square. The duvet now enveloped the sleeping beauty in the midst of its feathers. The weight made her wobble as she went back up the ladder, but then, with the balance of a tightrope walker, she slid it right up onto the very highest shelf. All that could be seen was the well-padded side of the duvet. Victorious, she closed the cupboard door and put away the stepladder.

"And now, the crate!"

In her zeal, she grabbed the cover and tried to break it up against the tiled floor in her kitchen, but the wood resisted. Should she take it outdoors, without being seen, and throw it in the first dumpster? She couldn't keep it in her apartment. In her cellar? Impossible with the elevator assistant, who'd have asked her what she intended to do with that . . . that . . . that great empty thing. Worse, he was bound to offer to carry it for her! *Disaster*. She couldn't think straight. *God, these smart apartment buildings, how dumb, always needing to have staff around.* She must buy a saw and cut the crate up into really small pieces, like with a corpse, bit by bit. She felt sick. Oh, she'd think about it tomorrow. The most important thing was that the painting was safe. *It's okay*, *it's okay*. Reeling, she went to bed . . . "*And then we'll stroll along Johannesgasse and I'll show you my father's house. What a splendid house that was! A real little palace!*"

"*Johannesgasse?*"

"*Yes, at that time, all the aristocrats of Vienna owned mansions overlooking the Stadtpark. And the Brombeeres were . . .*"

She sat up. The Brombeeres, Isidore's parents, but of course, she should start with them! She fell back onto her pillow, drunk and satisfied, she knew what she had to do. Forget Johnny, buy a saw, and book a ticket to Vienna.

12

Pearl had gone to the New York Chamber of Commerce to consult the Austrian professional directory. "Detective" is "*detektiv*" in German, too, and it hadn't taken her long to find what she was looking for. She had rung the first number on the list, and a young-sounding woman with a pleasant voice had answered. Pearl had asked:

"Do you speak English?"

To which the reply had been:

"*Einen Moment bitte . . .*"

Pearl had understood "moment" and waited until a man came on the line.

"Mr. Stauber here, what can I do for you?"

The accent was very strong, almost comical, but it turned out that Mr. Stauber's English was perfect, and Pearl felt immediately reassured.

Her enquiry was, seemingly, pretty standard. She said she was the daughter of a Brombeere who had emigrated to the States in the mid-1920s, and had died the previous year. Since her father had told her very little about his childhood, and was, sadly, no longer around to answer her questions, she now wanted to trace her Austrian forebears. Was there still a Brombeere alive? Or, if no living memory survived, could one find documentation, birth and death certificates, property deeds, letters, why not, any kind of document, and ideally photographs—she had emphasized those. She was convinced that, to understand why the stolen painting had been sent to her, she needed to discover the identity of the mysterious relative whose double she was.

She didn't know much, but enough for the private detective to start on his search. Isidore had told her one day that his father had died a hero during the First World War and his mother had passed away due to illness. They were rich, perhaps aristocrats, and lived in a big house on Johannesgasse, of that she was certain. However, Isidore had never told her exactly who had taken him in and brought him up when his mother died. Was it an aunt? A cousin? They would have to find the Brombeeres' family tree and pray that some descendant could tell her their version of events. Pearl had announced that she intended to come to Vienna in two weeks' time. Would that be too soon?

"No, no, you've given us plenty of information, this search won't be difficult. A few days in the archives at the city hall and the War Ministry, and I think we'll have what you require."

Mr. Stauber seemed confident. She pictured the gumshoe as a tall, very tough and very serious Austrian, in a checked shirt and mustard corduroy trousers. When she hung up, she was euphoric.

She had told no one that she was going to Vienna, except Adri, to whom she'd sent a deceptively cheery email. Adri knew her too well, if she'd spoken to him on the phone even for just a couple of minutes, he would have detected that she wasn't in her normal state. Euphoria wasn't the worst of it, the truth was that, since she'd opened up that crate, she'd been a nervous wreck. Swinging from excitement to anxiety, she'd consulted her dictionary to find a word for her condition. "Hysteria"? The definition didn't fit, well, not really.

And yet, she had good reasons to be in such a state. She was a brilliant attorney, her probity had to be beyond reproach, but she was hiding, in the folds of a duvet, a stolen painting that police worldwide were looking for. She could have walked into the first police station she came to and put an end to this situation, particularly since she was but the recipient and had done nothing wrong apart from opening a mysterious crate that had been delivered to her. But she was the double of the woman in the portrait, she couldn't hand the painting in to the police without raising questions about this resemblance. And indeed, she wanted to be the only one to ask those questions. And she had carefully destroyed the crate that contained that treasure, with the saw she'd bought specially for the job. She hadn't just destroyed it, she'd also made it disappear, like some criminal. Each passing day increased her guilt, it was no longer simply about a painting she'd received, but a painting she was fencing. She was so rich, she could have easily commissioned the theft. She was scared of ending up in prison. She was scared the portrait would be taken away from her.

Her paranoia wasn't unfounded, after all, whoever had delivered the painting knew her name and address . . . so could always return . . . As soon as she left her office, she would rush home to get back to it. She thought about it endlessly. She constantly felt like taking another look at it. The portrait exerted a fascination in her that was close to madness. She feared damaging it. Every evening, when she got home, she'd shake her head, no, she wouldn't climb up to the top of the cupboard to take her out of her cozy duvet. *Leave her in peace.*

She had begun to talk to the painting, attribute feelings to it. Perched on her stepladder, arms reaching up, Pearl would promise herself that this was the last time. And yet she couldn't stop herself from looking at her, and then she'd become totally absorbed, engulfed by the portrait.

Insidiously, she'd taken to checking and re-checking that the door to her apartment was properly locked. But when she turned the latch to see if it was locked, she thereby unlocked it and so had to repeat the procedure, several times, to feel reassured. She had let her cleaning lady go. No way could someone enter her apartment when she wasn't there and move things around and tidy her dressing room. Apart from Johnny, who had surprised her that dreadful evening, she'd let no one in anymore. Johnny, that drop-dead gorgeous rich kid who'd cheated on her (was he still cheating on her? She hadn't the slightest idea) with Rhonda, also privileged, and pretty ugly, to say the least. Was Pearl's heart broken? She avoided confrontation and Johnny couldn't fathom why she no longer wanted to go out in the evening, why she no longer wanted him to come to her place. Maybe he'd end up wondering whether she'd found out something? She didn't want to think about it.

She was ruminating on everything: Isidore, his Austrian childhood, Klimt the famous artist, the unknown woman in the portrait . . . Nothing made any sense. This secret was too big for her. Alone in her bed, she would imagine hundreds of hiding-places, each stranger and more unlikely than the last. Or then she'd think back to her cleaning lady, who might have got doubles made of the keys and, one of these days, as revenge for being dismissed without notice, would come back and help herself and rummage around and . . . But of course, while Pearl would be in Vienna! She expected so much of this trip. To think she was half-Austrian and had never set foot in Europe! She'd have to sew the canvas into the lining of her suitcase and take it with her, she had no choice. But how would she get past customs? She was getting all worked up about the checks at airports. Fifteen days and thirteen nights far away from *her*. Pearl couldn't even sew. In the street, she felt like she was being followed. And also, it was absurd but . . . she would leave her office desk ever more frequently to go and wash her hands. Even Barnett had noticed her feverishness. She had announced at work that she was taking two weeks off.

"Oh yeah? Where are you going?"

"To Paris."

Her colleagues had found it rather unlike her, but had

presumed she wasn't going away alone, since Paris was the city of lovers.

The days had gone by with her in this nervous, agitated state. She had her plane ticket, her suitcase was packed, and the portrait stayed put, perfectly still and cocooned. She'd considered adding a bolt to the cupboard, but decided against it. That would only draw attention to it, better that it remain inconspicuous. Or installing a safe, a real one, embedded in the wall, but her experience as an attorney had taught her that people with safes were automatically singled out by burglars. Best to do nothing at all. Her building had two porters, one daytime, one nighttime, so . . . She must calm down, calm down and get away. She didn't know whether she'd be capable. Capable of leaving behind that damned cupboard. The great departure day was approaching. She was going to fly in a plane and find herself thousands of miles away from *her*. The investigation, her curiosity, finally understanding this story, would that be enough? She untied a knot in her stomach the better to tie one in her brain.

On the morning she was setting off, she looked at herself in the mirror. She was hardly recognizable. Her sleepless nights had ended up circling her eyes with a mauvish shadow and there were red patches on her neck. *They're going to stop me at customs, I look like a druggie.* She really struggled with locking, unlocking, and relocking her door, and finally threw herself into a taxi as if into the void.

Once at the airport, she felt sick and rushed to the restrooms. When she re-emerged, new red patches had appeared on her cheeks. She handed over her passport to check in her suitcase, did so again to enter the departure lounge, and yet again to board the plane. She thought how these repeated checks weren't pointless: they prevented her from running away. *You're leaving, you're leaving.* The flight attendant who showed her to her seat in the plane was charming. Her skirt was straight and her pillbox hat wasn't. She offered her a drink.

"A whiskey, please."

Pearl was flying in first class. She let her head tip backwards and the plane took off, and then she thought of her portrait, nestled in its wadding. The two women were now as one, each in their cloud.

You're going to know where you come from. She tried to conjure up Isidore's smile again. What a weird story, having met her father too late to be able to be his daughter. And yet she had learnt to love him. *Ten years is enough to create some memories.* A ten-hour flight. A six-hour time difference. Up in the sky, she slept a dreamless sleep.

* * *

She landed in Vienna in the early hours of the morning. It was April and chilly, much chillier than New York. People didn't speak English. She reached the Hotel Imperial, the one Isidore had booked for them. The crystal chandeliers she'd imagined a few months earlier winked at her.

She had made an appointment with Ernst Stauber for that very day. Over the phone, he'd told her that he was making progress and it would be very good for them to meet all the same. At the time, she hadn't picked up on that.

She took a shower and changed her outfit. She slipped on some very elegant front-pleated gray trousers, a cream silk blouse, and a tweed jacket that the Bloomingdale's sales assistant had assured her was the epitome of English style, since she couldn't guarantee Austrian style. It was Isidore who'd often worn tweed. The jacket had been expensive, which was also important for her to feel strong.

She had given the address of the *Privatdetektiv* agency to the concierge and the doorman had hailed a taxi. She had sped through the streets of Vienna without even time to look out the window and soak up the city, and the taxi had dropped her outside a nondescript building with a glass door. With her heart racing, she had paid and thanked the driver. It had started to rain so she rushed under the porch and rang the doorbell.

The agency wasn't nearly as smart as she'd imagined it to be. Herr Stauber's office was more a storage room cluttered with dusty files and papers. Stauber shared this cramped space with his secretary, doubtless the pleasant voice Pearl had first heard on the phone. She wondered if they were husband and wife. Herr Stauber must have been in his forties, with green-flecked hazel eyes and an open smile. His skin was speckled with freckles, and as he held his hand out to her, he blushed.

"Ah, Miss Alvez! It's a pleasure to meet you. Welcome, welcome! Did you have a good trip?"

"Yes, very good, thanks."

"Please, do sit down."

She looked around for a chair, but the only one available was covered in a heap of papers that threatened to collapse at the first attempt to file them. Swerving an overflowing wastebasket and a phone placed on the floor, Stauber strode over to a stool, hidden behind three removal boxes, and held it up triumphantly.

"Please . . ."

"Thanks."

No, she really hadn't expected to be received like this. The man might speak good English, but he screamed amateurism.

"So, I've carried out the research you asked me to. And I have to tell you that nothing . . . worked out, yes, I'd say worked out . . . as expected."

Pearl felt huge disappointment tightening her chest.

"We did indeed find some members of a Brombeere family

who lived on Johannesgasse, at No. 24, a splendid house that today is divided into three luxury apartments. Unfortunately, no one who died for their country, either during the First World War, or the Second. And most importantly, no child with the name Isidore, or indeed any other name, who would have been born in 1909, or 1908, or even 1910."

Stauber's accent threw her.

"I'm not sure I quite understand what you're saying, sir . . ."

"It's very simple, your father said he was called Isidore Ferguson. Indeed, that's the name he gave when he arrived at Ellis Island on May 18, 1925, I checked. It's important to know that it wasn't rare for people to create a new identity for themselves as they stepped off the boat, and the name Ferguson recurs frequently in the immigration records. So, let's say your father was called neither Isidore nor Ferguson but his father was a Brombeere who lived on Johannesgasse . . . Well, that doesn't hold together either! On Johannesgasse there did indeed reside a Mr. Otto and Mrs. Hermine Brombeere, with their only son Franz Brombeere. And in 1909, the presumed date of your father's birth, Otto Brombeere was sixty-one, his wife Hermine forty-three, and their son Franz twenty-one, I checked it all. Since Franz wasn't married, if he was the father of your father, it would have made your father a bastard, which wasn't rare either. But since you told me that your father's father had died in combat, I searched in the military archives and found nothing whatsoever, apart from some documents signed by Otto Brombeere, who was close to the Emperor and in the diplomatic service, a most remarkable man, by the way. As for young Franz, he never got a sniff of military service because he was asthmatic. And no other Brombeeres lived in Vienna, there's a vague branch of cousins with the name near Salzburg, but I've not yet had time to look into that."

Pearl was speechless, it seemed nothing held together. And so? Had Isidore spun her a yarn all that time? And not just her, but Peter and Felicity, too? Did they also have a made-up surname?

"Could the name Ferguson not be that of his mother?"

"There's no Isidore Ferguson on the register of births from 1905 to 1915, I checked them all. But if the child was illegitimate, things were often vague, and with the destruction of archives during the Second World War, I can't guarantee to you that all this is totally flawless . . ."

"And you think my grandfather came up with the Brombeeres' name, but it could just have easily been the neighbors' name? That it's a false trail?"

Ernst Stauber paused awhile.

"Well . . . that's where it gets interesting, because in 1925, the year your grandfather left Austria for the United States, even if his ship did depart from Genoa, which I also checked, something occurred in the Brombeere family."

"Oh yes?"

"Their son, Franz, was murdered."

13

The private detective had looked deep into the young woman's eyes.

"A burglary that went wrong, according to the police. They never found the murderer."

Pearl instantly made the link. Even if Ernst Stauber didn't want to accuse anyone, he, too, seemed convinced that the business of a false identity and departure for the States was concealing something, but a murder?

"Would you like us to go for a walk?"

"Sorry?"

"I always think better when walking, don't you?"

This man astonished her, "vigorous" was the word that came to mind, it was like he was mounted on springs. He grabbed his raincoat, stepped over a cardboard box, and boomed:

"*Brigitte, wir gehen raus*!"—Brigitte, we're going out!

"*Sehr gut, mein Herr.*"—Very good, sir.

The secretary seemed perfectly accustomed to her boss's frenetic outbursts.

They walked for a long time. Pearl had the strange feeling that this city was familiar to her. Ernst Stauber talked and waved his arms around, without looking at Pearl and without stopping. He was imposing, must measure at least 6 feet, and walked fast. Bizarrely, she noticed that the rhythm of their steps synchronized perfectly. Just as those of very close friends would. She thought people in the street must surely take them to be husband and wife. Conversely, when she walked with Johnny, even if they were holding hands, Pearl could tell that people found them ill-matched. She'd reassure herself that it was because Johnny was too handsome for her, but she sensed that the way they were at odds went deeper.

"Let's recap. Isidore Ferguson is probably a false name, but the fact is that Isidore Ferguson disembarked at Ellis Island on May 18, 1925. He'd boarded the ship in Genoa and his nationality was Austrian. On his arrival card, it's written that he has no papers but is in good health and doesn't have lice. He also gives his date of birth, October 10, 1909, meaning he was sixteen at the time."

"But it's impossible to be sure-sure . . ."

"Impossible, but it's certainly *that* Isidore Ferguson who later added his wife's surname to his own and called himself Isidore Hoffmann Ferguson, and *that* Isidore who made a fortune in oral hygiene, and *that* Isidore who was your father."

"Yes."

"Right."

Ernst Stauber was square-shouldered. Maybe the word "vigorous", which had come to her to describe the detective, wasn't the right one.

In reality, the moment Pearl had walked in, Ernst Stauber had felt extremely nervous. He'd needed some air, needed to get out of the confined space of his office, needed, also, to be alone with her. They walked side by side, at a reasonable distance, but the air separating them could have been outlined, or almost colored in. And without realizing it, they each had exactly the same perception, the same almost palpable, and yet indefinable, certainty; that of having entered the magnetic field of the other.

"He told you that he'd spent his childhood in Vienna and his father was called Brombeere, and he lived in a big house on Johannesgasse, beside the Stadtpark."

"Yes."

"And when you asked him why his name wasn't Brombeere, he told you that he'd changed his name when his mother died."

"Yes, and I'd imagined that it was his mother whose name was Ferguson."

"The fact is that there was a family by the name of Brombeere who lived in a big house, No. 24 Johannesgasse, to be precise, and I think we should stick to that track. Your father could very well have been the illegitimate son of Franz Brombeere, who was twenty-one in 1909, and that would explain why he didn't have his surname. His mother was undoubtedly from a lower order than the Brombeeres, maybe a servant or a prostitute, I hope I'm not shocking you . . ."

Pearl wanted to smile. *If you only knew*, she thought. How strange it was that history should repeat itself this way, no wonder Isidore had a heart attack when Pearl's existence had been revealed to him.

"Having said that, this whole story about his father dying in combat doesn't stand up anymore, since Franz Brombeere spent the war working in the archive department, and indeed, made the most of that to get a book published."

"Really?"

"Yes, a translation of a collection of poems . . . by a French poet . . . Anyhow, all that to say that he didn't seem to be madly keen on weapons. I have a photo of him."

"Really?"

"Yes, at the office, I photocopied the police report on his murder. I'll show it to you."

Pearl really must ask Peter and Felicity about all this. Their father was bound to have told them about his childhood, there would surely be one thing, one detail, one sign.

"So, Franz Brombeere died, murdered, on the night of April 1-2, 1925. He was thirty-seven years old. The police report is really thorough. His butler discovered him in his study. He had been struck on the brow and temple with a paperweight, but the autopsy reveals that he almost certainly gave himself a rabbit punch by falling onto a marble console. He had bled profusely and the time of death given was around three in the morning. There was evidence of a struggle in the room, but no sign of a break-in in the house. And only his fob watch and his wallet containing a few banknotes were stolen. That's why the inquiry concluded that it was an interrupted burglary, and the burglar, before running away, had struck the master of the house who'd caught him in the act, you get the picture."

"Yes, yes . . . but . . . I can't see the connection with my father."

"I'm getting to that."

Ernst Stauber took a deep breath and turned towards Pearl.

"Come, we're going to cross."

He took her arm and she let him; this contact seemed to calm the detective, but it electrified Pearl.

"At that time, the Brombeere mansion had eight full-time servants, five of whom lived there, plus a groom who slept above the stables. The other servants lodged in the boarding house of a certain Frau Rathau. When poor Franz Bombeere was found with his face covered in blood, just one member of staff was missing, one Stefan Bauer. A young handyman who had entered into service there six months previously. He was the prime suspect. Clearly, since there was no sign the house had been broken into, it seemed likely to be someone who had means of access, as he did, and his killing of Franz Brombeere might indicate that he'd been recognized by his master. Do you follow me?"

"Yes, yes."

"It is plausible, one can just imagine the young man deciding to steal from his employers, doing so in the middle of the night, but, bad luck, coming face to face with Franz, who had insomnia. Fear grips him, a fight breaks out between the two men, he strikes his master and kills him almost by accident, before running away with almost nothing . . . it is plausible . . ."

Stauber shrugged his shoulders to indicate that it wasn't plausible otherwise. Pearl was lost.

"Yes . . . but I still don't see the connection with my father."

"The butler tells the police that young Stefan Bauer was nineteen and an orphan from Leobendorf, which is 25 kilometers from Vienna. So the police head to the orphanage, where there had indeed been a certain Stefan, not Bauer but Grün, who was seventeen and fitted the description of our young man. They set off in search of him, but when they find him, it's the wrong guy. The butler admits that he hadn't checked the references of this recruit and had lost the letter from the orphanage confirming his full identity; in short, the inquiry stalls, nothing is found. But personally, I did find something . . ."

Pearl was staring at Ernst Stauber with her big blue eyes, he'd stopped speaking, confident in the effect he was producing.

"What did you find?"

"I went to Leobendorf. The orphanage no longer exists, it closed down in 1952. But they kept the records at the town hall."

"Records of what?"

"Of all the war orphans whose fathers had died during the First and Second World Wars. And among all those little Kurts and Adolfs, I found the famous Stefan Grün, who doesn't interest us, but most importantly, I found . . . an Isidore Linde! And I can tell you, there aren't that many Isidores in Austria. Born in 1909, the son of one Martha Linde, who died of Spanish flu in 1918, and an unknown father, possibly killed in combat, he was taken into care at the Leobendorf orphanage until he was fifteen, in 1924."

"And that Isidore Linde would be my father?"

"And that Isidore Linde would be your father because your father told you that he was the son of Franz Brombeere!"

"And?"

"Franz Brombeere translated a collection of poems . . ."

"Yes, you told me, but . . ."

"The French title of the collection is *Les Chants de Maldoror*, and the poet is called the Count of Lautréamont, but that's a pen name."

"I still can't see the connection."

"Lautréamont's real name was Isidore Ducasse!"

Ernst Stauber was jubilant. Pearl couldn't deny that his enthusiasm was infectious.

"But you don't think that's . . . a bit far-fetched?"

"Not at all! It's the most fascinating investigation I've ever done! Everything holds together! Franz Brombeere gets that poor Martha Linde pregnant, they call the baby Isidore after Franz's favorite poet, in memory of an evening when he'd have read her some poems, who knows? Then he cravenly abandons mother and child to destitution and gets on with his life as a rich Viennese gentleman and culture buff. Unfortunately, poor Martha dies of Spanish flu, little Isidore is nine years old, he's placed in the orphanage but, as soon as he leaves the place, he has just one thing on his mind: finding his father to get his revenge!"

"You have a vivid imagination!"

"Not at all! Isidore gets himself hired by the Brombeeres, lies about his name and age so as not to be recognized, and a few months later, the dates tally, at the first opportunity, he kills his father! Do you see? It's anything but an accident, it's premeditated murder! But he makes it look like a burglary gone wrong and runs away to the New World, lands in New York, starts his life again under a different name . . ."

"While keeping his real first name?"

"Yes . . . I did think of that . . . I thought maybe his mother had spoken to him about the poet, or he was probably the sentimental type . . ."

Pearl thought of old Isidore, she'd known him so little.

"And he becomes chairman and CEO of Chloros and dies taking his terrible secret with him, would you like to have dinner with me?"

Pearl was totally stunned. She tried to think, she must get away from this absurd exposé and the eyes of this man who was staring so intensely at her. She felt the blood rushing to her cheeks.

"I imagine you'll need to think over all that, I . . . Would you like us to return to my office? I'll give you that copy of the police report, I had it translated into English for you, and also the photograph . . ."

"Dinner? But it's nowhere near dinnertime!"

"Yes, sorry, I meant, this evening, would you like to have dinner with me?"

14

Ernst Stauber had left Pearl at her hotel and she hadn't re-emerged all afternoon. She'd stretched out on the bed with the police report and had read it, very slowly, very carefully: the pool of blood on the floor of the study, the stiff corpse, the smashed objects, a broken vase, books scattered, Franz Brombeere had fought before dying. The photocopy of the sepia photograph was poor quality. She'd tried to find Isidore's features in Franz's, but genetics wasn't always as simple as a beauty spot under the left eye. A family resemblance? She'd closed her eyes to picture the violent scene more clearly and had fallen asleep. Who'd said that Isidore's mother was a prostitute? Stauber? Stauber had read too many novels. There was just the name Isidore, Pearl knew nothing about French poets. But whether the name was proof or an extraordinary coincidence, that had to be resolved.

When she woke up, she was in a sweat and convinced about the parricide. Even though it was the stuff of melodrama, the version of the wealthy young man killed by the son he'd abandoned at birth was viable.

The restaurant was a kind of brasserie serving beer and sausages called *wurst*. Pearl had changed outfit, she shouldn't have. After much dithering, she'd gone for a navy blue dress with white polka dots—all the rage in New York that spring. He was in the same threads as that morning, must have come straight from the office.

When he saw her appear, he stood up and very gallantly

pulled out her chair. He seemed less agitated to her, maybe because the place itself was so hectic.

Sitting opposite each other, elbows on the table and leaning forward to hear each other in the surrounding hubbub, Pearl found again that strange yet familiar feeling of intimacy. She thought of Johnny.

"Do you like schnitzel?"

"What's that?"

"A breaded veal escalope. It's their specialty here."

Her spotty dress definitely was ridiculous, but it didn't matter anymore, she thought how gentle this man's gaze was.

"Right, great, then I'll have that!"

"And a beer! Or do you prefer wine?"

"Wine, please."

They placed their order. To Pearl's ears, Austrian German sounded like an elfish language. They talked about the investigation, came up with all kinds of variations with more or less wild explanations. They had a wonderful evening. She thought of the painting; at one time she'd imagined that this Martha Linde was perhaps Klimt's model and the sought-after relation, but the possibility of murder was so shocking that it prevailed over all other considerations. Whatever conclusions Stauber might reach, she'd have to continue on her own to solve the mystery of the stolen portrait that had been delivered to her home.

The following morning, she'd woken up thinking clearly; "detached" was the best word to describe how she felt. This had reassured her. Not because she'd feared being the daughter of a murderer, but because this time, and for good, she accepted being the daughter of no one. Indeed, Stauber had been staggered at how unperturbed she'd remained by all their blood-soaked hypotheses. Together, they were looking into the past of Isidore Hoffmann Ferguson, and this story of revenge was the most fascinating of all, but she, Pearl, had nothing to do with any of it.

Isidore . . . she kept coming back to that name. If the mother had called her son after the favorite poet of the father, it could mean one of two things. Either the mother also liked the poet in question, or she'd done it out of love for the father of the child, and then Franz Brombeere could only have betrayed and abandoned them later on. This disillusionment fitted perfectly with the notion of the vengeful son, but contradicted that of the prostitute. Might Isidore's mother have been a well-read young lady from a respectable family, chased from her home by Puritanical parents? But if she had belonged to the same social milieu as Franz, he would have married her . . . And so Pearl stalled again. All the more since her knowledge of Viennese customs in 1925 was based on little more than Hollywood stereotypes.

On the third day, she went to the Shakespeare & Company bookstore, on Sterngasse, and bought the complete works of Stefan Zweig.

She'd reread the police report, and hadn't found it as clear-cut, but she wasn't familiar with such reports, things might have been different had she opted to be a criminal lawyer. An entire paragraph described the wound on Franz Brombeere's brow, and the paperweight he'd been hit with, a bronze toad. Could one force a boy to marry the girl he'd got pregnant? It all depended on her social standing. Pearl kept endlessly coming back to that.

She would see Ernst Stauber every day, and felt like admitting to him that she wasn't really the daughter of Isidore, that she hadn't been a desired child, either. More than anything, she wanted to talk to him about the Klimt portrait and her resemblance to the unknown woman, whom she now called "Martha."

They would go for strolls, stop at cafés, dine together. Pearl had planned on staying for ten days. She had gone to Leobendorf to see the orphanage building, now converted into a retirement home. She'd wished she could just touch the roughcast walls and they would reveal their secrets, like in some sci-fi film, in a flash she would have seen what had really happened.

Too impatient to wait for her return to New York, she'd phoned Peter. When she'd said the word "orphanage," she'd heard silence, and then Peter had asked, "Are you sure? Dad never told me he'd been in an institution . . ." She'd decided not to phone Felicity, what was the point? She was certain now that Isidore had revealed nothing about his past, even to his own children.

In the afternoon, she would take a nap. She'd been to the Leopold Museum and the Belvedere to admire the paintings of Gustav Klimt and, like millions of tourists before her, lose herself in contemplation before the bluish foot of the young girl in *The Kiss*. She'd trailed the artist, but had learnt nothing more than she'd already found in the monograph, each page of which she'd annotated carefully.

She had walked along the Ring as far as the former residence of the Brombeeres. A large metal gate protected the entrance. From the street, she'd seen the huge glass rotunda, but how could she have imagined that, seventy-three years earlier, when horseshoes still clattered on the cobbles of the courtyard, Isidore had cleaned the glass panes of that rotunda with utmost care? Old Isidore Hoffmann Ferguson, the feared and respected magnate, the American multimillionaire, as a boy handyman with a cloth in his hand?

With Stauber, she'd spent an entire day at the Vienna city-hall archives, looking for information on the Brombeeres. Their family tree struck them as sparse, to say the least: a line of only sons and some distant cousins near Salzburg, whom Stauber had contacted by phone, but not one object, piece of furniture, item of jewelry, or any photographs had survived the ravages of the Second World War. Admittedly, the cousins in question had chosen to rejoice in the Anschluss, and that hadn't brought them luck, as is well known. Stauber had spoken to a young Mark Brombeere, who had clearly explained to him that his family's past had been erased with good reason, and that no one was very keen to revisit it.

As for Otto Brombeere, Franz's father, his name did appear on a certain number of official documents. This high-ranking diplomat's signature figured prominently beside that of the Emperor, Charles I (who signed just Karl), at the bottom of agreements and other treaties until 1918, the year of the abolition of the monarchy, and the end of Otto's career.

Pearl had insisted that Stauber hunt through some newspapers. In the library, two were suggested to them: *Die Presse* and *Kleine Zeitung*. Maybe there had been a report on Franz's murder? Not reading German, she'd been reduced to scanning the pages for the Brombeere name, but found nothing. Stauber told her he wasn't surprised, that particular family wasn't the kind to accept the name of their darling son making the headlines. "Murdered in the middle of the night by his servant"—how ghastly!

She finally went to the Galerie Miethke, and then the Klimt Villa, the artist's last studio, but it was undergoing renovation so was of no help to her. She returned to the museum to see other portraits than the one she was obsessed with. It was one of the few things she'd kept of Isidore, these wanderings among paintings brought her a true feeling of calm.

On the sixth evening, Ernst Stauber had arranged to meet her at an Italian restaurant. Pearl was early. She refused to analyze the nature of their relationship. The work, of course, the investigation. She was the client, he was the private detective. She was attracted to him, but it wasn't clear the feeling was mutual. And yet Stauber always suggested that they see each other again, even when the investigation was stalling. But as soon as the detective walked into the restaurant, she could tell he was in the same state as when they'd first met, six days earlier, keyed-up, euphoric.

"I've got news!"

Pearl smiled, the childish joy of this man was like that of a treasure hunter. Her heart stirred.

"Tell me."

"You're not going to believe me! It's the craziest story! I went back to the archives at the city hall . . . and you'll never guess what I found . . ."

He left Pearl in suspense while he took off his overcoat and folded it neatly over the back of the chair.

"If I can't guess . . . you'd better tell me, Ernst . . ."

He blushed, it was the first time she was calling him by his first name.

"In the official journal for the week of April 6-15, 1925, there is indeed the announcement of the death of Franz Brombeere . . . and the publishing of the banns for his marriage!"

"Franz's marriage?"

"Yes! With a certain Liesl von Traum, the marriage was set for April 11! The publishing of the banns had to precede the marriage by ten days, and the person in charge of announcements didn't make the link between the two events, in fact they weren't even in the same section."

"Extraordinary!"

"Yes, and that's when I thought how right you'd been in telling me that this story of premeditated revenge was illogical, here we have a motive!"

So, Isidore Linde, the son of Martha Linde and Franz Brombeere, the pretentious rich kid who had cravenly seduced poor Martha with poetry and then abandoned her as soon as she fell pregnant; Isidore Linde whose mother died when he was nine years old and who was sent to an orphanage in

Leobendorf; Isidore Linde who, upon leaving the orphanage, had found his father and, under a false name, been hired by his family; well, Isidore Linde had discovered, after a few months, that his father was going to marry the pretty young daughter of rich and privileged aristocrats. That is why, remembering how his poor mother had suffered, he had gone to find Franz in the middle of the night to tell him all the harm he had done by abandoning them. Unfortunately, Franz had laughed in his face and that had been an affront too far, so, enraged, he had killed him and run away.

Yes, the story was becoming clearer. Ernst Stauber was waving his arms around more than ever.

And Gustav Klimt? And the painting in all of that? Pearl knew that a piece of the puzzle was missing. And yet she was incapable of telling the detective about the secret that haunted her. They had drunk schnapps to celebrate this ultimate version of the story, but not enough to rid them of their inhibitions entirely. She would have liked him to kiss her, tell her it wasn't just this investigation that fired him up. She no longer found Ernst Stauber's accent remotely comical. She wondered if he found her attractive. That she would never know, either.

For the day before her departure, Stauber had offered to take her to Schönbrunn Palace, and then, for one last time, they had dined together.

"What time is your plane?"

"Four o'clock."

"I can accompany you to the airport if you like . . ."

"Oh, that's kind, but it's not worth it, I wouldn't want to . . ."

"No, no, you're not bothering me, I'd really love to."

She didn't know what to think, was Ernst Stauber simply the most polite man in the world?

They had settled the bill. For once, Ernst Stauber remained

silent. They went outside. A taxi went by and the man's arm went up automatically.

"The airport is just thirty minutes from your hotel, would it suit you if I come to pick you up at . . . let's say, two o'clock?"

"Yes, that's perfect. Thanks so much."

"So, see you tomorrow?"

"Yes, see you tomorrow."

She had thrown herself into the taxi, full of schnitzel and regrets.

15

Pearl had arrived at the foot of her apartment building and looked up, at the rectangles of glass dividing New York's skyscrapers, the systematic way they were stacked, cutting the horizon into pointed rectangles. Europe felt so far away with its twists and turns! She had adored Vienna. Vienna had changed her.

When she'd turned the key in the lock, the immaculate calm of the apartment had made her feel like she was stepping onto virgin territory. She could have rushed to check that the painting was still in its place, untouched, but stopped herself from doing so. Out of fear, no doubt.

Ten days earlier, the hold that painting had on her was verging on madness, seeing it again might plunge her right back. Ten days earlier, she was a nervous wreck, obsessed by what she had hidden at the top of her tallest cupboard, and turning paranoid. Ten days earlier, she was disgusted by men, in particular, by a certain Johnny. And today? She was seriously considering that her genitor had committed murder, and she was in love with a wonderful man who hadn't attempted a kiss over five afternoons and six dinners. Her heart really was anyone's.

The only person she felt like talking to was Adri.

"Hey! You're back!"

"Yes, still a bit jetlagged."

"So, how was it?"

"Magnificent."

She told him about the old stones, the museums, the Schönbrunn Palace, and admitted that she'd hired a private detective to trace her forebears, the wonderful Ernst Stauber, who hadn't discovered much (she'd wisely decided not to reveal anything), but had shown her around Vienna's brasseries and . . .

"No! Are you getting married?"

She burst into laughter.

"I'd like to, but that's not remotely on the cards, we didn't even kiss!"

"Oh, I'm reassured, long-distance love isn't easy, you know . . . And the Klimt?"

Pearl controlled her voice and tried to sound believably casual.

"Nothing new there, no one knows who the young woman in the painting was and it's unlikely she had any link to my father's family, which was very wealthy. But I visited some amazing museums and saw lots of other Klimt paintings, you'd have loved it."

She hated lying to Adri, hesitated over telling him about her crazy investigation while remaining silent on anything relating to the painting, but managed to keep herself in check. Talking was putting oneself in danger.

"I'm so pleased you're back home. Do you have a free evening next week?"

"Yes, we could have dinner on Tuesday if you like."

"Perfect."

Adrian's voice was full of kindness. She smiled despite herself. How nice it was to have a friend like him, she thought. Adri knew her well enough to have immediately picked up that she was smitten. Would she ever see Ernst Stauber again? She let out a long sigh. *Get a grip*. On the way to her bedroom, she passed the wretched cupboard, but hurried off to bed without giving in to the temptation that tormented her.

* * *

She dug her high heels into the carpet at Barnett & Barnett the way small children dig their toes into warm sand. She returned to her files and her colleagues with pleasure. She'd almost forgotten how much she loved her work. She felt reassured, she was in her rightful place here. It was the feeling someone doing a jigsaw puzzle gets when gently pressing a small piece so the edges slot in, both on top and, miracle, on the side, and getting that light click under the finger confirming that it's a perfect fit. Mid-morning, her phone rang, it was Johnny, she steeled herself and thought of Ernst Stauber.

"Hello, Johnny."

"Hello, Pearl, I was wondering when you'd decide to call me."

His tone was sarcastic, which she found totally inappropriate, and she let out a long sigh in reply.

"When d'you get back?"

"Yesterday."

"Right, and was Paris good?"

"Yes, very good, thanks."

"D'you want us to meet up this evening?"

Pearl sighed again.

"Can you do something other than sighing, please?"

The boy was playing it offended.

"I'd like you to be straight with me, Pearl, if you want us to stop going out, just tell me!"

In her nicest possible voice, she replied.

"Yes, I wouldn't mind."

"Sorry?"

It seemed he was caught off guard. A heavy, awkward silence followed.

"You wouldn't mind what?"

"Johnny, I saw you . . . you and Rhonda."

"Ah . . . is that it?"

"That, among other things, Johnny."

"I'm sorry."

"Sorry you cheated or sorry you were caught cheating? Don't be sorry, I should have had the guts to leave you weeks ago, but it seems that . . . your cowardice is catching."

"So, you're leaving me by phone?"

In spite of herself, Pearl became glib.

"Yes, I really can't give it more time, it's me who's sorry, you won't hold it against me, will you? I have tons of work to do, you know."

She didn't know whether he'd listened her out, or hung up on her. She pictured his turquoise eyes foaming with rage.

It seems that your cowardice is catching, it was really good that she'd said that, she congratulated herself and perked up no end.

She spent a wonderful afternoon defending folks who swindled the taxman. She went home, pulled on some joggers, and poured herself a nice glass of wine. She felt like calling Stauber, but what would she have said to him? I got back to New York okay? I shut my boyfriend up? She hadn't even mentioned Johnny's name to him. She and Stauber hadn't broached any subject of a personal nature. She had simply asked him if he was married.

"No."

"A fiancée?"

"No, why?"

"Oh, nothing, I thought your secretary . . ."

"Brigitte?"

She'd smiled.

"Oh, Brigitte's wonderful but she isn't my girlfriend. I think it's a great mistake to mix love and work."

His smile had frozen, what went for Brigitte went for her, she mustn't get any ideas.

It was time. She put down her glass of wine and went to get the stepladder. Took great care. Placed the marvel on the bed and unfolded the duvet. The portrait was face down. Pearl had never paid attention to the security system, two copper wires, now severed, attached to the back of the canvas. Normally, cutting these wires triggered the museum's alarm. She didn't know how the thief had managed it, but clearly, the thing hadn't rung. He hadn't even removed the evidence of his theft, although, looking carefully at the wires, it must have been for fear of tearing or otherwise damaging the canvas that he'd left them there.

No, she'd never taken the time to study the back of the painting, and now started to decipher the two stamps of the Piacenza museum. The canvas was a gray linen, soiled over time and from the various journeys it had been subjected to. The wood of the stretcher was dark. It was undoubtedly paler originally. After all, it dated back to 1910, just after Isidore's birth. That gave her a strange feeling. There were even some stains that looked like splashes, not really like paint because they had no thickness, but they had soaked into the wood of the stretcher and circled the canvas. Maybe it was poor-quality fir wood.

With enormous care, she turned the painting over and the young woman with carmine lips appeared before her. *Here you are again*, she thought. *I missed you*. She gazed at the dancing shades of green, emerald green, forest green. A strange sense of foreboding came over her.

She turned the painting over again. The stains. On the back of the canvas and on the stretcher. They had darkened but retained a crimson undertone. Crimson red. *Blood*! She was instantly certain. Whose blood? Franz's? His murderer's? Isidore's? But this portrait had never belonged to Franz. Or at least, not that she was aware. Her hands started to shake. Her heart was racing.

She had to talk to someone. Stauber? Adri? Would Stauber understand? She looked at her watch, it was 7:30 P.M. in New

York, so 1:30 A.M. in Vienna, impossible, he'd think her crazy. Adri? She grabbed her phone, burst into tears, put it back down. She'd always believed that a real friend was the one you could call at two in the morning to help you make a dead body disappear. That was absurd. There were indeed people you could call at two in the morning to bury a corpse, but that had nothing to do with the friendship they felt for you. She now understood that certain people were capable of doing that kind of thing, and others just weren't.

A slight noise came from the walls of her room, like a cog turning, she lifted her head, incredulous, had the walls moved? Was she going to be crushed? She stared at the floor, and it, too, seemed to be closing in. It was dizziness. She had to kneel, and laid her hands on the carpet, but the woolen threads burnt her fingers. Panic-stricken, she straightened up, clung to the bed, and grabbed the painting. The young woman was there, peaceful, safe, tranquil. Tears kept rolling down Pearl's cheeks. Hypnotized by the painting, she couldn't move anymore. She stayed like that for an indeterminate time. Her pulse eventually calmed down and when she finally emerged from her torpor, she almost wondered what had just happened to her.

A parricide, a stolen painting, and bloodstains to join it all up. If she could get those stains analyzed, maybe the mystery would be solved. Like a hundred million Americans five years previously, Pearl had gone to the cinema to watch *Jurassic Park.* With a single drop of blood, Spielberg had worked wonders, but she had no idea whether these traces of spattering would be enough to identify a man, and anyhow, entrusting the painting to a laboratory was out of the question. So, she'd have to do the sampling herself and send a piece of the stretcher to some brilliant but mute geneticist.

She tried to think straight. *I've done nothing wrong.* How long could she go on? *I need to sleep.* She might also need to consult someone and be prescribed medication. That's it, she'd go to the first shrink whose plaque she spotted in her neighborhood. At Barnett's, colleagues often sought the help of a private detective. A fellow attorney there had recently been dealing with forensic police over some fingerprints, and had told her about this great investigator, yes, she remembered his name, tomorrow she'd call him. That man would know which lab to contact. And on that crazy thought, she went to bed.

The following day, in a trance, she walked into a psychiatrist's office and told him how she was living a lie and seeing the walls close in. He prescribed a strong tranquillizer in the form of green pills, and another gentler one, its pink tablets to be dissolved under the tongue. Pearl should take a green pill whenever an attack seemed imminent, and a pink one as soon as she felt the need to relax.

As for the genetical-analysis laboratory, they reassured her by saying that although DNA lasted barely ten days in full sunshine, it could endure for a century if it had remained in the shade. So she'd swallowed two pink tablets and gone to the hardware store on the corner of 134 West and 72nd Street. Hiding her nervousness as best she could, and with the advice of a kind assistant, she'd bought a bevel. She kept thinking of Stauber, if he'd been there, she wouldn't have felt so dreadful.

Back home, she'd found the strength to tackle the stretcher. With barely a cut, a sizeable sliver of wood had come away almost on its own. She'd wrapped it in Bubble Wrap and had enclosed the DNA-test results of Isidore Hoffmann Ferguson, carried out at the request of a Texas judge in a paternity suit ten years previously. Then she'd had it all delivered to the lab by a Barnett & Barnett courier. She'd taken a green pill and waited. The lab had told her she'd get no results for at least a fortnight.

She'd marked a cross in her diary, thinking they'd be likely to call her from that date onwards. She'd continued to think about Stauber and taken maybe more pink tablets than she should, but she didn't want to go through an attack like the other evening again, not at any price.

* * *

The day marked with a cross arrived and her phone rang.

"Ms. Alvez?"

"Yes, that's me."

"We have the results of the test you requested of us."

She'd have needed to sit down, had she not already been seated.

"We've compared the genetic fingerprints of the two individuals. The DNA sample on the piece of wood and the DNA supplied by you do indeed correspond to members of the same family."

"Sorry, is there more than one person's DNA on the wood?"

"No, excuse me, I expressed myself poorly. You supplied us with the DNA result of a certain Mr. Hoffmann Ferguson and a piece of wood from which we collected DNA in the form of dried blood . . . and it turns out that the second DNA result is that of the half-brother of the first DNA result."

"I'm sorry, I don't understand."

"What don't you understand, Ms. Alvez?"

"Who is the half-brother of whom?"

"Well, the blood sample on the wood is that of the half-brother of Mr. Hoffmann Ferguson."

Part Three

Silverly her image in the mirror
Looks at her strangely in the twilight-glow
And dusks sickly in the mirror
And she shudders before its purity.
—From "The Young Maid" by Georg Trakl

1

He gazed at the bare shoulders of the young girl and the curve of her nape was an invitation. Full of hope, he held out his arms to her. She nodded her head, smiling. Her curls began to dance and each lock lassoed the young man's heart to her service. They had developed a taste for each other, like milk and sugar. Martha was sixteen, Franz twenty-one. They were just two children sheltered by the night. In the room that was still in disarray from their love-making—it was in Franz's bedroom that the lovers frolicked—Martha straightened her blouse and then snuggled up against the pale chest. How soft his skin was! He wrapped his lean arms around her, his youth and his joy making him strong.

"Tonight, we're going out!" he announced.

She wasn't sure she understood.

"You're coming with me!"

"But where to?"

"To the Café Central!"

Her? To the café, with the gentlemen! She put her hand over her mouth to hide her laughter.

"No!"

"Yes! All my friends will be there, and you won't be alone . . ."

"How's that?"

Suddenly, he was all puffed up with pride.

"Come on, go and get dressed!"

Martha had nothing to wear and Franz hadn't considered

that. She owned only her maid's uniform and her Sunday-best dress. Franz said that that would do very well. The same outfit to go to Mass and to a café? Of course, nobody could care less!

She rushed up the stairs to her garret, four at a time. A few weeks earlier, she had bought a red ribbon, she who was so rarely coquettish. Fixing her hair into a chignon, she pinned the satin bow so its tails hung on either side.

When she presented herself to him, he gazed adoringly at her. She was his little Martha.

"You look perfect."

He kissed her on the neck and pressed himself to her breasts, two apples that fitted neatly into the hollows of his hands.

"You'll mess up my hair!"

"Your breasts drive me crazy."

She blushed. The very idea of saying such things.

"And what are we going to do at the café?"

"We're going to drink and we're going to listen to poetry! Georg will be there, and also Yvan, just back from a wonderful trip in the Black Forest."

The Black Forest. She imagined bedraggled trees, their branches crowded with thousands of scrawny crows.

"Martha! Martha! Martha!"

He grabbed her by the waist and twirled her around. A beautiful little doll. She laughed, not too loudly, the other servants were in bed four floors above, but the walls have ears. And so what? They could do as they liked. She put on her coat.

"Are you ready?"

"Yes, yes, alright, I am."

They took a carriage that dropped them off outside the café. It would be the first time that they'd be openly together. She hadn't expected that, what a surprise. Since arriving in Vienna, Martha had never been out at night. They went through the double doors. There was an almighty din, a mix of laughter and singing. Someone was playing the piano at the back of the café. They forced their way through in the smoke. She thought the women beautiful and, in some cases, their dresses very revealing. To think she'd feared being the only young girl, some here might be even younger than her, more shameless, at any rate, no doubt about that.

A man stood up in one corner and called out to Franz. They were a group of four boys and each had brought his grisette. Introductions were made. There was an actress with a heart-shaped mouth and a rose stuck in her bodice, another girl who didn't say what she did but was called Gretel and was so friendly, she made Martha feel instantly at ease. As for the last one, she seemed to be sulking.

Franz shouted out, "Here's the beautiful Martha!". She felt her cheeks blush. They ordered *Kaiserspritzer*s. Martha never drank. Franz's friends were looking her over, had he spoken about her to them? Waiters zigzagged between tables, it was a miracle their trays didn't tip over, with all the jostling and exuberance. Georg decided to recite a poem.

"On horrible reefs / The purple body is shattered / And the dark voice laments / Over the sea."[13]

He declaimed with hand on heart. Martha couldn't grasp the meaning but had never heard anything so beautiful. She felt like weeping. Franz also loved poetry, but was too timid to dare writing any, so he translated French poets. Martha was his first listener. She loved how words could move him, like this evening.

"Sister of stormy gloom, / Look, a frightened boat sinks / Under stars, / The silent countenance of night."

Franz felt almost jealous, seeing Martha lapping up his friend Georg's verses. With his coarse ginger hair, close-cropped, he looked like a hedgehog. And with his prominent nose and steely

[13] From "Lament" by Georg Trakl.

gaze, Georg wasn't handsome, but so powerful, so sad were his poems, they transfigured him.

For Martha, that evening was the most wonderful of her life. She was radiant with happiness. It was perhaps at that moment, and only at that moment, that Franz thought to himself that she might be worthy of being loved, not merely desired. But this thought evaporated before he could even clearly formulate it; it was unthinkable that Franz Brombeere should love a maid, those rules were too deeply entrenched in him. On the other side of the café, couples were dancing to the strains of a violin, a man had climbed onto a table, and drunkenness prevailed. Bursts of laughter combined with the knocking of glasses. The red ribbon in Martha's chignon bobbed and fluttered. Martha wasn't in love with Georg, no, how crazy of him to have thought that. Martha was all Franz's. The two youngsters exchanged feverish glances and, under the table, their hands joined. They couldn't stop smiling at each other.

In the carriage going home, they clung to each other without a word, but their symbiosis was total. Slightly tipsy, did Martha allow herself to imagine a different life for the two of them?

"Good night, Martha."

"Good night, Franz."

She never called him by his first name. He planted a light kiss on her forehead and watched her walk up the sweeping stairs, quiet as a mouse.

The servants' floor was plunged in darkness, she felt her way along it. When she saw a ray of light creeping under the door to her room, she thought how careless she'd been to leave her lamp burning, and yet she couldn't recall lighting it when she'd gone up to get ready.

He was sitting on her bed. Mr. Brombeere senior. He was waiting for her. She started back in surprise and clutched her throat.

"Oh! Sir!"

She remained at the door, not sure if she was about to be scolded. Servants weren't allowed to go out at night, so should she say that it was Master Franz who had asked her to accompany him? She lowered her head, ashamed.

"Sorry, sir."

"Might I know where you've been, Martha?"

The man's voice was quite friendly, which reassured her.

"I was with Master Franz."

"You went out?"

"Yes, sir."

"Everything going well with Franz?"

She said nothing. What could she have said?

"He's pleased with you?"

He had stood up and walked three steps towards her.

Martha's room was tiny. A bed, a chest of drawers, a ewer and its bowl.

Otto Brombeere was a corpulent man, he pointed his index finger in the air and began to draw a circle. He had raised his left eyebrow to look like some kind of ironic accuser. With his finger now pointing directly at Martha, he beckoned her forward. She complied. He closed the door and then placed his big square fingernail on the young girl's chin and pressed down on her jaw. It felt deeply unpleasant, but she kept still.

"And me? Will I be pleased with you?"

His voice was lugubrious. Martha shuddered. She felt the man's index finger move up her chin and reach her bottom lip, and before she could react, he pushed it into her mouth and hooked her bottom teeth. The young girl's tongue touched the revolting fingernail, and with an animal reflex, she closed her jaws and bit him. Maybe that was what he wanted?

With a cry of pain, he pulled his finger straight out and slapped Martha as hard as he could, making her head hit the wall. She put her hands over her face to protect herself from the second slap, already on its way.

"Little bitch! Don't you dare ever bite me again, do you hear me?"

"Sorry, sir, sorry!"

With her pupils dilated in fear, she remained huddled against the wall. What had she done? She'd bitten the master! They'd send her away! She thought of Franz.

Otto Brombeere was wearing a burgundy dressing gown wrapped over a white shirt. He was in slippers. Martha saw the man's bare calves, the hairs on them, and the prominent veins around his ankles. They disgusted her.

"You're going to be a good girl now."

That was the last thing he said to her. He had grabbed her by the nape, or the hair, she wasn't sure, but it was brutal and she hadn't fought back. He dragged her and she let out a whimper, but knew instinctively that she mustn't make a sound. She sat on the edge of the bed while he untied the cord of his dressing gown. She wanted to close her eyes, but even that she couldn't manage to do.

She was still dressed, he pulled up her skirt and petticoat, and the contact of the man's hands made her blood run cold. He widened the opening of the white-linen bloomers, cold flames danced in his eyes, the young girl's genitals were exposed. Then he shoved her roughly and threw all his weight on her. His big, fat, rancid man's belly. He lifted his shirt, and parted Martha's legs. She had turned to stone. He started fumbling furiously for his penis, grabbed hold of it, and thrust himself inside her. Then he kept writhing and writhing, and she tensed from the pain of his raw skin rubbing against her. The bed didn't creak, only the panting of the monster betrayed the silence.

He took forever to climax. She wished she could think of nothing, particularly not of Franz, not associate the terror of this scene with the gentle boy who also penetrated her. Was it the same thing? Would all the men who parted her legs and thrust themselves inside her now only ever be just one and the same thing?

The master finally ejaculated without a sound and heaved himself up. He retied the cord of his dressing gown and left, taking the lamp with him.

Distraught, Martha listened to the steady steps of the man going down the stairs, as if he were stamping each stair on purpose, and his steps were saying, "We will be back."

2

He couldn't remember his arrival at the orphanage. Someone had folded his meager things into his mother's gray fabric-covered suitcase, the one they would lug from one furnished room to another when they had to move because some men were nasty and they must get away fast. *Eyes down, Isi.* Someone had taken him up to the giant gates, but who? The neighbor? A policeman? Isidore had completely forgotten. The last image he'd retained was that of the bed and his mother's hair on the pillow, and then, with no logical transition, that of the office of the director of the orphanage, a bright office with a big window looking out onto plane trees.

The Spanish flu was raging through towns, and on the frontline, men were dying in droves, leaving behind legions of little kids with dirty hands and fallen socks. In the panic of the cataclysm, war orphans were mixed in with the rest. And so a particular kind of hierarchy had emerged, an aristocracy of misfortune. Right at the top, those whose fathers had died as heroes, then the siblings who stuck together, and finally, those who possessed objects. It could be a photograph, a letter, a card or picture, a scarf or a small toy. Isidore had no such thing and was at the bottom of the ladder. The others had soon singled him out. He had no one to watch over him and no one watched over him, nothing could be taken from him and he had nothing to lose.

Without a photograph of her, his mother's face would fade fast, but for a long time, the smell of her hair, the particular perfume that wafted from the heavy braid, would come back to him. He had always slept with her, it wasn't that she was particularly tender, but his contact with the slumped, warm body, that mass he was allowed to snuggle up to, had now turned into a longing that gnawed at his nights.

At the orphanage, he learnt that a mattress was something hard and cold. So he would curl up under the flimsy sheet, pull the scratchy blanket over him, and let his memories wrap their scrawny arms around him. He was nine years old, and already no longer slept like a child.

In the dormitory, clean as a morgue, fifty white iron beds were lined up. New arrivals appeared, lost, alarmed, hands black, shoes without laces, trousers patched, and sometimes even with mud in their tangled hair, but the director wouldn't stand for lice or vermin. Everyone's hair, without exception, was closely cropped from the start.

He was ten years old; they were fifty-odd naughty, snotty, loutish boys. Some spoke a dialect between themselves that Isidore couldn't understand, others were already adolescent and had big, red, chilblained hands and sounded like cockerels with colds. Those boys breathed malevolence and war at all times. Isidore had soon realized that he must be forever on the alert, forever doubting and anticipating traps everywhere. They hadn't allowed him time to be sad; he was instantly untranquil.

He was eleven years old when he finally made friends with his bedside neighbor, a stout boy of around twelve, strong as an ox and devoted as a dog, distinctive mainly for his hay-yellow hair, and who believed everything Isidore told him. This numskull had a facility for tears, red eyes and streaming cheeks, he blubbered as easily as others blow their nose, and if not a real ally, for Isidore he was a companion in suffering who cried for two. As for Isidore, he never cried.

During the day, they went to the classroom. On Sundays, they set off in serried ranks through the town's three streets to get to a place that they called the park, but was actually the edge of the forest. The bells rang out, the streets were full of people, young girls in pink bonnets and women in hats carrying baskets. Isidore sensed that the orphans, in their threadbare clothes, were being pointed at, and he felt ashamed. People felt sorry for them, but didn't want children of that sort around the place. Occasionally, a lady from some association would come to take a photograph of them, and once a year, an adoption ceremony would take place in the courtyard. Benches would be installed under the plane trees and a dais set up. But if Isidore had been hopeful in the early years, he'd soon seen that the older boys like him stood no chance of leaving the orphanage.

In class, he wasn't a bad pupil, was even very good at sums. But what he liked most was history lessons. Their teacher was a born storyteller. He would say, "Exercise books closed, textbooks shut!" The exercise books were poor quality and the textbooks old, foxed, faded and musty, with covers tattered and pages sometimes missing, but so what. Ink bottles, rulers, penholders were tossed any old how into desks. With arms crossed, the delighted children listened, wide-eyed, to how, long before the Empire, Magyar cavalrymen in shining armor had battled it out on the frozen steppes of the Urals. The account was served in a nationalist sauce that left little room for historic veracity, but those free and solitary warriors fired young Isidore's imagination, far more than the priest's stories, all about Heaven and goodness in pain and joy in suffering; Isidore didn't want to hear about that stuff anymore.

He was thirteen years old. There was confession to go to as well, particularly since Isidore, like the rest, swore like a street child and used the names of Jesus, Mary and God the Father himself in vain. It was enough to admit to superficial sins; his real secret he kept to himself.

"*Your father isn't dead but he doesn't know you exist . . . your father is alive . . . he has a big house . . . very beautiful . . . Johannesgasse, looking out on the Stadtpark . . . a house in*

Vienna . . . he's called Franz Brombeere . . . that's his name, you must remember it . . . repeat his name."

"*Franz Brombeere.*"

"*Promise me you'll never forget it.*"

"*Franz Brombeere who has a big house in Vienna on Johannesgasse.*"

Every night, to fall asleep, for nearly six years, or two thousand nights, Isidore would repeat that to himself as the only thing he could believe in and cling on to.

On October 10, 1924, Isidore turned fifteen and it was time, said the law, to hand back his gray overall of sadness and leave the orphanage. The institution's tradition was to organize a leaving ceremony—the director had a soft spot for formalities. Isidore would be the only one walking up onto the dais. The little ones, the latest arrivals, had looked flabbergasted as they watched him. What would remain to him of his time in this prison? The blows he'd received, the blows he'd delivered. The war was over, Austria had lost. Since peace had returned, the country was experiencing hardship and famine. The orphanage had been relatively well off because the Republic took care of its supplies. He'd been fed, he'd been made to grow up. He'd been taught how to sew and had put very little heart into his needlework. And yet it would be one of the only memories he'd keep of this miserable period, those mischievous faces, those bright, fearful eyes fixed on their sewing needles, those who were attentive, those who were distracted and pricked their fingers, and the whispering that would flow from table to table before the teacher shouted "Silence!" *Eyes down, Isi.* Upon leaving, the young men would be placed in factories or workshops, but he had absolutely no intention of working for a tailor.

The director had paid him a small compliment at the good-luck-in-life stage, "We hope you will be honest and upright, and show yourself to be worthy of all that we have taught you here . . .", and the wind had shaken the russet leaves of the plane trees above their heads. It was a lovely sunny autumn day. The director had then handed him an envelope containing three 100-schilling banknotes marked with the seal of the Oesterreichische Nationalbank, which was what the Republic provided for the good-luck-in-life in question.

"You told me that you intended to go to Vienna. Be careful because the big city is full of dangers and temptations, don't waste this money, and don't forget that we have taught you a trade."

"Thank you, sir, I won't forget."

The children had applauded without conviction and Isidore had smiled. He'd kept his good smile but no longer had any doubt that life was one big dirty trick. The history teacher had come forward and given him a package tied with red ribbon.

"Here, my boy, for the journey."

It was a new book with a stiff cover bound in fabric. The title was written in Gothic script, *The Sorrows of Young Werther*, and outlined on a blue medallion was Goethe's profile.

He'd slipped the volume into the gray suitcase, sole relic of his mother, and had walked through the high gates without looking back. The sky was laughing, the waters were green. He'd headed to the river, where large boats would sail past. He'd observed the bargemen passing nearby and singing, and decided to call out to one of them. The banks were dense with vegetation, covered in rushes and willows. "How much to take me to Vienna?" Isidore felt emotional. *Your father isn't dead but he doesn't know you exist . . . your father is alive . . . he's called Franz Brombeere . . .* The bargeman had let him come aboard and off they'd sailed.

That late afternoon, darkness was falling fast, along with a thick fog, when suddenly Isidore had seen lights shining from both banks of the Danube; they had sailed under one bridge and then another. *Franz Brombeere who has a big house on Johannesgasse overlooking the Stadtpark.*

He was finally going to know who he'd come from.

3

He had left his gray suitcase at the inn, taking only his letter of recommendation. He'd woken before the cock's crow (but did they even have farmyards in the big city?) and set off with a spring in his step. Forgotten were the horrors of childhood, his dead mother in her sweat-drenched nightdress, the creaking silence of the dormitory, gone the nasty little boys and the thread you had to wet to get it through the eye of the needle. His happiness fired his every stride.

Vienna, Vienna! At the orphanage, he'd thought back so often to that day when his mother had taken him to drink a hot chocolate! Even if he no longer recognized either walls or streets, he was too happy to be scared or disappointed. But he had to face facts and, once he'd arrived at the Stadtpark, admit that he was lost.

"Excuse me, madam, sorry to bother you, but I'm looking for Johannesgasse."

"It's straight ahead, my boy!"

Secretly, in his dormitory, he had developed his plan for months. He would present himself at the Brombeeres' big house and get himself hired as a stable lad. He couldn't give his surname for fear of his employer making the link with his mother, and wouldn't even give his real first name, out of superstition. He'd be called Stefan Bauer. Bauer because nearly every time they'd moved, they'd had Bauers as neighbors, as a caretaker, and even, once, a grocer, in short, because Bauer was a very common name in Austria; and Stefan after a boy at the orphanage whom Isidore had liked.

The previous day, when the bargeman had offloaded him and his pathetic suitcase, daylight had already gone. Isidore had entered the first inn he came to. He was a clean-cut young man and had good teeth, which wasn't that common in these post-war years. Most boys of his age had rickets and many had grown up crooked due to the privations. The innkeeper had given him a room, no questions asked.

He hadn't tampered with his identity papers, it was too risky, he'd just keep them hidden. But he had forged his letter of recommendation. Having understood that a good lie was never a new path, merely a truth that had branched off, he'd copied identically the letter he'd been given at the orphanage testifying to his training to be an apprentice tailor. He was determined never to touch another needle in his life, so had changed just the first name, surname, and vocation. Stefan Bauer, just like him, was a decent fellow who'd already worked for two years, but in the stables of the orphanage. Stefan Bauer had copied the director's signature, and his hand hadn't shaken because he knew that this lucky charm promised him a new life. A life that was rightfully his. He had got his smile back, the smile of a believer. His march was triumphal, a nightingale in his throat. On that morning of October 1924, Stefan Bauer was bursting with joy, his luck and his risk had joined forces, they were now one and the same.

His mother had said a big house . . . What to do? The section of Johannesgasse that faced the park wasn't that long. He pulled his brown-wool cap down, over his ears. He must stop someone on the sidewalk, a mailman, a deliveryman, and ask. Would he dare? He kept walking. *I must use a process of elimination, glean information, as if I were a spy.*

At a corner of the street, a tram went by, its bell clanging. Isidore had never taken the tram, but thought it a splendid vehicle. Perched on the rear platform, a stern-looking, mustachioed conductor in a kepi was adjusting one of the gilt buttons of his smart uniform. How great life was. An image came to him, or more a feeling, that of his mother's eyes resting on him. The air suddenly seemed lighter to him. He took that to be a kind of miracle.

Whenever he'd wanted to cling to his memories, when he'd made the effort to revive them so he could curl up and wallow in them, the summoning had invariably, and almost instantly, been followed by a feeling of loss, of emptiness. A memory can only be lived in the present, and that emerging present clawed his eyes. Isidore had ended up distrusting his memory, he wasn't even sure anymore that he'd felt that hot chocolate slipping down his throat. This lighter air was exactly what had hovered above his cup, he understood that now. He made his nostrils breathe in more deeply, had the crazy impression he was escaping time itself. He remained suspended, neither in the past, nor in the present, nor even in an anticipated near future, but confident in his joy. *The last time I was here it was with Mom and today I'm going to meet my father.*

He arrived in front of a row of very fine houses. He came across a woman carrying a basket of vegetables and herbs, with carrot tops and celery sticks spilling out on either side. She wore a rather ugly bonnet and a kind of shawl tied at her back but covering her shoulders. She looked every inch a cook and her fat belly inspired confidence in Isidore. Too shy to approach her directly, he barged forward, head down, and knocked into her basket, catching some celery on the way and handing it to her with his best smile.

"Oh! Sorry, madam!"

"No harm done."

"Here!"

The woman tucked the celery under a lettuce.

"I'm so sorry, I wasn't looking, I . . . I was retracing my steps . . . because . . . I think I'm lost."

"Where were you going?"

"I'm going to the Brombeeres' house."

"The Brombeeres?"

"Yes."

The woman looked suspicious.

"But it's there!"

Unfortunately, as she said that, she hadn't pointed at any particular house.

"It's just that . . . I've never been before."

"There!"

This time, she was pointing at the second house along, the biggest one. *It was meant to be*, Isidore thought.

"There?"

She nodded.

"What d'you want from the Brombeeres?"

"I've come for work, as a groom."

The woman widened her eyes in surprise.

"Did Herbert get you to come?"

Isidore was smiling so broadly, it was as if a metal rod went from one cheek to the other.

"Yes, Herbert did!"

"Right."

Isidore's enthusiasm was meant to be convincing. The woman grumbled something but gave him a vague wave and turned on her heel, swinging carrots to the right and celery to the left.

Isidore measured his luck, it was seven letters long, H-E-R-B-E-R-T. He walked up to the gate and pulled on the bell. A man in livery came to meet him.

"Good day, my name is Stefan Bauer, I'm here to see Mr. Herbert."

The man looked him up and down, dubiously.

"That's me."

"Good day, sir, I'm here to apply for the job of groom."

"But we don't need a groom, who sent you?"

"Ah, it was the cook who . . . I must have misunderstood."

"The cook? What cook?"

"Because I told her I was looking for work and . . ."

"We've never needed a groom. What's all this nonsense! We're looking for a waterer!"

Isidore pictured himself holding a big watering can. He knew nothing about plants or the upkeep of gardens, but he was ready to do anything to enter into the Brombeeres' service.

"Yes, sorry, not a groom, I must have got it wrong, a waterer, yes, that's it!"

He was smiling so much, his cheekbones were aching. He stared at Mr. Herbert's mustache, which was impeccably combed.

"Who sent you?"

"I'm looking for work. I'm called Stefan Bauer, I have a letter of recommendation."

He pulled the envelope from his pocket and held it out. Mr. Herbert took it from him, snootily, turned it over and saw the stamp of the orphanage.

"You come from Leobendorf?"

"Yes, I was born over there."

"Well, that's funny, me too."

"My name is Stefan Bauer. My father was a hero. He died in the war. My mother, she died of influenza. I was at the orphanage. I'm an honest and upright boy."

Isidore was repeating the pleonasm the director had drummed into them throughout their years at his institution, "honest and upright," the two adjectives always went together.

"I'm looking for work. I'll be really good at watering if you show me . . ."

The man laughed.

"D'you know what a waterer is, at least? It's the fellow who cleans the carriages, well, more of a young handyman really . . ."

"I'll be really good at being handy if you give me a chance. I'm honest and upright . . ."

"Okay, okay . . ."

As a rule, a waterer had several employers and would go from house to house with his bucket and cloths.

An orphan from Leobendorf. In these tough times, Herbert didn't have much hope for the kid if he didn't find a job fast, he'd end up on the street in less time than it takes to spell honest-and-upright. He looked more closely at him. Blue eyes, sweet face, this Stefan radiated youth. Well, they'd always find something to keep him busy, Mr. Brombeere often needed a messenger, and if the boy could also manage the horses, all to the good. Their groom was getting old, he'd been in the family's service for donkey's years, and Herbert had noticed him getting increasingly exhausted by this physical work. And then, an orphan wouldn't cost much, if he wasn't too clumsy, he'd even be a good recruit, Herbert would train him.

They were still standing on either side of the gate, Isidore on the sidewalk and Mr. Herbert on the gravel path that led to the steps of the house, when a tall beanpole of a guy suddenly appeared. Isidore noticed that his clothes were shabby and the cuffs of his sleeves grimy. The fellow addressed the butler tentatively.

"Mr. Herbert?"

"That's me."

"I've come for the position of waterer."

Herbert gave Isidore a knowing wink.

"Too late, pal, the position's taken."

4

So, on that first day, young Stefan got down to the work of the waterer, which meant cleaning the Brombeeres' horse-drawn carriage. Strictly speaking, it wasn't a barouche, but a landaulet (Isidore had never heard that word before) with two hoods, one at the front and one behind, folding on both sides and able to be closed, or half-closed. There were two regular seats and two jump seats facing each other, and the door had a "B" painted on it in a style evoking entwined bramble branches, since *Brombeere* means bramble in German.

It wasn't a massive carriage, like the mail coach that served Leobendorf, but certainly sturdy enough for long journeys. With it being autumn, the roads were muddy and the carriage was spattered, so the boy scrubbed, scoured, polished and shone, putting all his heart into the work. This young man was so keen to do well, it was touching, Herbert thought, congratulating himself.

He introduced Daniel, the old groom, to Stefan. The man looked more like a sailor lost at sea, in his thick woolly hat pulled down almost to his eyes, white straggly beard, sweater with holes at the elbows, and large calloused hands.

"This is Stefan, you can ask him to help you sometimes, he's already worked in stables."

There were three horses there. The two strongest-looking were Holsteiners, but Isidore knew nothing about horses, so he said nothing and looked silently at the third.

"He's splendid!"

He stroked the animal's rump. The groom observed Isidore, surreptitiously, and finally said, in a neutral voice:

"It's a Hanoverian, he's called Kuss, he's quite nervous but a softie really."

This horse sure was a thoroughbred! His coat was dapple-gray and his mane silvery. *This is my father's horse*, Isidore marveled.

When his work was done, Mr. Herbert had taken him to Mrs. Rathau's boarding house, which had a good reputation and where the butler usually lodged Brombeere employees who didn't need to serve the masters at any hour, day or night; such servants would naturally sleep on the fourth floor of the house. He had given Isidore his due wages and offered to take him on for a trial month. The two men had then shaken hands. Isidore went to fetch his suitcase from the inn and settled in at Mrs. Rathau's. His plan was working out brilliantly.

Lying didn't bother Stefan Bauer because he was himself the fruit of deception. His mother had told him that his father was dead, with no details, and had remained closed to his questions. So, when other children had heard of the death of their father in the war, he'd been relieved that he could latch on to their story. Who can get by without a family legend? This first deception (his father was alive) wasn't his doing, so wasn't as important as the second one, that of the hero who'd died for his country, which the child had fabricated knowing full well that it was unfounded. To explain his mother's truncated lie, he'd added a wedge, a prop, and since then, everything had stood up better. Which is why that particular lie was a part of him, he would love it like a familiar smell, would never really be able to let go of it.

His mother had brought him up with secrecy, forever looking down and changing landlord, always being wary of neighbors, but why? She had never given him a reason, but from it he would retain a form of defiance towards men. Not disturbing anyone, not crying, and preferring to swallow a pebble than admit he was hungry, all that had come naturally to him. The great shock, the turnaround, the shattering of the pretense, came about on the night of his mother's death. He had then understood that nothing could be explained or interpreted, that there was neither sense nor purpose, merely a fate that struck randomly and, by turns, favored or crushed your dreams. Just as a river's turbulent waters would crash against the piles of bridges before moving on, leaving no sign of their upheaval, so there was nothing else to do but just keep on living; he was nine years old and children are very good at doing that.

At the orphanage, his teachers hadn't been demanding, not academically, at least. Those kids weren't destined to study at a high level, they were taught a trade and that would be more than enough. Had they been more attentive, his teachers would have noticed that the young Isidore had abilities, a remarkably analytical mind and an astonishing memory for figures. But for stitching a hem or sponging the axles of a landaulet, what use were they?

On the second day, Herbert gave him the job of cleaning the outside of the windows on the ground floor. The previous day's rain had stopped. In the garden, up on their branches, the bronze leaves were reluctant to let go and dance with the wind and then die under the gardener's broom.

They were high windows made up of small panes. Three hundred and forty small panes in all, not counting the kitchen and pantry windows. The gardener showed him where the ladders were kept. Stefan picked up his bucket and sponge from the previous day, and the lady's maid gave him a can of white vinegar and a pile of clean cloths. Herbert told him to start with the windows that faced the street. The young man carefully stepped over the beds of azaleas and planted his ladder in the soft earth. Then, with his nose to the glass like some authorized voyeur, he could take a peek inside the Brombeeres' mansion. Persian carpets, velvet curtains, armchairs, window seats with embroidered silk cushions, vases overflowing with flowers, an accumulation of useless objects gleaming in the shadowy light . . . so was this luxury? To him, having known only bare walls and purely functional furniture, the opulence of these people became apparent in all its layers. The walls were paneled and lined with fabric on which paintings had been hung, the whole framed by drapes. And when he'd finished the windows of the drawing room, he moved on to those of the library, and that was another shock. Books, in their thousands, lined up from floor to ceiling!

Over the years, Isidore had attributed the qualities of a fairytale character to his father, but at this precise moment, and without being conscious of it, the possibility of any direct filiation became impossible. Isidore would never be worthy of being the son of Franz Brombeere who lived in a big house on Johannesgasse. This didn't cause him any suffering because he fell into a kind of idolatry that filled him with sincere joy. At the end of that day, his right arm was aching from going round and round in small circles. He must toughen up, the better to serve.

That night, his dreams were restless.

The days were very busy. Stefan Bauer learnt fast, but knowing how to clean and polish wasn't everything. Most important was the young man having the right attitude, at once eager and self-effacing. And respectful in the extreme. Isidore immediately picked up the particular way servants of the very rich have of being devoted without being obsequious, alert while remaining discreet, all with a deference that had every appearance of being sincere. This would prove useful to him throughout his life.

On the third day, the old groom, hat still down to eyes, handed him a shovel and told him to clear out the dung and get it ready for the man who came by every morning to collect it.

"And then you'll have to go fetch some peat!"

His tone wasn't friendly, but Isidore was used to rough treatment. Misfortune forces the person it strikes to invent a place in which to take refuge, to create an alternative truth, a more beautiful, more dazzling truth. People who are satisfied with their life, for whom reality is sufficient, can't develop their imagination. And so Isidore had enough imagination for two.

"Daniel!"

The old groom turned around.

"Get my horse saddled up, please, we're going for a ride."

It was him. Franz Brombeere.

Fine-featured, slender, with pale skin and dreamy eyes. His outfit was really smart and his boots perfectly polished. Isidore drank in this vision. With his aquiline nose and chestnut-brown shoulder-length hair brushed back, the refinement of this man's features was such that he could have been mistaken for a woman.

"Stefan! Did you hear what the master said? Go fetch the saddle!"

Isidore blushed, almost tripped over his shovel, and hurried off to the stables. When he returned, carrying the saddle the way a believer carries a sacred relic, he was beaming. Daniel was holding the Hanoverian by its bridle and talking quietly to Franz Brombeere.

"Thanks, Stefan!"

He knows my name.

Isidore kept on smiling, enough to seem like a half-wit, but felt too emotional to articulate the slightest polite response.

Eyes down, Isi.

He saw himself as a child again, when his mother would hold his hand as they climbed the stairs to their lodgings, and how she'd close the door without making a sound, with a whiff of fear. How he'd wished then that there was a father to protect them, his mother and him. But now Franz was already turning his back on him and talking again to old Daniel, as he adjusted the stirrups.

Deeply affected, Isidore found the strength to pick up his shovel and hold it with the blade standing perpendicular to the paving. The bucket made a slight grating sound and he just stayed like that, gripping the handle so no one would see his hands shaking in the fine rain that had begun to fall again.

5

Everyone was pleased with young Stefan Bauer. He actually saw very little of the masters, receiving his orders mainly from Mr. Herbert, Daniel, and occasionally the old gardener, when he was needed to sweep the leaves or help trim the hedges.

Isidore loved the atmosphere of the stables. He would stroke the rump of the Hanoverian, and the horse's coat felt like living piqué silk.

"There, there . . . gently does it . . . there, there . . . Kuss . . . my fine Kuss . . ."

He would brush the horse down with such care, it was touching. In general, whatever belonged to Franz became adored by Isidore, but he did his best not to show it. The other servants thought him very devoted. Even Daniel, having been wary of the young man at first, ended up recognizing that this Stefan cleared the dung, changed the peat, and filled the hay bags with an enthusiasm that put you into a good mood.

Every morning, Stefan would accompany the cook to the market and carry her baskets for her. He was increasingly sent on errands. He had learnt to find his way around Vienna, its wide avenues and grand buildings didn't intimidate him anymore. When he got back, he would scrub, clean and polish carriage, gates and flowerbeds with equal gusto. Then, at 6 P.M., he would return to his landlady, a charming woman. "Good evening, Mrs. Rathau," he would say, doffing his cap. The old woman wished all the youngsters in her boarding house were as polite and discreet! How could one not appreciate a boy with such a nice smile who never brought anyone back, not a friend or a girl.

There was also Mrs. Brombeere, who wore her platinum hair the way others wear a helmet. She had small dark eyes, beady and close-set, and held herself so straight, Isidore imagined she hid a suit of armor under her dress. This woman was rigidity personified, she'd never spoken to Stefan, not even a nod to indicate that she'd noticed his presence. Had she known that Isidore was her grandson, she would have keeled over backwards, like a domino, without bending her legs! Indeed, it had taken Isidore a while to make the link between Mrs. and Franz Brombeere, so different were they in every way. And Hermine Brombeere being his grandmother seemed so improbable to him that he didn't dwell on the thought.

"Stefan! Go up to Master Franz's apartments. He wants you to deliver a letter for him."

The butler had said it perfectly naturally, but it was no banal event because Isidore had seldom crossed the threshold of the big house, aside from going to the pantry or the kitchen. Indeed, the notion of "apartments" within a home was new to him, but he said nothing and went up to the second floor. He arrived in front of several high, dark-wood doors and knocked lightly three times on one of them. Franz emerged, holding a small envelope.

"Hello, Stefan, I'd like you to deliver this to Miss Liesl von Traum, she lives at No. 13, Schubertring."

"Right away, sir!"

Isidore gave him his biggest smile.

"Should I wait for a reply?"

"Yes."

"Very good, sir!"

At that, the young man charged down the stairs.

Before such eagerness, Franz couldn't help but smile himself.

Delivering little envelopes to Miss Liesl became one of Stefan's daily tasks. Franz Brombeere was courting the young girl according to the rules. At thirty-six, the time had finally come for him to settle down. In 1925, Austrian high society married its daughters early and its sons late. A good marriage demanded a big age difference, and no father worthy of the name would have entrusted his daughter to a twenty-year-old boy.

And so Isidore, with his cap pulled down over his ears, went back and forth between the two families, envelope in hand. He thought Miss Liesl very pretty, but saw her only briefly, their exchanges being limited to a "Good day, miss, Mr. Brombeere awaits your reply," and a "Thank you, you will deliver this to him."

Whenever Franz went out, Isidore would admire his elegance. Franz Brombeere wasn't strictly speaking a dandy, but did adopt the look of a Byronic hero. He always had a volume of poetry poking out of his jacket pocket and a flouncy scarf wound around his neck with studied nonchalance. Isidore owned just one book, *The Sorrows of Young Werther*, given to him by his history teacher when he'd left the orphanage. It was a difficult book, but the sentences lulled him and, after reading and rereading it, he'd ended up making this tale of impossible love his own, featuring not a woman, but rather his father.

How many hours, minutes, seconds had Franz and Isidore spent in each other's presence? Between two doors, a brief instruction, "Thanks, Stefan!", a smile, and then off he'd go. Did Franz know that the boy was an orphan? Had he shown any interest in his life, even just once? And yet they saw each other every day. Isidore didn't hold it against him, they weren't from the same world.

As the days went by, the plan to reveal to him who he was seemed increasingly absurd. Isidore didn't doubt for a second that his mother had told him the truth; Franz was definitely his father, but he would never be his son. He convinced himself that it didn't matter that much. Briefly being with him, breathing the same air as him, was enough to keep him happy.

Only someone extremely observant would have noticed that, since his arrival, Stefan had let his hair grow, that he'd started to pay particular attention to the cleanliness of his fingernails, that he polished his shoes every morning, although his role certainly didn't demand that of him; quite the opposite, the boy spent most of his time with his feet in the mud. One day, he was caught posing by Mr. Herbert. He'd brought his book with him, and he saw the butler staring at the edge poking out of the pocket of his drab jacket. Nothing worse than servants wanting to rise above their station and give themselves master-like airs. Mr. Herbert had said nothing, but Isidore had blushed from ear to ear.

* * *

It had been six months since he'd entered into the Brombeeres' service when, one fine day, the universe shattered.

Franz requested that young Stefan come up to his study. As usual, Isidore charged up the grand staircase four steps at a time. He wasn't as impressed anymore by the blue and gold lozenges on the carpet, or the heavy honey-hued velvet drapes that filtered the light, or the succession of austere portraits in their gilded frames, he was used to all that now, he was part of the household. There were still a great many rooms he'd never set foot in though—the apartments of the Brombeere parents, but also the fourth floor, where the best servants were lodged, and Franz's study, since he always remained at the door.

He knocked lightly three times.

"Come in!"

With his hands behind his back, he waited for Franz to give him the small envelope.

"Come in, Stefan!"

Franz Brombeere was sitting at his desk with his back turned from him. Isidore moved forward, the room smelt of tobacco smoke and leather. At its center, a splendid carpet in tones of crimson red, an ottoman (of course, Isidore didn't know the word) with faded cushions inviting lengthy naps; to the left, a light-wood pedestal table overloaded with books. There was a certain messiness in here that contrasted with the rest of the house, where everything seemed static and perfectly in its place. Franz folded the letter and slipped it into the envelope. Isidore noticed the golden fountain pen and the bronze toad used as a paperweight. Franz turned to him and handed him the envelope.

"Thanks, Stefan, you'll deliver it to Miss Liesl . . ."

He smiled kindly at him. Isidore put the letter in his pocket and looked up.

Without knowing what he'd seen, his entire being froze. Above the small bookcase, behind Franz, there hung a portrait, and the shock it caused the boy was like a stomach punch that makes you double up with pain. Within a fraction of a second, he felt a fire raging in his blood. The young woman with the carmine lips was captured in three-quarter view and her sad blue eyes were looking straight at Isidore. He wanted to scream.

His mother had died when he was nine, today he was fifteen and he'd endured those years without a photograph of her. Only his memory of pain had conjured an image that, little by little, had faded. Really, he'd only been able to retain a hazy impression, a sensation, that of snuggling up to a mother without a face, and now here she suddenly was, with her rosy cheeks and her sad smile. A portrait! He'd completely forgotten the end of that afternoon in Vienna, their stop at a gallery, but it was coming back to him now. And yet he could have almost sworn that the portrait he'd seen as a child was different to this one. What was this painting doing in Franz Brombeere's study? A thousand thorns pierced his heart. So it was true? This man had loved his mother! Otherwise, why would he have hung her portrait in his den? His thoughts were racing and burning him in silence. It was the most hideous feeling, the most extreme. All the wounds his child's mind had managed to stitch up had been ripped open again, gaping, raw. He suddenly began to shake, which brought him back to reality. He must get away, immediately, because Franz would notice his distress any moment now. He must find the strength to drag his eyes away from his mother's eyes. His mother who seemed to be looking only at him.

Isi, I'm here . . . Isi, you can see that I'm here . . .

And so, not knowing how his legs were still obeying him, he turned on his heel and bolted.

6

He went to see her every day, several times a day. And just as initial passion sometimes gives way to sincere and tender affection, the power of the portrait evolved; its intensity subsided and Isidore could finally love it without trembling. One grows accustomed to everything, even to love, which is just as well since this was certainly all about love. At the start of his rapture, the portrait seemed so beautiful, so extraordinary to him, he could barely look straight at it and withstand her gaze.

If time can be compared to sediments that, after successive layers, end up covering in dust all that was bright and shiny, then the mind of the young man had sought to shroud the portrait in all sorts of veils so it would cause him less pain, so its effect would soften. And so his mother appeared less dangerous to him, less fragile, too, and her face became increasingly reassuring. Knowing that she was there, close by, now brought him inexpressible relief.

When he walked into Franz's studio, he would get that same calming feeling as when one enters a cathedral. He couldn't help but think that if she had pride of place in his father's study, it was because they had loved each other. Isidore didn't really know the facts of life, he knew how babies were made, but barely how they were born. However, still being a virgin didn't mean he was naïve. At the orphanage, lots of boys told jokes on that subject. All through his adolescence, Isidore had asked himself the question; now, before his eyes, he had proof that he was the fruit of love, and that filled him with great joy.

Meanwhile, things between Franz and Liesl were coming along nicely. This suited Isidore because the more Franz had letters delivered to his betrothed, the more opportunities he had to see the portrait. But soon, this back-and-forth to the study was no longer enough for him. So, in the calm of his room, he came up with a plan. Franz had a very fine collection of art books and Isidore pretended to be interested in them. Surprised, the master asked the servant if he liked painting and sculpture.

"Oh, no, I know nothing about them, sir, it's just that you've got some mighty big books there!"

Franz laughed.

"Yes! And I also have catalogues, look . . ."

He went to fetch the latest that an Italian gallery owner had sent him. Isidore took it carefully.

"I own just one book, myself."

"Oh yes? Which one?"

"*The Sorrows of Young Werther.*"

"Aha! Goethe!"

"Yes, what I liked at the orphanage was when they'd read poetry to us."

It was the first time father and son had a conversation. Isidore's heart was beating hard enough to burst.

"If you like poetry, Stefan, I could lend you some anthologies."

Isidore didn't reply, but Franz was touched by the kid's smile.

"You see that shelf? All the greatest poets are on it. You can borrow those books whenever you like."

"Really?"

"Absolutely, as long as you promise to take great care not to damage them and to borrow just one at a time, I have no objections."

Isidore was in seventh heaven, his father had looked at him and spoken to him differently than when giving him an order.

His father had accepted to share his books with him, his father trusted him! He might almost have forgotten that he'd wanted Franz to lend him books so as to have more frequent access to his study.

From that day on, if a servant found Stefan in the study, he would say, "I'm just returning sir's book." Like that he could contemplate the portrait almost as much as he wanted to.

At first, he merely looked at her. Then he began to speak silently to her, and, miraculously, his mother's voice had come back to him. She would say, *Take care of yourself, it's cold, wrap up warm, be good, be a fine little man*. She would warn him, *don't take the wrong path, Isi*. She liked it when he smiled. *You have such a good smile, my son*. She had even admitted to him how happy she was that he'd found her again. It was so real.

"*I'm so happy that you've found me again*."

When she had said that, he'd realized that it wasn't just a voice inside his head; he couldn't have explained it, but he knew that his mother had spoken with all her soul. He had stammered, "Oh, Mom, so am I, so am I, Mom! I'm so happy that we're back together again."

It's a strange thing, belief. If paintings didn't speak, how come this one spoke to him? Isidore watched the parted lips closely, no, they hadn't moved, it was more a breathing out, an emanation from the canvas that made the air vibrate, and his mother's soul would come and settle inside Isidore's head. He didn't fear that others might hear her. He knew that these words were addressed to him alone, audible to him alone, intelligible to him alone. But they were real. There was something comparable to an act of faith about this. He accepted that reason couldn't explain it, but he knew that she existed, like the Holy Spirit.

He remembered the priest at the orphanage who had said that his mom had gone to Heaven, up in the sky. He would look upwards, but the sky was so very empty. No, his mother wasn't in the sky, she was here, vibrant, before him, in a frame.

7

And why, may I ask?"

"You know very well why, Franz."

"Mother, don't put words into my mouth, it's a work by Gustav Klimt! I know you're not keen on painting, but for goodness' sake, everyone agrees that he's one of our greatest artists!"

"Isn't he dead?"

"Yes, he is dead, but today, his paintings are worth a great deal and are highly sought-after."

"So much the better, you'll have no difficulty selling it then."

"But I don't want to sell it!"

"Why not?"

Hermine Brombeere eyed the painting with disdain; fortunately, it was rare for her to enter this room.

"It has sentimental value, perhaps?"

Franz sensed that his mother wanted to wound. He shrugged his shoulders and tried to look indifferent.

"Absolutely not. This painting has great artistic value, my dear Mother. It's a magnificent painting, I'd even say that it's the finest that we own!"

"Are you making fun of me?"

"Not at all. I'm not asking you to be a painting expert, not asking you to embrace the ideas of the Secession movement, but simply to trust me. I tell you, this portrait will keep going up in value over time . . ."

"Have you forgotten of whom this painting is a portrait?"

She had said *of whom* in a mocking tone. And yet she wasn't a woman to speak of that kind of thing. Franz suddenly felt uncomfortable.

"No, no . . . that has nothing to do with it . . ."

He couldn't have said where his mother sat on the scale of prudishness. After all, it had been her idea to employ that girl to keep Franz away from brothels and venereal diseases.

"Nothing to do with what, may I ask?"

"With the fact that that young woman worked for us, if that's what you're insinuating."

"Worked, you say?"

Hermine Brombeere's close-set eyes were two pinheads, ready to pierce their own sockets. She glared at her son with malicious glee.

"Very well, if it doesn't bother you that your future wife should have, in her home, the portrait of a woman who *worked* for you . . ."

She left her sentence hanging in the air. Franz thought it hateful.

"Mother, please . . ."

"And if nothing bothers you, I imagine that you won't mind learning that that little tart also *worked* for your father."

Franz's face contorted with incomprehension.

"Wh . . . wh . . . what do you mean? What do you mean, 'worked'?"

The mother was seemingly delighted with her turn of phrase, her thin lips cracking a nasty smile. She knew Franz too well not to see that he was suffering, but she couldn't stop herself.

Didn't they say that revenge is a dish best eaten cold? Hermine had also suffered when her personal maid had informed her that her husband went to Miss Martha's room every night after the young girl had left Master Franz's bed. "Oh, I didn't want to mention it to madam . . . but it's just that the other servants find it really shocking . . . I'm totally devoted to madam and I really hesitated, but . . . things always get out, people are so snide . . ." she had stammered, wringing her hands.

"Thank you, my dear Albertina, you did well to warn me. We're going to put a stop to it," Hermine Brombeere had muttered through gritted teeth.

She had thrown out the little slut, a word she'd never said out loud but had screamed silently to herself hundreds of times. The little slut who spread her legs for the son and the father in turn. Her husband and her child inside the same little slut. The little blubbering slut she'd thrown out, pointed at while clenching her jaws so hard it hurt. She had waited for Franz and Otto to be out of the house and had got the other servants to witness her chilling hatred. The little slut who'd implored her on her knees. She deserved to be beaten to death, that little slut. Let her go back to where she came from, let her die on the sidewalk like a dog.

Franz was flabbergasted. Martha? Young, innocent Martha, with his father? With the father *and* with him, who loved her so much? It was disgusting. He looked at the portrait of the young girl, she was forever besmirched. The artist had been right to paint her in the get-up of a prostitute, what a fool he'd been to ask the great Gustav Klimt to remove her hat and stole! All his sweet memories of love erased, lost, sullied.

Hermine could see in her son's eyes the abjection of the man for the sinning woman. She also realized now that Franz had never known, that only her husband was guilty, and she felt immense relief for that.

"Franz?"

He didn't reply.

"Franz! Are you going to get rid of that painting?"

He banished the obscene visions that were sickening him.

"Yes, Mother."

"I'd remind you that your marriage banns will be published next week, so the sooner the better."

"Yes, Mother. It will be done today."

Satisfied, Hermine Brombeere turned sharply to leave the room and, in doing so, almost banged into the stable lad who was standing stock-still at the door, looking dazed. She let out a small cry of surprise. Young Stefan hastily flattened himself against the wall to let her pass by.

"Sorry, madam . . ."

Isidore kept his head down, incapable of knowing whether what he'd just heard could be true. Mrs. Brombeere had asked her son to get rid of the painting and Franz had agreed to do so.

8

How could he bear to part with her? He was left with no choice. He'd heard it very clearly, or at least, he'd heard enough. Franz would marry Liesl von Traum and, because of this, would sell the painting. Isidore was a big dreamer, forever having to match reality to his imaginings. He'd allowed himself to believe that his father was deeply in love with his mother. Keeping the portrait, the ghost of the deceased, was unthinkable. If Hermine Brombeere had intervened, it was out of respect for this Miss von Traum, it was because keeping evidence of that passion would have brought misfortune upon the young married couple. It made sense and, mainly, it reinforced his conviction: he was the fruit of a love that was morganatic (Isidore didn't know that word, either), born of Desire, even if he hadn't been desired.

That very day, Franz had made a phone call to Italy. Isidore had deduced that it was to the gallery that sent him its catalogues. Franz didn't want the painting to remain in Vienna, and this need for distance corroborated the theory that they'd been madly in love. The gallery owner had agreed on the spot. He and Franz had settled on the sum of 25,000 Italian lire, equating to 1,100 Austrian schillings. Gustav Klimt was a highly rated artist, and the Italian wasn't going to miss such an opportunity; he hadn't even negotiated on the price. He had asked Franz Brombeere to deal with the transportation of the painting. Nine hundred kilometers separated Vienna and Milan, so Franz had found a Vienna-based courier company.

By an irony of fate, he asked Isidore to go to the company's office to ask that they come to Johannesgasse. Which he did, and then he remained in his master's study while the two men discussed the details of the consignment. He learnt that an employee would come to the Brombeeres' to collect the painting on the following Tuesday and then do the journey to Milan by train.

Isidore was succumbing to panic, not knowing which course to follow. For a moment, he imagined that if he told his story, if he described how destitute he and his mother had been, deprived of his protection, he might manage to move Franz. He'd ask for nothing other than to be allowed to keep the portrait, and Franz, overcome with pity, would agree to it. But that would require him to reveal his identity. Now, with his back to the wall, he knew he was incapable of doing so. Deep down, Isidore had long abandoned the idea of admitting who he was; that dream had been wiped away one morning while he was cleaning the windows. Cloth in hand, he'd realized that he was nothing at all.

He was preparing to commit a theft, and yet he was honest and upright. He was ashamed, would have liked to feel ashamed of being ashamed, didn't know what to think anymore. At the idea of being separated from her, all his childhood anxieties had resurfaced. The flame of his candle was flickering once again in the stairs and casting its wretched shadows. He imagined his mother hanging on the wall in the house of strangers, surrounded by portraits of ancestors who would look down on her. Once sold, he'd never find her ever again. To lose her for a second time was intolerable.

His plan was simple. The Brombeeres' house was big, very big. He'd ensure that the door to the pantry, leading to the back garden, was left unlocked, then sneak in, in the middle of the night, wait for the right moment, enter the study, take down the painting, and run to the railway station, where he'd board the first train. And then he'd go to America! He'd always wanted to go there. At the orphanage in Leobendorf, once a year they'd all be photographed, full-face and in profile, so that some kind ladies in America would adopt them. Unfortunately, he was already too old, the kind ladies only liked orphans who were under five. Yes, he'd set off for America with his mother under his arm. She would give him courage.

To reach the port of Genoa, he'd need to take several trains. He had a little money put aside. The 300 schillings, with the Oesterreichische Nationalbank seal, he'd been given upon leaving the orphanage and had hardly touched, and his wages of the past six months—Isidore was thrifty. But still, he had no idea how much a ticket to cross the Atlantic cost. He would improvise. First, steal the painting as discreetly as possible, then run away, one thing at a time.

He steeled himself against the thought of never seeing his father again. How he'd longed to become close to that man! But seeing as Franz was incapable of defending the love of his youth against his new wife, seeing as he'd made the choice to abandon Martha once again! Isidore's heart bled at this thought, *abandoned, she'd been abandoned, they'd been abandoned.* He cursed him and gave himself reasons to hate him. The legend, the wonderful tale of lovers thwarted by destiny and separated by evil forces, had, in the end, not withstood this ultimate cowardice. Yes, he did hold it against his father. What would it cost him to leave Martha a little corner of his study? At least he, Isidore, would be able to defend her and protect her. He hadn't been able to do so when she'd been ill, but now that he was grown up, he wouldn't let her down. The dead woman's voice rang louder and louder in his head. *Isi, stay with me*! *Give me your hand, my little man, don't let them take me far away from you*! And he would promise, and he would swear.

He could clearly see that it saddened her, Franz wanting to get rid of her this way. How he wished he could spare her that.

It would be tonight, or never.

Very wisely, Isidore chose not to do the masked-burglar routine. Quite the opposite. If he was caught inside the house in the middle of the night, he would say that he'd got back too late for his landlady, so he'd preferred to sleep on a chair in the pantry, rather than get an earful from her. It was a good idea. Once he had the painting under his arm, he'd have to head straight for the station and take the first train for Salzburg, the 5:03 A.M. one.

When he'd finished his day at the Brombeeres', he'd gone to buy his train ticket, and then on to Mrs. Rathau's, where he'd packed his bag. He'd left his gray suitcase under the bed; although it was the only thing that had belonged to his mother, he wasn't attached to it. That suitcase had carried only suffering. From the Brombeeres' kitchen, he'd taken a sturdy canvas bag that could be slung over the shoulder, and which he often used for shopping. Into it he had slipped two shirts, two pairs of socks and two of shorts, his savings, his copy of *The Sorrows of Young Werther*, and his bottom sheet, neatly folded. Then he'd waited for Mrs. Rathau to be away from the door, busy in the yard or somewhere else, and had left with the bag hidden under his jacket.

He'd had supper at an inn to kill time. The servants would always complain that Franz got home late from evenings spent hookah smoking with friends while seriously arguing for Total Art. Isidore caricatured him as a spoiled, rich kid, the man deserved to be robbed. He wanted to believe that his decision was irrevocable, but feared losing his nerve at the last moment. He prayed to the Holy Eels, they'd always favored his future. The courier would be collecting the painting the day after tomorrow.

Tonight or never, he kept repeating it to himself. But if tonight went awry, he'd still have one last chance.

9

"Have you ever heard of Stendhal syndrome, Henry?"

"No, sir."

Isidore had summoned Henry Hogan to his apartment, having put a lot of thought into how to present the thing. The two of them had known each other for a long time. A life of good and loyal service. On behalf of his boss, Henry Hogan had schemed, wheedled, intimidated, threatened, sometimes even blackmailed. Despite seeming impassive, Henry was far from an angel, but what Isidore was about to ask of him was far more serious and dangerous than just causing problems for a competitor.

"Stendhal syndrome is when a work of art triggers physical and psychological symptoms, Henry."

The employee raised an eyebrow, a sign that he wasn't really bothered.

Isidore leant hard against the back of his armchair and continued in a voice he wanted to sound firm.

"Pearl came to see me the other day and she showed me an article from *The Guardian*. A painting by Klimt is making headlines in the Italian press these days because a student discovered that it was a repaint."

"A repaint?"

"A work that's been painted twice, do you see? Those paintings that are X-rayed and it's discovered that, under one image, there's another hidden image?"

Yes, Henry saw, and nodded.

"Right, well that Klimt painting, currently in a museum in Piacenza, Italy, I would like to get it back."

The two men exchanged a cautious glance. Then Henry asked, with exaggerated politeness:

"Get it back, sir?"

Isidore paused a moment to control his nervousness. He so wanted to appear calm and detached.

"I think stealing it will be the simplest thing. Do you think you could do that for me?"

Would Henry Hogan have stolen the painting without knowing more about it? Just because his boss was asking him to? He remained silent, alert. Isidore knew that the moment Henry saw the painting, he would make the link. For the rest of his life, Isidore would remember those few seconds when Pearl had stood at the door to his drawing room in her baggy checked shirt, and how she'd slowly turned to face him, and the lightning bolt that had ripped his old man's heart, the revelation of those grayish-blue eyes and the beauty spot high on the cheek; the resemblance was too glaring, Henry would know. Isidore decided to go for broke.

"That painting marked the end and the beginning of my life. It's the portrait of my mother and to protect it . . . I killed my father."

What does a man feel as he confesses to a secret kept for so long? A thousand times, over his lifetime, he had held back from saying it, to Lotte, to his children, to strangers. And now he had uttered the accursed words, *I killed my father*, and nothing had happened, neither tempest nor hurricane. No monster had suddenly appeared from the bowels of the earth to swallow him whole with a roar, nothing. This left him stunned, disappointed perhaps.

"I was sixteen, it was an accident."

His confession could have ended there, but as he said these words, the old man began to tremble.

"I was born of an 'unknown father,' and my mother was most probably a woman like Pearl's mother, not a prostitute . . . no . . . but a woman of toil and hardship. Things were different in Vienna in 1909. We lived in misery, you know, whereas my father, he was rich, very rich. Can you see the irony of my situation?"

Henry Hogan said nothing.

Isidore had asked this question calmly, but a real anxiety could be detected in his voice. The old man took a deep breath and wiped his forehead with his hand.

"When that attorney sent me that letter . . ."

He broke off, perhaps to register the actual significance of his words, then, after thinking for a moment, he said:

"When I became Pearl's father, I also became what my father was."

He'd understood that: those Holy Eels, in the twisting and turning of their coils, had only been able to make and unmake the same loops of fate. And sure, by endlessly beating you, life can simply end up beating you down, but that event had brought some deeply buried issues back to the surface. Upon receiving the DNA test results, he'd seen his son Tommy again, drowned in a lake one summer morning, and cursed the fate that took one beloved child away from you, only to give you another child you hadn't desired. Once again, Henry Hogan, his good old Henry, had dealt with everything, using Mr. Hoffmann Ferguson's heart attack to manage the negotiations quietly, avoiding public proceedings and the scandal that the other side's attorney was hoping and praying for, to up the ante. Yes, Henry had enabled them to come out of it with heads held high. Isidore thought of how absolute the confidence he'd placed in Hogan was, and how he'd always admired his composure, just as he was showing right now.

Henry was waiting for the rest of the story. Isidore coughed to clear his voice and continued, sounding calmer.

"I don't think my mother knew much about painting . . . I mean, she posed for Gustav Klimt, she would have posed for anyone . . . it was just to earn some money. The portrait was painted in 1910, just after my birth. I've always imagined that my mother must have been on the streets and needing money to meet our needs . . . She was what was called an unmarried mother, she was sixteen when she had me. I was born in Vienna, then we went to Leobendorf, she worked at the factory, and then there was that terrible epidemic."

In spite of himself, Isidore was now sounding plaintive.

"My mother was carried off by the Spanish flu. She'd always told me that my father was dead, but with her last breath, she admitted the truth to me, saying, 'Your father isn't dead, but he doesn't know that you're his son'."

Henry Hogan didn't move, merely murmured:

"That's awful . . ."

Isidore gave a start, but immediately recovered.

"Yes . . . it was awful . . . I was nine years old. I was put into an orphanage. When I got out, I was fifteen and had just one idea in mind, finding my father."

Isidore started to speak faster, he must get to the end of his story.

"My father lived in Vienna but I didn't want to tell him who I was. I passed myself off as someone else and entered into his service. I thought I'd reveal my identity to him later, or maybe never, I wasn't sure, it takes a lot of courage to say to someone, 'I was told that I'm your son'."

He no longer even tried to hide his febrility—how had he kept going for all those years without weakening?

"And then one day, I came face to face with that painting, the portrait of my mother. My father had hung it in his study and it gave me such a shock. A real shock, Henry! That's when the famous Stendhal's syndrome struck me . . . Of course, at the time, I didn't even know it had a name. It was as if I'd got my mother back. The portrait spoke to me, it comforted me, it became essential, I loved it like an actual person, like a real person!"

On the rare occasions when Isidore had allowed himself to think back to that episode in his life, he considered it one in which he'd only just avoided the asylum.

"And then I discovered that my father wanted to sell the portrait because he was about to get married. Most probably, he didn't want this evidence of a past love. I imagined all sorts . . . I never knew why the portrait was in his study, or if he'd loved my mother, or whether the two things were, or weren't, linked. When I learnt that he was going to sell it to a gallery owner in Milan, I didn't hesitate, I had to steal it . . . and I stole it. But I was young and clumsy."

He pushed open one side of the large gate, having oiled it the previous day, and placed his bag under a bush in the garden. He opened the door to the pantry. Not a soul around. He settled on a chair as if about to spend the night there. He didn't want to steal the painting before 4:30 A.M., so he could run off immediately and jump onto the train. It took barely fifteen minutes to run from Johannesgasse to the station. He asked himself, was he determined to go ahead? Yes, he was. The big clock in the kitchen showed just a few stars past midnight. The silence inside the house was supple, broken by grating and creaking. Isidore sensed that outside, the night was alive. But the whisperings of the trees, the echo of carriages and hooves in the distance, all those sounds would gradually be swallowed up.

The night dragged on and finally the clock showed 4:00 A.M. Through the window, the moon seemed to be staring into the void.

Isidore, his hands clammy, stood up from his chair, alert, ears pricked like those of a lynx. Before him, in the main entrance hall, the staircase stood out in the half-light, he placed his hand on the banister and the feel of the polished wood calmed him. He climbed the steps and arrived at the first floor, outside the door to Franz's study. He tried to control his breathing, but that had the effect of stopping him from breathing. Holding his breath, he turned the handle, which squeaked slightly.

The study was plunged into total darkness because the curtains had been drawn. Isidore felt his way forward, sliding his hands along the wall, avoiding the small varnished-wood bookcase, and finally touching the frame. The painting had been hung quite high up. *Isi, are you there*? Hearing his mother's voice in the darkness filled him with anxiety. *I'm here, Mom, I'm here*. He started to tremble, tried to lift the painting to free it from its nail, but his hold was hindered by the furniture, he should have climbed on a chair, but instead, continued to feel along the cord stretched behind the canvas until he reached the point where it was attached. He raised the portrait vertically and, with relief, felt something give way. But simultaneously, since he was on tiptoe, the painting dragged on him, so, to regain his balance, he stepped backwards and struck a pouffe. He stumbled and slowly toppled over, risking twisting his ankle, but still clinging to the canvas. And so, with a thump, he found himself on the floor, holding out the portrait to protect it.

He jumped up. Had he hurt himself falling? Well, no. *What an idiot*! It was time to clear off, yes, but just then, from the other side of the wall, he heard Franz calling:

"Herbert?"

The study was connected to Franz's bedroom via a small door. Isidore shouldn't have stopped to think, should have bolted like a rabbit with the painting under his arm. But he stayed right there, still as a statue. *If I don't move*, he thought, *he'll go back to sleep and all will be fine*. He didn't know that, on the other side of the wall, Franz was sure he'd heard a noise in his study. Franz hadn't been asleep. He'd even recognized the door handle turning when Isidore had entered. He'd turned the light on. He was already out of bed.

"Stefan?"

Holding a lamp, the master stood there in his nightshirt, in front of his young servant. The halo of light from the flame gave him a magical aura. Isidore stared at his incredulous father.

Was this young lad he found so charming, this fine boy, just a good-for-nothing? A thief? The two men looked hard at each other. If Franz called for help, staff would rush to him in a minute, and then it would be all over for him, the orphan from Leobendorf, the bastard, the scum. But Franz made an error, that of being confident that he was well within his rights.

"Let go of that painting!"

He had spoken with the contempt that comes from unmerited authority. He put the lamp on the table and moved a few steps closer.

To Isidore, time seemed to have stopped, but he saw in his father's eyes a disdain mixed with pity, and that look, thrown at him since childhood, torpedoed his heart.

"Stefan, give me that painting immediately!"

* * *

Seventy years later, the memory of that night was mystifying to him, the images forming it were frozen, with no real continuity, no longer able to flow or follow on to form a fluent account; it was barely coherent.

"My father surprised me, so I hit him . . . the painting ordered me to. Said like that . . . obviously . . . Henry, you know me . . . you know I'm a rational fellow, I know very well that paintings don't talk, but I was hearing *her* voice, my mother's voice, I'd become demented, and I was so scared he was going to damage it, snatch it from me! I beat him . . . or maybe we beat each other . . . I don't know anymore, but there was blood everywhere and then he fell backwards and his nape smashed against the desk. I knew that he had died instantly. I took the painting and legged it."

* * *

His feet were barely touching the gravel path in the garden when he'd grabbed the bag he'd hidden under the bushes. He had run through the streets, breathlessly, carried by the wind; the avenues were completely deserted and the moon cast a wan light over the city.

Just before reaching his destination, he stopped in an alley to catch his breath. His hands were stained with blood. He took his landlady's sheet out of the bag and unfolded it, wiping his hands on a corner, then wrapped it around his darling mother as best he could. *Holy Eels, protect me*! Pulling his cap down over his ears, he wedged the swaddled painting under his right arm, threw his bag of provisions over his left shoulder, and set off at a pace that was meant to be energetic.

Vienna's grand railway station appeared in the breaking dawn, lit up by dozens of gas lamps. He hurried along the platform without meeting anyone's eye and climbed onto the spluttering train.

A few minutes later, seeming like hours to him, the train whistled and its wheels finally moved with a screeching clatter.

* * *

"I got on the train for Salzburg, and then another for Villach, I crossed the Italian border, I don't know how, I'd become a shadow of myself, and then caught another train in Udine and yet another in Verona. I'll remember those trains and those stations, and my anxiety, all my life. I had palpitations, my heart was pounding so hard it hurt, it felt just the same when I had my heart attack, you know?"

And feels just the same now, he could have added, since his speech was now racing at the pace of his crazy escape. As he continued his account, the old man sensed his pulse quickening and blood throbbing in his throat. Henry Hogan, usually not ruffled by anything, struggled to hide his alarm.

"It was on the train from Milan to Verona that my bag was stolen. I'd not slept for forty-eight hours, I was exhausted, I'd been endlessly terrified, endlessly catching trains . . . Fortunately, I'd slid the sheet-wrapped painting under the seat. But I'd placed my bag, containing all my savings, on my knees and someone took advantage of my being asleep to swipe it. I remember my arrival in Milan, I was in despair, I didn't even have enough money now for the ticket to get to the port of Genoa, let alone cross the Atlantic. And it was *she* who provided me with the solution."

Isidore went quiet, aware of the absurdity of that last sentence, but then continued:

"My mother, well, my mother's voice speaking through the painting. It was she who told me, 'Go to the gallery, sell me, take the money, get that boat to America, and we'll find each other again one day.' I do know, Henry, that that voice was but a symptom of my hallucinations, but I've thought about it many times since then, and it was the only way I could accept to part with her. It had to be the painting's decision, like some trick of the mind. Do you understand? Because it was indeed the thing to do to save myself, but it was unthinkable for it to be my responsibility, so my brain fabricated an order that I was forced to obey."

Slowly, Henry Hogan unclasped his hands and nodded almost imperceptibly, yes, he understood this madness.

"The Galleria Scopinich, on Via Casati, I can still see myself there. I went with my painting under my arm, made out I was the courier. The gallery owner told me I'd been quick, he'd not expected me until two days later. He spoke very bad German and I spoke no Italian, he said, '*Bella*! *Bella*!', when he looked at the painting, and handed me the money. He and my father had already arranged everything in advance. He was perhaps surprised that the painting wasn't protected, in a crate or whatever, but the language barrier helped me out there. I left without further ado. I went to Genoa and boarded the first ocean liner. It was a British ship of the White Star Line. I was sixteen, imagine it! The young today, what have they lived at sixteen? But I already had several lives behind me."

Henry was looking at the old man with such intensity that Isidore got scared. Had he got him wrong, would Hogan be capable of denouncing him to the police?

"I'm sorry, sir, but why would you want to steal it today?"

Isidore exploded and started screaming:

"Because that face . . . that face is my daughter's face! When I saw Pearl for the first time, I thought she was the ghost of my mother, she looked so like her. And the painting is stained, Henry! Because history repeats itself and the blood that could be mistaken for carmine paint in 1925 would today be identified and analyzed and traced back to me! Because of Pearl! And then everyone would know that Isidore Hoffmann Ferguson is not just a father who doesn't recognize his children, but also a bastard and a murderer!"

Hogan considered contradicting his boss. After all, even if the painting was headline news in the Italian and international press, even if experts scrutinized the canvas and suspected there were bloodstains, if they'd even survived after all those years, and even if those bloodstains revealed anything, there was very little chance they would trace them to Isidore Hoffmann Ferguson, whose DNA was recorded by a Texan judge on the other side of the ocean. But he'd never seen Mr. Hoffmann Ferguson in such a fragile state and he understood that what was at stake went beyond the weighing up of probabilities. He looked at the old man and saw how fear was making the whites of his blue eyes glisten. His daughter Pearl telling him about that painting had made him lose the plot. Stendhal syndrome or not, this painting had come back to haunt him, and, once and for all, maybe irremediably, he had to get hold of it.

And so, regaining his usual composure, Henry Hogan said to his boss:

"Very good, sir, it will be done."

Epilogue

A scientific truth will always be undone by a truth born of fiction. Did Martha suspect that Isidore was Otto Brombeere's son rather than Franz's? Had she lied to her child the better to convince herself? In fact, what did a DNA result change? Everything, and in the end, nothing. Pearl was living proof of that. Whether parricide or fratricide, Ernst Stauber's intuition was correct, it was, fundamentally, a family matter.

Pearl had turned then to Henry Hogan. Who else but the man who dealt with everything for her father? He alone would have been capable of getting that painting stolen and delivering it to her apartment building, one evening in May.

When she had asked him the question, Hogan had almost appeared relieved and had admitted to it without beating around the bush. He told her how it hadn't taken him long to make up his mind, it seemed obvious to him, that painting was the portrait of Pearl and it was to her alone that it should return. Together, they had put the pieces of the puzzle back together again. And as soon as Pearl had known the portrait's story, the spell had been broken, the painting had no longer had any hold on her.

But the awkward question of its hiding-place remained. She couldn't keep, hidden under a duvet at the top of her cupboard, a work of art being hunted for by police worldwide. Once again, Henry had offered to take care of it, and he'd had the painting sent to the free port of Geneva, which promised "safe storage under thermic and hygrometric control in high-security strongrooms." The problem remained intact, but it did change continent.

And so Pearl let twenty years go by. Then, on December 8, 2016, an article appeared on the BBC website headlined, "The mystery of the stolen Klimt" (it remains online). Pearl had added "Gustav Klimt" to her Google alerts and the notification had arrived just as she was drinking her third cup of coffee.

It said that the Italian police had just received fresh information concerning the theft committed in Piacenza in 1997: the painting would soon be returned! It would take a few weeks, at most a few months.

Pearl put her cup down, her hands were shaking. The article also gave a totally fanciful version of the story of its repainting:

"Klimt had fallen madly in love with a young girl from Vienna, it was said, who had quickly become his muse. Then, when she suddenly died, he painted over her portrait to forget the pain of his loss."

That was stupid! If Martha had effectively been Klimt's muse, there would have been a great many drawings or sketches of her, and several paintings featuring her. But Pearl was sure, nowhere else within the artist's oeuvre was there any trace of that face. What's more, if Klimt had wanted to erase his grief, he wouldn't have just removed a hat and a stole to replace them with a shawl and a chignon, that made no sense.

As for the person who promised that the painting would soon be returned, he was some kind of Arsène Lupin, a local mafioso whose name the article hadn't revealed. He had admitted theft of the Klimt to the police in exchange for his immunity. His revelations seemed confused, to say the least, because he said he didn't know the identity of the person who had commissioned the theft, but bragged that he'd received "a large quantity of money and cocaine." Pearl felt nauseous reading these lines. He claimed that the painting would return to Piacenza for the 20th anniversary of its disappearance, meaning February 2017.

Henry Hogan hadn't revealed the name of the person who had committed the crime to Pearl, but had assured her that all necessary precautions had been taken. There was absolutely no way it could be traced back to him, let alone to Isidore Hoffmann Ferguson. He had total confidence in the people he had dealt with.

So, once Pearl's initial terror, of being denounced or discovered, had passed, she was left pensive by what she'd read. Despite the crazy claims of the thief, there was a question that needed to be asked: wasn't it time to return Martha to the light? And what if the predictions of that nutcase were a lucky opportunity?

She prevaricated for a few more months, all the same, then decided to get a 28- by 24-inch padded cover made, which she could conceal in the lining of a suitcase bought specially for the purpose.

She had no fixed plan, just the intuition that it was best to do the journey accompanied by her husband and children. And so she booked tickets and they set off in August, like any model American family, to vacation in the Swiss mountains.

* * *

It was hot in Geneva. Adri had taken the boys for a swim in the lake. Pearl had claimed that she had shopping to do before their departure, that very afternoon, for Milan.

She presented herself, along with her wheeled suitcase, at the gates of the free port. It was a high-security set-up. She had an appointment, and was led along the neon-lit earthquake-proof concrete corridors. After a series of red latches, she was shown a door and left alone to tap in her code and insert the key into the lock.

She entered a small, gray, bare room, which displayed a constant temperature of 20 degrees centigrade and an ideal level of 50 percent relative humidity. Standing at its center was the insulated double crate in which the marvel had been stored. Very carefully, she removed the cover and then lifted the acid-free paper. Martha's water-blue eyes jumped out at her.

After all these years, Pearl had aged, she no longer resembled quite as much this evergreen girl who cast her melancholy gaze on the spectator. The indescribable grace of the painting took her breath away. She closed her eyes to stop herself from being swayed by such beauty. She laid the suitcase down flat and unzipped it. She picked up the painting like someone who fears getting burnt, and then, quick as she could, slid her sweet little young girl of a grandmother into the padded cover.

She could still change her mind. The thief had proclaimed that the painting would be returned in February 2017, and it was now August 2018 . . . No, she'd delayed too long already. *There's the statute of limitations, come on*! But much as she chided herself, the big-shot attorney she'd become was dead scared. Her ears were buzzing, had she heard a voice? She's not sure how she found the strength to return her key and get herself back to the hotel. She felt as if she'd just been torn apart.

The boys were splashing each other in the pool and gleefully squealing. Adri had dozed off in his deckchair with an open book on geopolitics over his nose. She went up to their room, repacked her suitcase with her neatly folded clothes like an exemplary mother, put aside whatever they'd need during the journey, checked in the bathroom and under the beds that they hadn't forgotten anything, closed the suitcases again and called reception for help with loading up their car. It was a gray rental car. Pearl felt nauseous.

"Darling! We must go!"

Adri was driving. Before and after the Mont-Blanc Tunnel, she feared there'd be customs checks, but not a single policeman indicated for them to stop. She put on some music to drown her anxiety, and the children had the great idea to sing their heads off. After four hours of driving, they arrived at a five-star hotel, a Relais & Châteaux kind of place in the countryside surrounding Piacenza, with a pool and purple sun loungers, looking out over Romagna olive groves.

In the first supermarket, she bought a roll of large garbage bags and some sticky tape. She isolated herself to wrap the painting up carefully, *do it, do it without thinking about it*. They would be leaving Piacenza the following day, they'd planned to visit Florence, and then Rome. So she'd left herself no choice, she had to get rid of the painting before tomorrow morning.

She parked her car on the lot behind the museum. The heat in the streets of the small Italian town was overwhelming. A static sun disturbed the blue of the sky, ricocheting off the ochre and yellow walls of the villas lining the deserted roads. It was two o'clock, siesta time, when the cicadas sing.

The museum looked like a small palace, with arcades and a square patio. It was self-contained, and all at ground-floor level. A huge entrance hall with a disproportionately high ceiling led to a central gallery, with other galleries branching off it here and there, some of them octagonal, making the paintings seem to be in dialogue with each other. It was a very fine museum, nothing flashy about it, a touch faded.

Perhaps due to its pervading silence, the gallery made her think of a sleeping beauty. She imagined her grandmother here and thought how perfectly in her place she would be.

On the graying-white walls, rosy young girls, docile in their gilded frames, tilted their heads for all eternity. The museum was virtually empty and Pearl heard her every step, click, click,

click, ringing on the herringbone-parquet floor. She walked past arrested sunsets, a woman sewing, a man on a bench reading the paper . . . Distractedly, she read some labels, *Man in hat*, *The Turin Royal Gardens after the March rains*, *Man dragging sled in snow*, *Children in the sun*, *Morning prayer*, *Portrait of the artist's mother*. Had these people existed? What were the stories that were hiding behind each one of them?

At the end of the central gallery, a double door led directly out of the museum and on to the lot she had parked on. To the left, large trees, to the right, a gravel path running along the brick walls covered in ivy and Virginia creeper. She couldn't stop herself from constantly turning around to check that she wasn't being followed.

There seemed to be an adjoining single-story building, closed to the public. Perhaps the residence of the museum's director? What to do? Leave it outside the door, the way babies are abandoned on the steps of churches? But what if someone dishonest found it and kept it for him- or herself? That would be worst of all. She looked around for security cameras and saw none. The railings were too high, climbing them was out of the question. No, doing it at night was a bad idea, she must have the courage to do it in broad daylight, *the courage or the recklessness.*

Pearl was finding it increasingly hard to think. She was fighting with all her might not to be overwhelmed by the fear gnawing away at her. And then she spotted, in the wall, about 12 inches up from the ground, a door, a small, black iron door, a hatch door, to be precise. She knew immediately that this would be perfect. She wouldn't even have to go back round.

She went straight to her car and opened the trunk. *I'm crazy, I'm completely crazy.*

In the distance, she heard a police, or maybe an ambulance, siren; since this morning, she'd felt as if all the carabinieri of Italy knew what she was preparing to do and were waiting for their moment to seize her. She could feel herself succumbing to panic, the dogs were unleashed, this time she could barely control her movements, and for how much longer? If she got caught, all that she'd fought for, all would be destroyed. And yet she had to give up this painting, she had to.

She grabbed a white floral shawl, bought specially, from the back shelf, picked up the garbage bag and wedged it under her arm. She tried to hide the painting under the shawl, but it was hopeless, her hands were no longer obeying her. She felt the blood rushing to her cheeks and thought her heart might catch fire. There wasn't a soul around, she hurried on.

Kneeling down at the foot of the wall, she checked that the hatch wasn't dirty or damp, and that no critter had set up home in it, and then placed the painting, wrapped in the garbage bag, inside it, nice and flat. She shut the door firmly, stood up, shaking all over. *Done.*

Automatically, as if her knees were on springs, she strode off. Despite the heat, she covered her shoulders. She must get away as fast as possible now, on the crunching gravel.

She went back along the path, through the gate, and into the deserted parking lot. As she put the key into the lock of the car door, she jumped and stopped herself from crying out. Reflected in the silvery window stood a ghost.

Martha.

The shade resurfacing from the past. It took Pearl just a moment before she understood. It was the shawl, of course; it was remarkably similar to the young girl's in the painting. She gazed at the familiar specter facing her. *That's funny.* And yet, when she'd bought that shawl, she hadn't made the connection, she'd chosen it instinctively.

As soon as she'd recognized herself, she'd got a grip. It sometimes happens that we come across our own reflection in a mirror unexpectedly. The surprise at not having instantly grasped that it was our own image is almost always accompanied by a kind of disappointment. *So that's me, that person*? But in Pearl's case, it was an eye-opener, she discovered another identity for herself, something she'd actually always known, a truth deeply buried that was finally surfacing. This feeling was so dizzying that it reverberated in her reflection. With a lump in her throat and yet strangely calm, she plunged her eyes, for one last time, into those of her mirage. And then smiled at the spectacle of herself.

At that moment, Pearl became the granddaughter of Martha; even more, she became her own story.

* * *

On Wednesday December 11, 2019, as he was about to cut back some ivy, the gardener at the Piacenza museum found, secreted in a ventilation hatch built into the wall, a garbage bag containing the Klimt painting, in perfect condition.

Today, Portrait of a Lady *can be admired at the Galleria d'Arte Moderna Ricci Oddi every day of the week apart from Monday, when the museum is closed.*

Acknowledgments

This book required a good deal of research, reading, documentation, and many encounters.

I would like to thank my publishing house, Calmann-Lévy for allowing me to go and investigate in Vienna and Piacenza, on the trail of my heroine.

All of my gratitude goes to the exceptionally kind and helpful staff at the Galleria d'Arte Moderna Ricci Oddi, in particular to its director Lucia Pini and to Leonardo Caro, who afforded me the great privilege of remaining tête-à-tête with the *Portrait of a Lady*, even after the museum had closed its doors to the public.

To Margaux Bouaziz, doctor of public law, associate professor at the University of Burgundy, for looking into my Texan-law problems.

To Professor Thomas Bourgeron, a brilliant geneticist, who solved my DNA problems.

To Philippe Esperança, bloodstain morphoanalyst, for his enthusiastic advice and the precious time he kindly dedicated to the reconstruction of my crime scene.

Finally, to my editor, Delphine Mozin Santucci, who has shared all of my commas for such a long time.